Chinaberry Summer

Enjoy your visit in Slippery Branch, Georgia!

CARROLL S. TAYLOR

New Plains Press

Sept 8, 2017

Library of Congress Control Number 2013937564

ISBN 9780985770327

Published by Summerfield Publishing,
New Plains Press
P.O. Box 1946
Auburn, AL 36831-1946
Newplainspress.com

In memory of my aunt,

JoAnn Barnett Pierce:

A friend, mentor,

and keeper of

our family history.

Table of Contents

Page 11. . . . . The Continental Divide

Page 18. . . . . Mashed Potatoes and Gravy

Page 25. . . . . The Order of All Things

Page 33. . . . . The Orb Weaver

Page 37. . . . . The Adventure Begins

Page 41. . . . . Turtle Soup

Page 47. . . . . Old Pearly Fangs

Page 50. . . . . A Haunted Night

Page 56. . . . . No Bones About It

Page 64. . . . . A Mostly Silent Night

Page 77. . . . . The Burning of the Greens
(Collards and Christmas Trees)

Page 81. . . . . Destination Unknown

Page 89. . . . . Miss Cold Germ 1960

Page 95. . . . . The Great Poetry Writing Contest

Page 103 . . . . A Curious Visitor

Page 106 . . . . The Old Clock

Page 115 . . . . Chickens and Dickens

Page 126 . . . . **Toad's Adventure**

Page 131 . . . . **The Wild Plum Bush**

Page 134 . . . . **The Garden of Miss Information**

Page 140 . . . . **Grandpa Spills the Beans**

Page 149 . . . . **Chinaberry Summer**

Page 154 . . . . **A Come to Jesus Meeting**

Page 165 . . . . **Shall We Gather**

Page 179 . . . . **Troubled Waters**

Page 191 . . . . **Gone to Glory**

Page 205 . . . . **The Rose of Sharon**

Page 218 . . . . **White Sugar Sands**

Page 228 . . . . **Turtles and Gators and Snakes**

Page 240 . . . . **Home at Last**

CHAPTER 1

The Continental Divide

> *"This world is a very big place, and you are all
> in for a grand adventure."*
> *– Mrs. Clara Sue Martin*

I figure some teachers like to make their students' heads spin by filling eager, unsuspecting little brains with perfectly useless information, the kind that will probably never do anybody any good. In those teachers' ordinary classrooms, each student's education is a lot like an empty paper bag with a department store's name stamped right across the front of it. At the end of the school year, when all the students leave the classroom to begin summer vacation, they take their paper bags home with them, still empty. At least the name on their bags proves that they must have gone somewhere.

But then there are those rare, amazing teachers who are far from ordinary – the ones who give out knowledge like colorful pieces of chewy candy wrapped in shiny, red cellophane. Their students want to take home a bagful – and, sure enough, they do.

On a very ordinary autumn day, on the first day of my fifth grade year in 1959, once again I carried my paper bag to

Slippery Branch Elementary School to begin another ordinary year of grammar school with another ordinary teacher. But, at last, I wasn't disappointed, because by the end of that afternoon in geography class, my new teacher, Mrs. Clara Sue Martin, had already made her first deposit of candy into my empty bag of knowledge.

She stood at the front of the classroom and held up a copy of our geography book. Then she said the words that I never will forget: "This world is a very big place, and you are all in for a grand adventure." I reckon that's exactly when my adventure began.

I immediately sat up straight in my desk and listened to every word she said.

That day she taught our class about the continental divide. She said the western divide runs right through the state of Colorado in the Rocky Mountains, and it forms a natural dividing line up and down the whole United States.

"Of course, you can't see the line, even if you're in an airplane," she explained, "but you still know it's there. The rivers to the west of the divide head toward the Pacific Ocean, and the rivers to the east of the divide eventually end up in the Atlantic Ocean or the Gulf of Mexico," Mrs. Martin continued, as she moved the end of a wooden ruler up and down a huge wall map of the United States to show us exactly where to find the invisible line.

In my mind I could see all those rivers, running freely every which way in all directions, until God told Mother Nature, "Get them all organized!"

Mother Nature obeyed. Leaning way over toward the north and hunching up her great rippled spine, she extended one arm to the west and the other arm to the east and said, "This is it! This is the moment when you find your true direction. You rivers flow to my left and you other rivers flow to my right. Now do y'all understand?"

My idea about Mother Nature's simple solution made perfect sense to me.

But I would soon discover that life is not geography, and its directions are not always quite so simply and clearly marked for us by some kind of invisible dividing line or even by the points on a compass.

Up until then my little corner of the world hadn't felt complicated at all to me, a girl growing up in a small brown house on a dirt road in Georgia, surrounded by practically all of my family. However, Mrs. Martin knew how to explain things in a way that I understood, and I sensed that what she was teaching us was very important. I suddenly realized for the first time in my life that I was like one of those rivers. I was searching for my own true direction. *I was on a journey.*

I didn't really need Mother Nature to show me the way to go, though – lots of adults were already willing to do that for her. Most often they weren't able to read the points of life's compass very well for themselves, much less for somebody else. But looking back, I guess my moment, the time when my own version of the continental divide at last was able to point me toward the right direction for my adventure, occurred during the summer of 1960.

But on that first day of school I had never been anywhere in my life –unless I considered the one time that Daddy's red and white '56 Chevy carried the four of us up U.S. Highway 27, and we ventured across the state line into Tennessee for a two day trip to Chattanooga, Lookout Mountain, and Ruby Falls, before scurrying right back into Georgia.

So Colorado was just a distant square on the big wall map that Mrs. Martin could roll down during geography class. I knew that in the evening, if I faced the sunset, Colorado and the Rocky Mountains were way over in that direction someplace. And if somehow I ever went to Colorado and kept on going, I would eventually reach California and the Pacific Ocean.

The other place on Mrs. Martin's map that especially struck my fancy was that long southern state, the one that hung down like a pendulum into the Atlantic Ocean and almost swung right into Cuba. Mrs. Martin taught us a wonderful new word: peninsula. I loved to pronounce it and to write it in black, inky cursive. But my sights were actually set on all that blue surrounding the peninsula. Or more specifically, on the edges of the blue. The beaches.

How I longed to see a real beach. Not a fake manmade beach meandering around a muddy lake, but a real, honest-to-God ocean beach, complete with sand and foamy waves and seashells. The kind that I had only seen in books or at home in black and white on our television screen. I didn't much figure I could ever get to Colorado or California, but, heck, I knew that maybe I had a shot at seeing a beach in Florida.

During the hot, sweaty summers of my life, when a bath made me feel even more sticky and miserable, and flipping my pillow over at least a dozen times at night still didn't make my white cotton pillowcase feel a bit cooler on my skin, I had often imagined what it might be like to walk on an ocean beach. I'd be holding my colorful plastic inflated beach ball lovingly under my right arm and my empty sand bucket in my left hand, waiting expectantly for the wonderful seashells I would find on the shore.

The ocean breeze would feel cool on my skin, and the sugary white sand would crunch softly under my bare feet. At least, that's how I imagined it would be, because that's the way Gemma described it. She and her sister, Aunt Pearl, had been to Florida before, and she had brought back the souvenirs to prove it. She had taken lots of pictures while she was there, too, but, of course, they were black and white.

On top of the bureau in the front bedroom of Gemma's house, an ashtray that looked like a white porcelain toilet sat proudly on a lace-trimmed doily. It proclaimed in black print *Park your butt here. Souvenir of Florida.* Of course, no one was allowed to park cigarettes in it, just safety pins.

And on Gemma's kitchen table sat The Napkin Holder. Not just any napkin holder, mind you, but the one that no one but Gemma was allowed to move. It was pink sparkly plastic, decorated with little pink dyed shells, a jaunty flamingo, and a palm tree, all of which was sprinkled with a good dusting of glued-on glitter. *Florida* screamed at an angle across the little scene in black cursive.

"Now don't move my napkin holder, you hear? You might drop it," she warned us all. Even Grandpa.

That napkin holder was always on the table, and it sparkled proudly when she added the extra table leaf, hunted up mismatched chairs, and spread out her best white, patched, tea-stained tablecloth so that we could all gather around for Sunday dinner at her house.

So Florida had to be an exotic place. It just had to be.

One day after a heavy rain, I sneaked into the cabinet in our kitchen and swiped a box of shell macaroni from the cabinet over the sink. I raced out the back door and around to the front yard, where the rain always formed a large, sandy puddle in our dirt driveway. I opened the box and scattered the hard, dry shells around the edge of the puddle. Then, pretending that I had never seen the shells before, I looked at them in amazement as I began collecting the wonderful seashells that had washed up on the shore of my private beach.

"Sissie, you've gotta stop stealing my macaroni. It's wasteful," Mama's voice called out to me. She had pulled back the kitchen curtains and was looking at me with disgust through the screen of the open window. Mama always had a way of bringing me back to reality. But my little shell game wasn't really wasteful, because it transported me someplace besides my little brown house on that dirt road. I could almost hear the waves.

Besides, I took exception to her accusing me of stealing. She knew perfectly well that I had never stolen anything in my life except one time in the second grade, and that really didn't count, since I stole something from myself.

* * * *

I was so excited about my new deluxe box of forty-eight crayons that Mama had bought me at the five and ten cent store. The crayons were lined up in neat, perfectly pointy rows, like a church choir ready to sing joyfully for the Lord. I couldn't wait to get to school and see what special pictures I might need to color in my reading class. I showed my friends my new crayons, put the box back into my desk, and headed to lunch.

When I returned to the classroom, my box of crayons was missing. I complained to my teacher, Miss Maude Jones. "Miss Jones, someone stole my box of colors."

She looked at me like I was a worm on her prize tomatoes. "Was your name written clearly on the box?"

"No, ma'am. I haven't had time. I only got 'em yesterday and…"

"Well," she informed me with a nasty tone in her voice, "there is absolutely nothing I can do about the situation. Just about every pupil in this classroom has a box of crayons. I cannot possibly know which box belongs to you. You should have written your name on the box."

She shrugged her shoulders, turned her back on me, and started fussing at Julian Swanson for chewing with his mouth open during lunch. In my opinion, stealing was a much worse offense than letting people see food in your mouth. Besides, Julian always had a bad cold and a runny nose, and he had to breathe when he ate, for Pete's sake. So I persisted.

"But, Miss Jones, they're *new*," I protested. "They still have the points on 'em." She walked away and sat down at her desk, never once acknowledging my dilemma.

Maybe she hadn't heard me right the first time, so I tried again. "But Miss Jones, I want my colors back. What am I s'posed to do?"

Her eyes bored into me. "This is *your* problem to solve, not mine. And I might add, you ask way too many questions for one little girl. The world does not revolve around *you*, Miss Stevenson."

I took her response as a sign that it was time for me to take action on my own and locate my stolen property myself.

Later on when Miss Jones led the class outside for afternoon recess, I lingered in the classroom for a few minutes, pretended to retie my shoes, and peeked into the desk of my prime suspect, Joe Borders. He was a sneaky boy who had a habit of taking things that didn't belong to him. And there in his desk, under some workbooks and sheets of red construction paper, lay a deluxe box of forty-eight brand new crayons. So I stole them back, put them in my desk, and went outside for recess.

Since Joe never complained to Miss Jones that his crayons had gone missing, I figured I had hit pay dirt. I also never asked Miss Jones to help me with anything again. The rest of that school year if I didn't know the meaning of a word in my assignment, I looked it up in a dictionary on my own. If I had a problem, I figured it out for myself.

Even though I guess Miss Jones indirectly helped me with my reading and vocabulary skills, I don't believe she ever appreciated the fact that I was a person with a lot of questions that needed answers. But she did help me to learn that sometimes I had to take things into my own hands, especially when adults refused to intervene.

All of my teachers from the first through the fourth grade had left their own kind of mark on my life, mostly not favorable, and I responded in kind. At the end of each school year, I left their classrooms disappointed, carrying home my empty bag of knowledge and feeling a bitter dislike for school. However, it was Mrs. Clara Sue Martin and her first geography lesson that helped me set my life on the right course – due east, then south, straight down to Florida.

CHAPTER 2

Mashed Potatoes and Gravy

"Money can buy a lot of things, but it can't buy you a good name."
– Mama

On one side of my house, through a field and down a sandy path lined with June apple trees, stood the old house of my father's parents, Gemma and Grandpa. It was a simple white country house with two porches, one in the front and one in the back. On each porch a wide wooden swing hung from a rafter. The house was surrounded by all sorts of flowering bushes – altheas, azaleas, camellias, Christmas honeysuckle, forsythia, flowering quince, and bridal veil. In fact, in the spring the yard looked a lot like the pictures in Gemma's flower seed catalog.

Tall oak trees near the house commanded the respect of everything that was growing in the shadows of their great height, including crape myrtles with their pink ruffled clusters of blossoms. Vines holding miniature pink roses spilled over a rock wall near the front porch. A good place for copperhead snakes and scorpions to hide. Red flowering quinces, with their long sharp thorns, dotted the edges of the yard.

In the back yard, pear trees sheltered the patch of land near Gemma's chicken coop and the old outhouse. Sometimes I helped gather eggs from the small straw-filled hen boxes, and I loved the feel of the smooth, warm brown eggs in my hands.

"Now, Sissie, don't you put your hand under that little red hen in the fourth box. She's settin' and she will peck you!" Gemma didn't really need to warn me, because I had already made that mistake once. And once was enough.

In the spring, I loved to stand under the pear trees and let their tiny white flowers rain down on me, leaving petals in my hair, like I was a fairy tale princess. Grandpa's scuppernong vines grew along his homemade grape arbor, and near the arbor, his weathered, gray wood smokehouse stood to remind us of days gone by. Now it was just used to store his yard tools. And along the side of the smokehouse, Gemma had created a small flower garden where every year she planted her sunflowers and the seeds of various other annuals that caught her eye in her flower seed catalog.

Gemma's clothesline was in the backyard, strung between two thin leaning wooden posts, and a huge white oak shaded her when she hung out her freshly washed laundry. In the spring and summer the field between our two houses became a maze of corn, tomatoes, beans, squash, and okra that Grandpa planted and Gemma canned or froze.

A lot of what Grandpa raised in his garden was given to neighbors, sort of as a way to show his appreciation. "The Good Lord gave me a fine garden this year, Sissie, and I'm gonna show Him how grateful I am by sharin' some of it with my neighbors," he explained as I helped him put fresh ears of corn and sacks of butter beans into empty cardboard boxes from the grocery store. The tomatoes, right off the vine, were sweet and delicious, still warm from the sun, and Gemma slipped a few of those in the boxes as well.

I guess Gemma probably was a strange name to call my grandmother, but there was a very good reason for her special name. My grandmother was born in February, and so her mother named her Amethyst. It was my sister Biddie who actually gave her the name Gemma.

One day Biddie asked, "Grandma, what's an *athemyst*?"

"You mean an *amethyst*? Why, it's the name of my birthstone."

Grandpa chimed in, "That's your grandma's real name. So that makes her a real gem, I reckon."

So Biddie started calling her Gemma. And later when I came along and learned to talk, I called her that, too.

On the other side of our house a deserted cotton field overgrown with tall weeds and briars provided me ample space to hunt for ripe blackberries, seek out maypop vines, and generally press my luck at not getting snake bitten. I loved finding the maypop plants—lifting their vines carefully and looking to see if they had any flowers hiding on their leafy vines that had curled and twisted among the surrounding tall grasses and weeds.

Their blooms created a circle of purple fringe surrounding their centers, which bore the shapes of the fish and loaves of bread, just like the story in the Bible about the little boy who helped Jesus feed the multitudes. Often their vines held another treasure - large, smooth green fruit the size and shape of an egg. Sometimes I liked to crack open a maypop fruit just to touch the seeds neatly lined up inside its gauzy white lining.

Directly across the street from our house, a white house and a huge barn with a hayloft presided over the farm of Uncle Toolie and Aunt Pearl. Grandpa called it a valley house. Their farm had been there since the thirties, one of the farms created in the Valley during the Great Depression by President Franklin Delano Roosevelt as part of his New Deal.

Grandpa told me all about Uncle Toolie's farm. "Times was hard everywhere. Toolie and Pearl got the house, the barn, thirty acres of land, and a mule and wagon. In exchange, he farmed the land and made payments to the government."

Uncle Toolie and Grandpa had both met Mr. Roosevelt when he lived at Warm Springs. "He was a fine man, a fine man. It was a pleasure to shake his hand. He was a good Democrat," Grandpa said, beaming. Grandpa never criticized the Democrats.

A red, dusty, and sometimes very muddy dirt road formed a ribbon that looped us together and tied us to a paved road three miles away. The front yard of my house looked out over that dirt road, and the best place to be was in the huge, sheltering mimosa on the front lawn. I loved to climb that tree and sit on one of its many sturdy limbs that created a wonderful place to hide. Its smooth bark encouraged no climbing mistakes, and any person who was of a mind to climb a mimosa had to be extra careful, or he'd wind up on the ground with a broken arm.

But once I was settled onto my favorite perch, I could sit for hours and watch people go by without being seen under the tropical branches of the tree. The tree's flowers in the summer were a pastel pink, and they smelled like a soft perfume. I often picked a few of the feathery flowers and brushed them on my cheeks, because they reminded me of powder puffs.

Sometimes when I was sitting high up in my mimosa tree, tiny hummingbirds would fly right up close to me, searching for the sweet nectar in the flowers. I wanted to catch one of the speedy birds, with his ruby throat and sparkling feathers, and hold him in my hand, just to admire him and then set him free, but I never could catch one.

Gemma once told me, "If you can ever get close enough to sprinkle salt on his tail, you can catch him." I never thought to carry a salt shaker with me when I went climbing, and so I never caught a hummingbird. Actually, I wasn't too sure I believed her advice about catching hummingbirds with salt anyway.

On the other side of the yard near the driveway stood a tall chinaberry tree. It was a straighter, more stately tree than the gnarly chinaberry growing in the backyard. It seemed to brag, "Look at me. I'm in the front yard. I have to keep up a good appearance." In the spring, clusters of fragrant lavender flowers with tiny purple trumpets filled the chinaberry trees. Then after a couple of months or so, the flowers became clusters of hard, shiny green berries, just right to pick and use for ammunition in a chinaberry fight.

When the tree bloomed, I liked to put some of the flowers in my bedroom, and, of course, I had to shinny up the rough crisscrossed bark of the tree in order to pick them. Although the tree wasn't very friendly to climbers, I stubbornly put my bare foot in a low fork of the tree anyway, hoisted myself up, gathered a handful of the fragrant flowers, and took them into the house. Those flowers were worth the scratches on my arms.

I once tried to get Daddy to like the chinaberry flowers, too.

"Look, Daddy. Aren't these beautiful?" I held up my lavender bouquet to him so that he could appreciate their beauty and fragrance.

"Sissie, get those things away from me!" he fussed. "Chinaberry flowers make me sick at my stomach if I smell 'em."

Well, they didn't make *me* sick. So every year when the chinaberry flowers appeared, I tucked away a small bouquet of them and put them on my dresser in a little milk glass vase that Gemma had bought at the five and ten cent store.

During the times when I was sitting in the mimosa tree watching cars drive by, pining away for a hummingbird to hold in my hand, or when I was climbing the chinaberry tree gathering its flowers or its shiny green berries, I had a lot of time to think. There was just something about climbing way up in a tree that made me want to think of more questions that needed answers. Maybe being higher up gave me a different perspective on life.

Through the branches of the trees I looked across the street toward Uncle Toolie's farm. Now there was a strange and interesting family. How in the world did Uncle Toolie end up married to someone like Aunt Pearl? Why would their daughter want to leave the big city of Atlanta and come to live here with them in the country? How could Grandpa and Uncle Toolie be first cousins, act like brothers, and yet be so very different?

Toolie was not really my great uncle's name. It was more of a nickname, because he had almost every kind of tool imaginable in his barn. His real name was Herbert, but Aunt Pearl refused to call him by his given name, since it reminded her of President Hoover.

"I still can't understand why in the world your mother named you Herbert. It's especially a shame to have the same name as President Hoover, what with the Depression and all. And besides, he was a Republican."

Even though Uncle Toolie's mother had died long ago, Aunt Pearl still loved to criticize her, never mind the fact that Uncle Toolie was born in 1895 and his mother had been unable to predict the future.

Uncle Toolie loved to work on everything, from farm equipment to television sets, and Aunt Pearl put up with his clutter as long as none of it found its way into her pristine house. Their oldest child, Sharon, and her husband Jamie lived in Atlanta. I hardly knew Sharon, and I had never met her husband or two sons. Uncle Toolie and Aunt Pearl's middle child Mitchell had died in France during World War II, and they still kept a folded American flag in a special box on the mantel over the fireplace in their living room. Their youngest child, Rose McKenna, who was a widow, still lived with them. Even though she was my cousin, I often called her Aunt Rose, because she was my chosen aunt. But the best person of all who lived in their house was Rose's son, Spud.

Living in the house with Aunt Pearl, Spud had to find some place to go where he could be himself, and that place was Gemma and Grandpa's house. Somehow it was as if Gemma was his grandmother, and not Aunt Pearl.

Uncle Toolie and Grandpa were first cousins, and Aunt Pearl and Gemma were sisters. That meant that Aunt Pearl was not only Gemma's sister, but she was her cousin by marriage, so Daddy and Rose were first cousins and second cousins. I didn't really worry about whether Spud was a first, second, or third cousin, because whatever order he was didn't really matter to me. Spud was more than my cousin – he was my best friend.

None of my family members ever seemed to be who they really were anyway. Everybody was hiding behind something, even if it was only a nickname. Biddie wasn't my sister's real name either. Everyone started calling her Biddie because she loved baby chickens so much, but she spelled her name with an -*ie*, because she didn't want anyone to ever refer to her as an "old biddy." And since I was the sister born later, I became Sissie.

Mama often told Biddie and me, "We don't have a lot of money, but that's okay. Money can buy a lot of things, but it can't buy you a good name. Always be proud of your name and have a good reputation. A good name is what counts."

Well, if a good name is what counts, then why did we all have nicknames?

I tried to convince Spud to remember what Mama had said about a good name, but he wouldn't listen. "I don't have a good name, Sissie. I *hate* my real name." His real name was Homer. For a long time when Spud was very young, everybody in the family called him by his given name, but that didn't work, because his name never seemed to fit him right. Spud just wasn't a Homer.

One afternoon Spud and I were sitting on our favorite limbs in the mimosa tree. Spud was holding on to the limb above him, looking off in the distance, like he was really thinking hard about something serious. "Sissie, why in the world did Mama name me Homer?" He must have asked me that same question every single week, mainly because he was teased on a regular basis by the boys in our school.

"Spud, you know the answer to that question. She's told you a thousand times. Homer was the name of a famous Greek poet," I explained as I softly brushed an ant off my arm.

"That still doesn't answer my question. Why do you reckon she would name me after someone from Greece? That may sound all fancy up in Atlanta, but around here, that name don't mean a thing. I'm just a joke."

"Spud, you are *not* a joke. You can't help what your mama named you." Well, unfortunately for Spud, his *nickname* was the joke. When he was five, he got really sick and had to have an operation. When he finally came home from the hospital, all he wanted to eat was mashed potatoes. Mashed potatoes for lunch, mashed potatoes for supper. He would have eaten mashed potatoes for breakfast if Aunt Pearl and Rose had cooked them for him. Then, when he started feeling even better, he asked for gravy on his potatoes.

One day while we were all eating Sunday dinner at Gemma and Grandpa's house, Uncle Toolie looked over at Spud and watched him as he gulped down his mashed potatoes. "Boy, if you don't stop eatin' so many potatoes, you're gonna turn into one. Maybe we should just start callin' you *Spud.*"

And so Homer became Spud, and his nickname stuck. In fact, it stuck to him like gravy on mashed potatoes.

CHAPTER 3

The Order of All Things

*"Now, boys and girls, I want to remind you that the earth does
not revolve around you. It revolves around the sun."*
– Miss Maude Jones

Spud and I were in the same grade in elementary school,
but while I had suffered in Miss Maude Jones's second grade
classroom, Spud was lucky – he had the new teacher, Miss Emily
Dew. Miss Dew wore gray skirts and pastel pullover sweaters, and
she tied a matching pastel scarf into a bow around her neck. She
smelled like flowers, and she always smiled, causing a little dimple
to form on each side of her mouth. She liked Spud's real name, so
she insisted on calling him Homer in class. Miss Dew meant well,
but Spud just got teased even more mercilessly at recess.

"Homer, would you please erase the blackboard for me?"
she asked kindly, giving him a pearly white smile in dimple
parentheses.

"Yes, ma'am." Spud slipped out of his desk, trying his best to
be invisible to the rest of the class, but giggles started up among
the girls and turned into outright laughter among the boys.

That afternoon another student in Miss Dew's class, Rusty
Jackson, punched Spud in the face at recess. Rusty turned around

to his friends who were watching and bragged, "Looka there, boys. I just hit a homer." They bent over double laughing, and the painful expression I saw on Spud's face was not so much from the hurt of the punch as it was from being humiliated by Rusty and the other boys.

I wanted so much to kick the daylights out of Rusty's shin, but I knew I couldn't get in trouble at school or I'd be in worse trouble at home. How I hated seeing that defeated look on Spud's face and the look of triumph on Rusty's face as he laughed and turned to walk away with the other boys, slapping them on the back, proud of the terrible thing he had just done.

I wanted to explain to Spud that the boys weren't actually laughing at his name, but I couldn't do that, because then I would have to tell him the truth – they were laughing at *him*. Spud was smaller than the other boys his age, and they never chose him to play sports, so he always ended up playing with the girls. Besides, Rusty didn't have any reason to laugh at Spud's real name, because Rusty's name was a nickname, too. His parents had named him Elmo.

Every time Rusty picked on Spud, I tried giving Rusty the special evil look that Mama always gave me when I did something wrong, but it didn't have any effect on him whatsoever, except to make him give me a dirty look in return. I guess his mother never tried to make him feel guilty, or else the guilt just rolled right off him like pond water off a duck's feathers.

"Don't you worry none, Spud," Patsy Stephens instructed in her motherly-sounding voice, trying her best to make him feel better. "You're just fine the way you are. Don't you ever act like those boys. They are up to no g-o-o-d." Patsy was my best friend, but she had a really annoying habit of spelling out her words entirely too o-f-t-e-n.

Third grade hadn't been a bit better for either of us. Spud's teacher was Miss Flora Hickey. She was tall, thin, and very pale, and she had a big dark mole right above her lip, and it definitely wasn't a beauty mark.

Spud had his own opinion. "You know, Sissie, I swear when she's talking, that mole moves up and down. Sometimes I can't concentrate in class for lookin' at that mole."

On the playground some of the students in her class liked to say, "Holy moly!" when she was out of earshot standing in the shade talking to other teachers, which didn't seem to happen very often.

Miss Hickey's students had to fold their homework papers long ways and write their name and the date on the first and second lines on the front of the folded sheet. If they forgot – no recess. They also had to obey about a zillion rules, and if they forgot to obey a single rule – no recess. If they stepped out of the line on the way to recess – no recess. Actually, I think Miss Hickey didn't really like to take her class outside for recess, and all of her rule-breaking students gave her an excuse to stay indoors. Her pale skin made her appear sickly, and for some reason, she always smelled like cigarettes and moth balls.

My teacher, Miss Hazel Montgomery, was also a very strange lady. The expression on her face made her look like she might be smelling something really bad. So the right side of her upper lip was always pinched up higher than the rest of her mouth, which was all thickly painted with bright red lipstick. She had a nervous twitch that was bad on Mondays and five times worse by Fridays. Miss Montgomery wore high heeled shoes with her skirts every day, and not to be outdone by the weather, in the dead of winter she wore rolled down, heavy white socks with her high heels.

Some days she was very sweet, and other days she was so mean that no one dared to ask her a simple question. On those days, we tried to stay busy and pretend we were reading. We didn't dare look her in the eye. I used those opportunities to work on my homonym collection I had started writing in the back of my notebook. Then when the bell rang and our line reached the door, we headed out for the playground like rats jumping out of a burning ship. In the classroom our teacher's name may have been Miss Montgomery, but on the playground we had a special name for her.

"Phew, Witch Hazel is in a bad mood today," I said, doing my best imitation of Miss Montgomery's nervous twitch. "I think I actually saw a black cloud over her head this morning."

"Yeah, I think I saw a flash of lightnin'," added Becky Turner, who had been the unlucky recipient of a fiery tongue-lashing by Miss Montgomery in front of the class the day before. Becky's lip was curled up just like Miss Montgomery's, but I don't think she was doing that on purpose.

"I know, sometimes she is just so m-e-a-n." Patsy Stephens spelled. "I declare, I believe she must eat nails and thumbtacks for breakfast."

Maudie Dinsmore spoke up – I swear that girl lived in a fog. "Did you notice she has on red today? Like I've told you before, my brother Cecil had her as his teacher two years ago, and he says when she wears red, she's mean, and when she wears black, she's nice."

"Humph," Becky countered. "She was wearing black yesterday, and I didn't notice a lick of difference. She nearly snapped my head off for asking if I could use the restroom."

We looked up, and I noticed that the students in Spud's classroom were headed out to join us for recess. I put my hand above my eyes to shade them from the sunlight while I looked for Spud, but he was not among the group of Miss Hickey's students who filed out the door and down the stone steps before dashing across the grass to the playground like freed chickens. I caught the attention of Richard Davis, who was lining up behind a dozen students, waiting his turn on the high slide.

"Richard, where's Spud?" I asked.

"Oh, he won't be coming out for recess." He started to chuckle, and some of the boys standing near Richard started laughing, too.

"And why is *that*?" I demanded, ignoring the laughter that often started up after Spud's name was mentioned.

"Uh, he had a little toilet problem, and Miss Hickey is making him clean the whole entire restroom."

"Oh, no!" Not at school, Spud, not at school. My cousin Spud was a wonderful cousin and my best friend, but he did have a few faults. One of them was that he always sat with the girls in the lunchroom, and they loved to make him laugh, because he would laugh so hard that he would blow milk bubbles through his nose. I failed to see the humor in that.

Another one of Spud's shortcomings, and probably his worst, was that, whenever he came to my house to visit, he almost always had to use the bathroom for serious business. And he almost always stopped up the toilet, causing an overflow of murky water on the floor and a frantic run for the plunger Mama kept hidden in a closet.

"I declare, I don't see why he can't do his business at home." Mama always fussed after one of Spud's flooding visits, but she never complained to the right person: Spud. It's just that Spud had never come to realize that he didn't have to use half a roll of toilet paper at one time.

Spud's toilet woes were bad enough, but at least he had kept them in the family. Now everyone at school would know about his toilet paper habits, and he would be teased even more. If Rusty found out – which he did – he would tease Spud even worse than the other students did.

I declare, Spud was his own worst enemy. Flooding the boys' restroom earned Spud a new nickname: Plunger.

Miss Maude Jones moved up to teach fourth grade, and this time Spud was the really unlucky one, or at least, he was unluckier than I was. He had such a hard time with the multiplication tables that I thought he never would get to go out to recess again. And if he couldn't pronounce every word in his reading lesson, Miss Jones made him write his name on the blackboard and stay in during recess and write any words he mispronounced twenty-five times each. She did that to all of her students.

I overheard Miss Jones in the hallway one day when she had her class lined up to go outside. An unfortunate victim, Davey Morris, was backed up against the wall, his eyes so big they were about to pop out of the sockets, and Miss Jones was shaking her finger in his face. "Just who do you think you are, talking in this line? The world doesn't revolve around *you*, Mr. David Morris. *I* am the teacher, not you."

Davey never said a word back to Miss Jones, but he didn't forget the embarrassment of the scolding he had received in front of the class. A few days later Miss Jones was lecturing her class on the subject of spiders.

One of her students, Belinda Jackson, who everybody knew was the teacher's pet (and Rusty's first cousin), raised her hand and asked, "Miss Jones, what exactly do spiders prefer to eat?"

What a stupid question. But Miss Jones smiled sweetly at her and began a lengthy explanation about spiders' daily diets and their favorite foods.

Just exactly how did Miss Jones know what their favorite foods were anyway? Had she ever actually asked a spider that question? Maybe some spiders preferred lady bugs instead of crickets and flies.

Davey passed a note to Spud. "I wonder if they like to eat teachers?"

Spud wrote back, "It would take a mighty big web to catch her."

My teacher was Mrs. Melba Colley. She had blue cats-eye glasses with little sparkly stones on each corner, and she wore a pearl chain that was attached to each side of her glasses. When she put on her glasses, it looked like pearls were growing out of her ears. She let us know right away that she wanted her students to sit in their desks, listen to her, and keep quiet.

"When I'm talking, boys and girls, I want to be able to hear a pin drop." Unfortunately, she was always talking.

I raised my hand – I couldn't help myself. "Miz Colley, what good is *that?*"

"What good is *what?*" she asked, peering over her sparkly glasses at me in disgust like an offended Siamese cat with pearls sticking out of both ears. Because a student had actually dared to ask her a question, she had turned toward me so quickly with such surprise that her head was bobbing on the end of her thin neck, making her pearl chain quiver.

"Hearing a pin drop," I answered precisely, just like a school teacher. "Who cares about hearing a pin drop?" I spent my afternoon recess writing five hundred times *I must not ask the teacher silly questions in class*. So after that, I always managed to keep a Webster's dictionary on my desk, and while Mrs. Colley droned on and on with her useless information, I improved my vocabulary by looking up interesting new words. I even found a few to describe Mrs. Colley: *loquacious tyrant*.

When I got home from school, I complained to Grandpa about Mrs. Colley. "She is flat out mean, Grandpa. What am I gonna do? Dang it, I'm stuck in her class all year."

Grandpa studied me for a moment with his deep blue eyes. "Humph, you don't know the meanin' of the word mean, Sissie. When I was your age, I went to a one room schoolhouse. And we all had to go sit on a long bench in the front of the classroom to answer questions about our lessons. The teacher had a big hickory switch in her hand. If she asked a student a question and the student got the wrong answer 'cause he hadn't studied, the teacher switched us all with that stick."

I looked at Grandpa and just shook my head. I knew he wasn't making that story up, because he always told me the truth. "Well, at least, I guess that made everybody study extra hard."

"Yep, it sure did, 'cause if we got a whippin' in class, there was gonna be a extra whippin' for somebody after school, too."

* * * *

Finally, in the fifth grade Spud and I were in the same classroom, which probably may not have been such a good thing, because lots of times we got into trouble for talking to each other in class or passing notes. But the notes were good notes – well, mostly, except when one of our classmates acted a fool, which was pretty often, since Rusty Jackson was in our classroom.

Mrs. Martin planned lots of things for us to do. She made arithmetic fun, and we wrote stories, studied mythology, and learned how to read music.

One late September day during recess, the fifth grade girls were jumping a long, heavy rope on the playground's dusty red dirt. Patsy and Maudie were standing at each end of the rope, holding the rope and swinging it hard, causing it to slap the ground in a sort of rhythm as it kicked up dust. One by one each of the other girls took her turn running in, jumping a few times, and running back out, never once getting tangled in the rope.

Once I got in, I could jump up a storm. The problem was, I could never run in. I lined up and waited nervously. When it was my turn, I gave it my best try. I honestly did. But my feet tangled in the dirty rope, and it jerked out of Patsy's hand.

Maudie rolled her eyes, "Lord, here we go again. You still haven't figured it out, have you, Sissie?" she whined.

Suddenly, from out of nowhere, Mrs. Martin appeared beside me – dressed in a pink blouse, a gray skirt, and black high heels. She took my hand and said, "Count the beats, just like in music. Don't run in *on* the beat. Run in right *after* the beat. Let's go!" The girls began to swing the rope, and we ran in together, after the down beat, the two of us jumping rope and laughing just like a couple of friends.

On other days she took off her high heels and put on a pair of socks and navy blue tennis shoes so she could take our class for walks outside to learn all about different plants and animals.

In fact, during one of our morning walks, a shiny, striped garter snake slithered across the ground right in front of Mrs. Martin, but she didn't act the least bit afraid. Two boys standing near her started picking up rocks, getting ready to murder the unsuspecting snake. But before they could throw a single rock, she whirled around and spoke up firmly, "Don't you dare harm that snake, boys! He's a very beneficial animal. We don't kill snakes."

There was my absolute proof: Mrs. Clara Sue Martin was no ordinary person. She was *extraordinary.*

Miss Maude Jones had once explained to our second grade class how the earth was spinning on its axis and revolving around the sun at the same time. I suspected that secretly she really believed the world was revolving around *her*.

But Mrs. Martin helped me to understand that, in the middle of all that spinning and revolving, most of us are just trying to figure out which way to go, the same as that garter snake.

On that single day in the autumn of 1959 in Mrs. Martin's geography class, when she taught us about the continental divide, yes, I learned that I was on a journey to find the true direction of my life. But Spud and I realized something else that was very important: We both had Mrs. Clara Sue Martin as our teacher, and, at last, we knew that together we had found the teacher who would stuff our empty bags with knowledge.

CHAPTER 4

The Orb Weaver

"I never have understood why people kill spiders.
I think it's just because they can."
– Spud

The first day of October started off the month with heavy rains and a horrible thunderstorm. But when gusty winds finally blew the dark clouds farther east two days later, a wonderful chill in the air let us know that the summer heat had at last turned us loose and autumn weather had officially arrived. Of course, autumn was not the only thing on our minds. Halloween was only four weeks away, which meant that Spud and I had to plan our costumes.

Spud wanted to dress up like a ghost, and I wanted to be a spider. An orb weaver, to be exact. I liked to watch those spiders make their webs in Gemma's garden in the summertime. Their webs always looked so beautiful when the dew settled on them in the early morning sunshine, and the strands of the webs looked like tiny strings of sparkling diamonds. I couldn't imagine that a creature so small – and feared by so many people – could create something so wonderful and complicated, like the work of a miniature artist. I had once found enough courage to touch an orb weaver, but she didn't much care for being touched, so she scooted farther over on her web.

Now Spud and I really had to be creative with our costumes, because the PTA had planned a big harvest festival for Halloween at school, and we could wear our costumes that night. Teachers were also selecting students from each grade to appear in a play for the program, and after the play the PTA was sponsoring a contest for the best costume. I really wanted to win the contest, and an orb weaver costume, if it was well made, might be just the right idea.

I was puzzled about Spud's costume idea. As much as he loved spiders, why didn't *he* want to go as an orb weaver? So I asked him, between bites of my peanut butter and grape jelly sandwich. "Why do you want to go dressed as a ghost? I mean, that's easy. Everybody dresses like a ghost. For Pete's sake, Spud, use your imagination. Can't you think of something more interesting for your costume?"

"Nope," he answered right away, without a moment's hesitation, after swallowing another bite of his sandwich and burping.

"Why not?" I just had to ask.

He wiped grape jelly off the corners of his mouth and onto the back of his shirt sleeve. "Well, for one thing, Grandma believes Halloween is evil. I heard her tell Mama that she doesn't even want to go outside that night. And another thing is, who's gonna help me make a fancy costume? Mama doesn't sew, and Grandma won't do it."

"Maybe Gemma can help you somehow. I can ask her," I offered.

"Never mind, Sissie, it's no use," he sighed deeply, and the tone of his voice let me know that he had made up his mind and there was no need to try to talk him out of dressing up as a ghost.

That next Saturday I started putting a lot of extra thought into my costume. I figured an orb weaver might be pretty complicated, whereas a ghost just mostly needed an old white sheet with two holes cut in it for the eyes.

I wanted to call Spud and get some suggestions from him for my spider, but if I told Mama it was about a costume for a holiday almost a month away, she would tell me to finish my homework and wait until tomorrow. Well, since my costume was for school and I had to make it at home, it sort of was homework.

"Mama, I need to call Spud about a homework assignment," I lied.

"You shouldn't be calling him so late. They've probably all gone to bed. You can ask him tomorrow." She was busy cleaning out the refrigerator and didn't even look up while she was talking to me.

"I just have one question to ask him." Good grief.

"Lord, Sissie, you always have a question." She kept wiping off shelves. The refrigerator couldn't have been that dirty, but she was scrubbing it like it was infected with deadly germs.

"Mama, it's Saturday night, and their living room lights are still on." Not only that, but I could see the light of the TV screen through the front window of the living room. No doubt Uncle Toolie was watching *Gunsmoke*, and Aunt Pearl was fussing at him, telling him to turn down the volume.

I picked up the telephone and heard the distinct sound of Aunt Pearl's voice on the four family party line. I could barely hear Marshall Dillon and Miss Kitty talking in the background. I needed to talk to Spud *now*, and, besides, all Aunt Pearl ever talked about was what particular joint was hurting or what person at the church had found a way to offend her in some way.

Offending her wasn't particularly difficult to do anyway. I decided that she would probably never get off the phone, because most likely she was sitting back in her favorite arm chair, sipping a cup of instant coffee between complaints. I decided to take a chance. Aunt Pearl's voice always had a preachy tone, so I couldn't help but hear every syllable clearly.

"...And I told your father that it's time for you to take some responsibility for the boy. And besides, you need to spend time with your family down here. You can't continue to hide out in Atlanta with all your high-fallutin' friends, acting like nothing ever happened." Before the other person who was receiving Aunt

Pearl's tongue-lashing could respond, I jumped in.

"Uh, 'scuse me, Aunt Pearl, is that you?" Of course, I knew it was.

"Who is this? *Sissie*? Have you been listening in on our conversation?" she asked, continuing to talk in her preachy tone of voice, while angrily stressing every syllable.

"No, ma'am, I just need to…" I tried to respond politely.

"You are interrupting two adults having a private conversation. I know your mama taught you better than that."

"Yes, ma'am, she did. But I have an important homework question for Spud."

Aunt Pearl apparently thought she was the queen bee.

"Well, Spud can't talk to you right now," she snipped back at me. "When I get finished talking, *if he hasn't already gone to bed*, I'll tell him you called. Now hang up *this instant!*" As I hung up the receiver, I couldn't help forming another question in my mind: How in the world could Aunt Pearl be Gemma's sister?

By the time the lights finally went off in Uncle Toolie's house, Spud had never returned my call.

CHAPTER 5

The Adventure Begins

*"If you go back to school too soon after having a sore throat,
you might die of a relapse."*
— Aunt Pearl

The following Monday I woke up with a terrible sore throat. It had started hurting the night before, and I had foolishly hoped it would get better. Instead, it throbbed every time I swallowed and hurt like crazy between swallows.

I must have looked terrible, because Mama took one look at me and said, "You can't go to school today, Sissie. You'd better stay with Gemma and Grandpa while I'm at work." She felt of my forehead with the cool palm of her hand.

"Oh, no, Mama, I *can't* be out of school. I'll lose my apple."

"Well, I'm sorry, but you have a fever and a sore throat. You need to stay *home*." She turned and walked out of my bedroom, and I knew there was no need for me to argue with her.

I couldn't believe I was going to miss school. I had been hoping to get a perfect attendance certificate at the end of the school year, and now my apple would fall off the huge paper apple tree on Mrs. Martin's bulletin board.

Spud's apple had already fallen. In late September he had been helping Uncle Toolie rake pine straw, and he forgot that he had laid the rake on the ground. He put a handful of straw in the wheelbarrow, turned around, and stepped on the upturned teeth of the rake. His mistake produced immediate consequences.

I wondered why he didn't come to Gemma's to play Parcheesi that afternoon like he had promised, so I went to his house to check on him. He was sitting on a pillow on the couch, watching one of Aunt Pearl's afternoon soap operas with her, so I knew something serious must have happened.

"What happened to you, Spud?" I asked, talking over the noisy actors who appeared to be in the middle of another daily crisis.

"I accidentally stepped on my Grandpa's rake," he answered with a sheepish look on his face.

"What happened then? Did you hurt your foot?" It never once occurred to me that what had happened to Spud might not have been any of my business.

"Well…" Spud actually turned several shades from light pink to deep rosy red as he thought for a moment. "No, the handle flew up and conked me on the head. And it also hit me you-know-where." I was able to fill in the blanks.

So the next day at school Spud's red paper apple had slipped right off the tree to the bottom half of the bulletin board where it landed softly in a pile of orange and gold construction paper leaves.

* * * *

My sore throat got worse during the day, and Biddie became sick as well. Grandpa had to go pick her up at the high school. Mama came home from work early and marched us right into Dr. Frazier's office, where we were both given bad news. We had strep throat, and we would have to have penicillin shots. How I longed for a day in the future when maybe we might be able to just take a pill and feel better. Instead, Biddie and I became human pincushions, and we both claimed to have the sorest behind.

Mama kept us out of school all week, just to be sure we didn't have a relapse. I hated it when Mama took Aunt Pearl's medical advice. Biddie was okay with being absent from school, though, because she had just finished reading *Little Women* and she didn't want to end up dying like Beth March. So she stayed at home, covered up with a quilt, reading one book after another.

By the end of the week, I was feeling good and bored, so I asked Grandpa if I could go with him when he went turtle hunting. The weather was warm for October, Mama was at work, and Gemma and Aunt Pearl had gone into town. So Grandpa and I seized the opportunity to escape without asking anybody's permission.

Grandpa picked up his cedar walking stick by the back door, and we headed out to his car before anyone could see us. His old Mercury had once been gray; but now the paint was dead, giving the entire car a whitish powdery look. He tried to crank the car with one foot on the clutch and the other one on the gas. Finally, after four or five tries, the engine made a grumbling noise and started up. Grandpa shifted the car to first gear, sort of, and it made its usual grinding sound as we lurched forward.

As the car slowly ground past the front fence of Uncle Toolie's farm, something caught Grandpa's attention that made him put on the brakes and roll his window down to get a better look. "Would you look at *that!*" Across the barbed wire fence hung a long, still, dark grey ribbon: A dead grey rat snake with a bloody, mangled head.

"Why did they do that, Grandpa? That's just a poor old rat snake. He isn't even dangerous. That's mean, Grandpa. *Just plain mean!*" I couldn't believe my eyes.

"Well, Sissie, we don't really need any more rain, so I reckon they did that just to warn other snakes to keep away or they'll suffer the same fate. Maybe they was just tryin' to teach that old snake a lesson."

"What kind of lesson, Grandpa? That he shouldn't have been born a snake?" The sight of that pitiful snake made me clinch my teeth with anger.

"I reckon so, Sissie. You know, snakes are like people. They can't help it they was born snakes, any more than we can help the way *we* were born. So I'm not exactly sure what lesson that poor old snake learned. Unless it was that he should've moved faster or crawled someplace else."

"Maybe he had just enough time before he died to warn the other snakes to stay away from Uncle Toolie and Aunt Pearl," I said, with hope in my voice, even though I knew perfectly well he didn't.

"Your Aunt Pearl, most likely." He eased the old Mercury down to the crossroads before the car ever made it to second gear.

I thought for a few moments, and then I looked over at Grandpa, who was keeping an eye on the road while concentrating on trying to shift the stubborn gears. "She's mean, ain't she, Grandpa?"

"Who?"

"Aunt Pearl."

"Well, Pearl's had a hard life, Sissie," he answered in a matter of fact way.

"What d'you mean?" I couldn't imagine Aunt Pearl ever having a hard life. Uncle Toolie and Rose always looked after her, and Spud tried to stay out of her way as much as possible.

Grandpa was quiet for a moment as he pulled up to the stop sign and looked both ways. He crossed the road, and the car picked up a little speed, grinding and complaining all the way. "Someday I'll tell you about it. When you're a little older. You need to be older to understand."

"But, Grandpa, I'm…" I protested, but he cut me off in mid-sentence.

"This hadn't got a thing to do with bein' smart for your age," Grandpa answered firmly. "It has to do with bein' a grown-up and knowin' about heartache. You have to trust me, Sissie. I'll tell you all 'bout it one day, I promise. Now let's head to the mountain. I might even find me a fat turtle today."

I was quiet for the rest of the way, thinking about what Grandpa had just said and thinking about that poor murdered rat snake. I was glad to be heading to the home place in the mountain with Grandpa, but I was secretly hoping that all the turtles would lie low, safely hidden out of sight.

CHAPTER 6

Turtle Soup

"Even an old turtle knows there's just some times when
he has to stick his neck out."
— *Grandpa*

Grandpa knew the mountain property like it was all mapped out on the back of his leathery, sun-spotted hands. He had walked the creek banks for years, stepping over mossy rocks and looking for signs of turtles.

Often we had heard the distant sound of grinding gears as his old gray Mercury sputtered to a stop down at the crossroads. He just never could get that old car to get in the right gear. He would pull into our driveway, blow the horn, and wait proudly for us to come outside.

"Come see what I got," he would call to us as he slowly got out of the car, leaning on his walking stick. Then he'd open the back door of the car, and there, once again, on the floorboard would be one of the biggest turtles I'd ever seen. He just had a way of finding them. Unfortunately, they were destined for turtle soup. None for me, of course -I would never eat a turtle. Why, that would be like eating one of my friends. No reptile or amphibian meat would ever cross my lips.

But on this day turtle hunting was not our only plan. I

wanted to go scout out Christmas trees, even though Christmas was almost two months away.

We drove up the old dirt road until we were almost at the mountain. Well, we called it the mountain, because it was certainly higher than the valley where we lived. And the hardwood trees, with their layers and layers of old cast off leaves on the ground beneath them, gave the woods a special smell like no place else I had ever been. It smelled like Earth.

We turned down the road toward the old home place. At least, it once was a road. It was mostly two long rocky ruts now. But when Grandpa and Gemma had lived there years ago, Daddy had walked that road to and from his school bus every day.

Sheltering tree limbs brushed the top of the car and the windows as we drove along, their branches hanging low over the road. I rolled down my window and breathed in the smell of autumn. At one point, we reached my favorite spot, a place in the road where a stream of crystal clear water, a branch, as Grandpa called it, crossed over the road. On summer days, he usually stopped the car, and Biddie and I would hop out of the car and take off our shoes to wade in the cold, shallow water.

Every now and then we found an arrowhead among the many small stones that lined the bottom of the branch. One day in the mountain two summers before, while I was busy looking for frogs and lizards, Biddie and Grandpa were picking up little white rocks in the stream. Grandpa picked one up and gave it to Biddie. "Here you go. I'll bet this one has a lot of stories to tell. Sort of like me." It was a perfect arrowhead.

Biddie turned the arrowhead over and over on her palm, studying the markings carved in the stone by someone long ago, someone who had probably hunted in the woods around us. Then she slipped the arrowhead and a few other smooth stones into her pocket and took them home, where she gave them a place of honor on her dresser.

* * * *

I longed to get out of the car once again and wade in the branch, but today was not the day. The water was too cold, and

I was finally feeling better. I didn't want to take a chance on getting sick again.

Besides, I could just hear Aunt Pearl's preachy voice ringing in my ears: "I *know* your mama raised you better than that. You should have *known* better, Sissie Stevenson. Now you've done gone and had a *ree*-lapse."

Grandpa pulled in under a huge water oak tree and parked near what was once the site of the home place. The old house was not there anymore, and two stacked rock chimneys rose sadly out of the brambles and bushes to remind us of that fact. Dried weeds and brush broom grass were everywhere, and brown oak leaves were swirling down on the breeze. Even with the wind, though, it was a very warm, sunny day.

Grandpa reached in the trunk of the car and took out his homemade turtle hunting stick, which looked like an old broomstick with a large iron hook attached on one end. As we headed toward the creek, Grandpa warned, "Now watch where you're steppin', Sissie. It may be October, but a rattlesnake or a copperhead don't care. If a snake's hungry, it'll hunt. Be 'specially careful if you step over a log."

I paid attention to what Grandpa said. A snake hiding alongside a log might think my foot was a nice, warm little animal for his lunch. We went past holly bushes loaded with berries, and I made a note in my mind to come back with Grandpa in December to get some holly branches for Christmas.

We walked down a rocky incline that sloped gently towards the water, and as we got closer to the banks of the mountain branch, Grandpa pointed out a small tree, almost like a very tall bush, with bright red leaves and white berries. "Whatever you do, don't touch that. That's thunderwood. If you get that on you, you'll break out so bad you'll wish you just had poison ivy." I steered clear of the tree, almost afraid to breathe when I passed by it.

"Come over here, Sissie. I wanna show you somethin'." We stepped over some foot logs crossing the small, clear branch and headed up the other slope through oaks and sweet gum trees, their castoff leaves crunching under our feet.

We knew we were at the edge of Grandpa's property, because a rusty barbed wire fence marked the line through the woods. Looking ahead across the fence, two separate barbed wire fences met Grandpa's fence straight on, both running in the same direction, but with a distance of about ten feet between them.

"Grandpa, why are there two fences instead of one? That space isn't big enough for farm animals."

"That's the Devil's land," he said, shaking his head.

"The *Devil's land*. What d' you mean?"

"Cuddin' Hester owned the property next to ours. And when she died, her children, Cuddin' Tobias and Cuddin' Flo, inherited the property from their mama. In her will she had asked her lawyer to divide the property in half for her children, and the deeds for the two properties told where the land was, but the land boundaries weren't clear. And the courthouse maps didn't agree neither. Tobias and Flo argued about that property line for years. Finally, Flo's husband Ben said, 'This is *enough*. You two are squabblin' like a couple of heathens over a piece of dirt.' So Ben and Tobias put up the two fences five feet back on either side of the disputed property line and said the land in the middle belonged to the Devil. Nobody ever argued over that property line again."

The Devil's land. I wouldn't be crossing the fence and setting foot on *that* piece of land.

"Let's hunt some turtles, Sissie." We followed the branch downstream and headed toward where it fed into the creek. There we began walking along the creek bank, carefully watching the brownish sand for tracks. We saw roots and ferns, but no tracks. How I longed to look for crawfish in the chilly water, but I couldn't do that today. And Mama was going to give me the evil eye for going turtle hunting when I had been so sick.

Finally, a few tracks appeared in the sand along the bank, and Grandpa started carefully scanning the water. "Here we go, a nice big one."

The snapping turtle was in the water next to some overhanging rocks. Grandpa extended the turtle hunting stick into the water. After slipping its hook under the edge of the turtle's shell, he started pulling the snapper slowly onto the bank. The turtle was really heavy, and he did not want to be caught. But he was no match for Grandpa's hunting skills or the metal hook.

"I don't suppose you'd think about just looking at him and putting him back, would you, Grandpa?" I could always hope.

"No, Sissie. I don't ever kill any animal 'less it's for food." He caught hold of the turtle on both sides of his shell, making sure the turtle's head was turned away from him.

"I want to look at him, Grandpa." I squatted down so I could see the turtle better.

"Don't go near his head. That mouth o' his could take off your finger."

I studied the turtle for a few moments and rubbed my hands over his shell. I looked into his unsuspecting eyes. "I wonder how many things he's seen in his life. I'll bet he's got some stories to tell." I loved Grandpa, but I didn't agree with him about killing turtles.

Grandpa carefully loaded the turtle into the floorboard of his car, and the old Mercury made its usual stubborn noises as it refused to crank four times before finally giving in and starting up. Grandpa dropped me off at my house and headed next door with his prize catch. I gave him plenty of time and leeway to take care of his turtle-killing.

Not long afterward, I heard his old car crank up again. I looked out the window and saw him slowly pulling out of his driveway. *Now* what was he up to? Later when I looked out the side window across the field toward his back porch, Grandpa was sitting in his swing, probably rolling a cigarette. What a perfect time to head out, sit in the swing, and have him tell – or retell for the umpteenth time – one of my favorite stories.

Now I have to explain this fact: By trade, Grandpa was a farmer. If anyone ever asked him what he did for a living, he would say, "I'm a farmer." However, it was common knowledge that earlier in his life Grandpa had been a moonshiner as well. He never bootlegged his liquor, and he never got in trouble with the law. The location of his moonshine still was top secret, and, to be perfectly honest, he had been his own best customer.

Mama and Daddy had finally put an end to his alcohol drinking during World War II. Daddy told me all about it one day. "It was a time of rationin' and short supply on many household items, includin' sugar. We were all tired of your grandpa's love for alcohol, and we wanted to see that sugar put to good use. So your mama and me, we secretly visited his still, broke it to smithereens with a pickax, and brought the bags of sugar to our house under cover of the night. Your grandpa cussed for days, but we had plenty of sugar after that. Now don't you ever tell." Since Daddy had never told Grandpa who really broke up his still, I wasn't about to tell him either.

Grandpa had a temper and he could get all riled up, especially if politics was involved. "Those d-blank revenuers broke up my still. It was a beauty, too. I just can't figure out for the life of me how they found it. It was hid good, too. D-blank revenuers. I blame the Republican Party. They had to be involved somehow. Why can't a law-abidin' man have his liquor?" According to Daddy, Grandpa must have really pitched a fit, but at least he finally gave up moonshining.

I'd never heard Grandpa talk that way in all my life, but Daddy explained, "When your grandpa was younger, he was a colorful character, a regular *rounder*," whatever that word was supposed to mean.

I guess that probably explained why one of his favorite stories to tell was about his Grandpa John's encounter with Old Pearly Fangs. And I could listen to him tell that old story a zillion times, because if there was anything Grandpa and I loved and appreciated, it was snakes.

CHAPTER 7

Old Pearly Fangs

"The only good snake is a dead snake."
– Aunt Pearl

The old growth forest had been in our family for generations. Once it was the home to early inhabitants whose spirits still haunted the shadows. Some said the forest was mystical. Winding through the forest was a slow-moving creek, and its waters were deep enough to sustain fish – bream, crappie, and an occasional catfish. It was shallow enough to be the ideal spot for a moonshine still. To my Grandpa John, it was a perfect creek.

Along the creek bank, an outcropping of rocks here and there provided an ideal spot for a fisherman to drop his fishhook in the murky water and patiently wait for the bite of an unsuspecting fish. The rocks were warm and sunny. The fisherman, Grandpa John, could also pass the time reflecting on life, planning his future, and estimating how many pints of moonshine his still could run off before cold weather set in.

But even our perfect forest had its darker side. Snakes – copperheads, water moccasins, and rattlers. But the granddaddy of them all was Old Pearly Fangs, a timber rattler whose legend was bigger and longer than his scaly body. And the outcropping of rocks provided the perfect place for a reptile to warm up in the sun and reflect on life, plan his future, and estimate how many frogs and rodents he could catch before cold weather set in.

Now Grandpa John never made any money off his moonshine. You see, he drank it all himself. Occasionally he would offer a pint or two to a trusted friend, but mostly his moonshine business was a closely guarded secret.

"One day, John, you're gonna get caught by a revenuer or get snake bit, and I'm not sure which is worse," my Grandma Bess warned as Grandpa John headed out the backdoor. He just smiled and whistled, carrying his fishing pole, a bucket of freshly dug worms, and a pint jar of moonshine in his overalls pocket, letting the screen door close behind him.

Stories of Old Pearly Fangs had been told for years. He was an old, fat snake with an ornery disposition. Everybody wanted to kill him because, well, he was a snake. But he was fast, and he was smart. He could charm the death wish out of the meanest farmer. Some said he could even stare down the farmer's wife who had a garden hoe, poised to bring it down on his neck. She would just lay down the hoe and walk away.

No one was sure where he lived, but everybody always looked twice before stepping out their back door at night. Some said he was as big around as a grown man's arm. Some said he was bigger than a man's thigh. But his business end was what scared everyone the most – a cavernous mouth holding two pearly white fangs sharp as rose thorns.

With Grandma's usual warning still ringing in his ears, Grandpa headed for the sanctuary of his favorite fishing spot. The morning was cool for early September, and he found himself a sunny spot on the rocks and started baiting his hook and taking a few swigs of his moonshine. As he fidgeted with the squirming bait, the unmistakable sound of a shaking rattlesnake's tail began to fill the air. Where was it coming from? With a rattler, it was hard to tell, and moving around to look could result in a well-placed bite.

Grandpa slowly cut his eyes to the right. Nothing there. He looked to the left. A timber rattler. And not just any rattler – it was Old Pearly Fangs. He was so dark green that he was almost black, and he was every bit as big as legend said he was. He was coiled on the rock right beside Grandpa. Seems that Grandpa had beaten Old Pearly Fangs to his favorite sunny spot that morning, and that snake wasn't happy at all. His head was raised, ready to strike.

"Well, Old Pearly Fangs, it looks like it's gonna be me or you. And I ain't got a thing to kill you with." Now Grandpa wouldn't have killed him anyway, because he knew that snakes were on the earth long before people were.

Without thinking twice, Grandpa grabbed Old Pearly Fangs by the neck, squeezed it until the reptile's mouth opened wide, and emptied his open pint of moonshine down the snake's throat. Old Pearly Fangs flicked his forked tongue, and then he got really quiet. Grandpa carried him way downstream, laid him on some soft dry moss, and returned to the rock. He'd had a close call, but there was no reason not to keep on fishing.

He sat there on his sunny rock and dipped his baited hook into the creek water. He caught three big catfish. He wouldn't have to lie today about the one that got away. All of a sudden he felt a gentle tap on his back, and he froze on the spot. Who could it be, and how did whoever it was slip up on him? Was it a revenuer?

Slowly he turned, and he couldn't believe his eyes. Old Pearly Fangs! And in his mouth he held the fattest, sassiest bullfrog that Grandpa had ever seen. He'd come back for more moonshine, and he was prepared to pay for it.

Now Grandpa John used to tell some stories that we just couldn't believe, but he always swore that this story was true. In fact, he even started carrying two jars of moonshine in his overall pockets when he went fishing.

CHAPTER 8

A Haunted Night

"Don't sweep any of your hair outside the door of your house,
because if you do, a witch might get it and put a spell on you."
– An Old Stevenson Family Superstition

October inched along slowly, and day by day the valley changed clothes from its summer green to its autumn red, yellow, and gold. Colorful leaves drifted down like someone was shaking them out of a gigantic flour sifter overhead. Dried seed pods, flat and brown, lay scattered all around the ground underneath the mimosa on the lawn, and the tree had spread its empty branches out as if it were giving a final blessing over the dead leaves that had fallen together on the lawn.

The chinaberry tree added its opinion to the fall season by dropping its leaves and allowing its hard, shiny green berries, the ones high enough up that Spud and I hadn't been able to reach them, to start turning a soft, dull, wrinkly poisonous yellow-white. Meanwhile, in Grandpa's garden, flocks of noisy crows visited daily to see if they could pick at any remaining dried ears of corn or sunflower seeds.

Spud and I had been counting the days until Halloween. Instead of marking off the days with a check or a gigantic X, I drew a pumpkin or a leaf on each day's square after that day had passed.

In the afternoons, when school was over and we had stepped off the bus onto our dirt road, we tried to stay outside as long as possible. But the days were getting shorter and shorter, making night fall sooner. Once the sun went down, the evenings were too cold to sit out on the porch with Grandpa. So we moved inside to our favorite place: Gemma's warm kitchen.

Two nights before Halloween Uncle Toolie and Grandpa sat at the kitchen table, playing a game of Parcheesi. Uncle Toolie was dressed in his usual flannel shirt and overalls, just like Grandpa. He was taller and thinner than Grandpa, and that was saying a lot, because Grandpa was thin and over six feet tall. Uncle Toolie seemed really happy, and he smiled as he and Grandpa played their game and drank cup after cup of strong black coffee.

Come to think of it, Uncle Toolie didn't smile that much when he was around Aunt Pearl. He seemed quieter somehow, too, as if he didn't have too much to say. Who could blame him? Even if he had something to say, he could barely get in a word edgewise between Aunt Pearl's complaints and her preachy prattle.

But he came to life when he and Grandpa were sitting around Gemma's kitchen table, swapping stories, with Uncle Toolie telling fish stories and Grandpa telling stories about turtles, each of them trying to outdo the other. So Uncle Toolie rolled the dice and told his latest fish story, while Grandpa occasionally interrupted him to get more details. Then Grandpa started telling him about his turtle hunting adventures.

Spud and I were sitting at the table, watching Uncle Toolie and Grandpa play their game. Gemma was puttering around the kitchen, putting dishes away in the cabinet.

"Didn't you go turtle hunting earlier this month, Woody?" Uncle Toolie asked as he moved his blue Parcheesi piece along the board. Suddenly I had a horrible sinking feeling in the pit of my stomach. What if Grandpa slipped and mentioned that I had gone turtle hunting with him?

"Yeah, I did. I caught one of the biggest ones I have *ever* seen." Grandpa answered, as he watched Uncle Toolie make his move on the game board before taking his turn to roll the dice.

Gemma stopped in her tracks, holding a blue coffee cup in

midair. "You did *not* catch a turtle this month. If you did, why didn't I know about it?"

"Uh, well, he got away. He escaped from my car," Grandpa answered, kind of sheepishly, scratching the back of his head and making his wispy white hair look like it had just developed a cowlick.

"Got away? Are you crazy, Woodrow?" A look of uncertainty was on her face. "How could a turtle escape from the floorboard of your car?"

"Well, I drove over in the Valley and pulled over at Mount Olive Creek. I got out to look at a big dead snake by the road, and for some reason I left the door of the car open. I guess the turtle must've escaped. 'Cause when I got back in the car, he was *gone*."

Uncle Toolie and Gemma looked at each other in disbelief. Then a grin suddenly started up on both of their faces.

"My Lord, that's one of the best tall tales you've ever told us, Woody. The big one that got away. I guess you're lucky that turtle couldn't drive. He might've taken off in your Mercury and left you standin' by the road," Uncle Toolie snorted, laughing and slapping the table. "I wonder how well he could've shifted the gears. Maybe almost as good as you, I bet." Uncle Toolie kept on laughing.

Grandpa looked over at Spud and me and winked. Maybe what I had said about that turtle had caused Grandpa to let him go free after all.

Mama and Gemma never did find out about the day that I went turtle hunting with Grandpa. First of all, Grandpa and I didn't tell them. And Biddie was so happy to be left alone for a little peace and quiet that she simply didn't happen to mention that I had been gone all day.

* * * *

At last, the day before the school's harvest festival arrived, with the following day being Halloween, which happened to fall on a Saturday. All day Friday in our classroom we had a terrible time keeping our minds on our lessons. The only thing we could think about was the festival the next day. After lunch Mrs. Martin allowed us to start setting up our booth, which was The Fish Pond.

Throughout the month of October our class had been collecting small prizes to give as "fish," and we sorted the items in boxes lined up in our classroom, which would be hidden behind a blue curtain over our classroom door. For ten cents, each fisher could drop his cane pole, with a clothes line string and clothes pin attached, over the curtain, and someone in the classroom would help Mrs. Martin attach one of the prizes to the clothespin. Mrs. Martin asked Spud to be that someone.

The fourth grade was sponsoring a ring toss and an apple bobbing. Somehow I had no desire to stick my face in the same metal tub of water where other people had been dunking their faces and bobbing, too. The upper grades had created a complicated haunted house connecting all of their classrooms by a special passageway in the hall. They had hung up bed sheets that had been dyed black to make the passage even spookier.

On Saturday night, right on cue, a harvest moon appeared in the chilly sky, and we made our way to the school. Spud rode with Rose, Gemma, and Grandpa. My family followed in our car.

Rose had offered to drive Gemma and Grandpa to the school. "I'll drive you all in my car since Mama and Daddy aren't going. Y'all know they don't like crowds." Actually, we all knew that Aunt Pearl just didn't want to go out on Halloween night. I couldn't imagine why she was worried, because no self-respecting wicked witch or goblin would want to mess with Aunt Pearl. Heck, she acted like one of their own.

Gemma and Rose had put together a pirate costume for Spud. I guess that even though Aunt Pearl thought witches, ghosts, and goblins were evil, she was comfortable with Spud dressing up as someone who robbed and murdered people at sea. Dressed in old cut off pants and a tee shirt, he was wearing a red scarf on his head, and one of Gemma's old screw-on hoop earrings hung from his ear. Rose had bought him a toy eye patch at the five and ten cent store. I liked him better as a pirate than as a ghost running around in an old bed sheet with holes in it.

Even though I really had my heart set on going to the festival dressed as an orb weaver, Mrs. Martin had changed my mind. Earlier in October she had pulled me aside one day as the class lined up and headed outside for recess.

"Sissie, the teachers are planning a special Halloween program, and we need someone to play the wicked witch. Someone who won't be afraid to get up on stage, recite some lines, and sing a song. Would you like to do that?"

Would I like to do that? My heart jumped up and down into my throat at least three times. "Yes, I would, Miz Martin. I'd *love* to do that."

"Good, then, you'll need a costume – a long black dress, a cape, and a black pointed hat."

"I'll ask Mama tonight," I promised, almost breathless.

"Let me know if I can help," she smiled, putting more candy in my bag of education, not realizing how much she had already helped me.

"Yes, ma'am." I practically floated out to the playground. I wasn't in any mood to go play silly games, because I was now a stage actress. I sat beside Spud on the rock wall under an oak tree and told him my news.

After the fifth graders, most of us sweaty and thirsty from running around playing Red Rover, filed back in from the water fountain and took our seats, Mrs. Martin asked, "We need a cauldron. Does anyone have an old black wash pot that we can borrow for the Halloween play?"

I looked around and no one said a word or raised a hand. Finally, I slowly lifted my hand. "My grandmother does," I stammered. "She used to use it to wash clothes in the back yard."

A few of the students covered their mouths with their hands to keep from giggling out loud.

Rusty Jackson blurted out, "That's funny, hasn't your grandmother ever heard of a washing machine?"

Before I could say a word, Mrs. Martin's eyes bored into Rusty. "That will do, Elmo. I don't believe I was talking to you. A witch needs a black pot, not a washing machine." And so the cauldron, otherwise known as Gemma's old black iron wash pot, made its way to school in time for rehearsals.

* * * *

At last it was time for me to make my stage appearance as a witch. Mrs. Elizabeth Williams, the school principal, stood on the stage in front of the curtain and introduced the play. We could only hear her voice, but I could imagine how she looked, because Mrs. Williams never laughed. She was always very proper, always dressed in a straight skirt, a pastel blouse, and high heels.

Finally the heavy red stage curtains opened on our production. When my big scene arrived, I stood at my cauldron and stirred its imaginary brew with my broom stick. I had a nice big mole on my nose that I hoped didn't offend Miss Flora Hickey. My black hat was perched upright on my head, and Mama had scattered dusting powder on my hair to make it look gray.

Dressed in the long black dress and star-covered cape that she and Gemma had sewn for me, I recited my lines without hesitation. I had to inform the audience that I had seen three boys trespassing outside my house in the woods. Then I burst into a song about boiling the boys alive for dinner:

> *"Double, double, toil and trouble.*
> *When my cauldron starts to bubble,*
> *I'll throw three boys into my pot*
> *As soon as the water is nice and hot.*
> *I'll stir and season and cook and brew,*
> *And then I'll have a tasty stew.*
> *I'd really rather cook some more,*
> *But I'll settle for the three outside my door."*

Mama wasn't too happy about the song I was singing. But since one of the three boys was Rusty Jackson, the words to that song were okay by me. I sang with great feeling. Of course, by the end of the play, the boys managed to escape the wicked witch, so once again Rusty got away.

We didn't even bother to tell Aunt Pearl that I was a witch in the school play. I, for one, didn't want to hear that I was going straight to hell.

CHAPTER 9

No Bones About It

"A thesaurus is not the name of an extinct dinosaur. You should use one every day to improve your vocabulary and writing skills."
— Mrs. Clara Sue Martin

The following night, the excitement of Halloween had died down, but my bagful of trick-or-treat candy lived on. Mama and Daddy were in the kitchen, where Mama was wiping down the cabinets and Daddy was drinking a cup of coffee. I was just about to reach for my bag of candy that I had left on the counter, but Mama's hand was quicker than mine.

"You don't need to eat a bunch of candy. You've already had too much tonight." If it wasn't already bad enough that Mama never would allow Biddie and me to eat much candy, I had to listen as Daddy gave me his usual speech about learning to put things away and save them for later. I called it his *squirrel speech*.

"Sissie, you need to think about tomorrow. All you think about is today. If you eat all your candy today, then tomorrow you'll wish you had it back." He continued, "Why, when I was a child durin' the Depression, I was lucky to get an apple or an orange, much less candy." I nodded politely, but all I could think about was a milk chocolate bar in my bag that was calling my name.

Mama interrupted. "Depression or no Depression, it's not good for your teeth to eat all that candy. Here, eat this instead." She handed me a shiny red apple and put my bag of candy in the cabinet, right next to a box of shell macaroni. I got the message.

"Besides," Daddy continued, stirring milk into his second cup of coffee. "Halloween is over and now it's time for us to make plans for Thanksgiving." Daddy didn't notice the sudden look that appeared on Mama's face, but I did, and it wasn't a happy or excited look.

She would be at work all day the Wednesday before, and then she would be in the kitchen half that night and most of Thanksgiving Day baking a turkey, making dressing and giblet gravy, fixing all kinds of side dishes, and when dinner was over, she would be in the kitchen trying to find a place in the refrigerator for all of the leftovers.

And last, as her final reward for all of her hard work, Mama would get to wash the dishes. Biddie and I would help, of course, but Mama would do most of the work. Daddy would be in his usual place, in his favorite chair in the living room, working hard at reading the newspaper and watching television. How could Mama be happy and excited about Thanksgiving? How could her day be any *worse*?

"Uh, and I thought we might invite The Preacher and his wife," Daddy added.

Oh, that was better. Now Mama would go into full speed cleaning the house from one end to the other, and Biddie and I would have to help. I was beginning to feel less and less thankful, and I wasn't too sure how much Thanksgiving spirit I would have left when we finally gathered around the table to eat our meal.

"Well! Why don't we just invite *everybody*?" Mama's eyes looked fiery. "If I'm gonna work myself to death, why not include your whole family?"

Somehow Mama's sarcastic tone of voice had no effect on Daddy. It went right past his ears like one of those whizzing bullets in a cowboy movie. "Hey, that's a good idea," he replied.

She gave him one of her looks, but when it came to Mama's evil eye, Daddy was like a king snake. He could take on the meanest rattlesnake without a second thought, because the venom didn't seem to hurt him one bit. He was completely immune.

* * * *

The luster of the full moon shining down over the harvest festival now had given way to dark nights and windy days as Mama went into her Thanksgiving overdrive, and she shifted gears from Halloween to Thanksgiving much like Grandpa shifted gears in his old Mercury.

As for school, the month of November never seemed to get out of first gear, with the biggest bright spot for me being Mrs. Martin. She could see through Rusty Jackson just like he was lemon gelatin, and she never looked the other way if he did something wrong. I think she even delighted in calling him Elmo. Sometimes when she called his name, she almost looked as if she had just said a dirty word.

"*Elmo*, please move your belongings to this desk." She stood beside the front seat next to the classroom door. "The next time that I ask you to move, *Elmo*, it will be out of this door and on to Mrs. Williams' office." He reluctantly left his seat and moved forward, accidentally on purpose hitting Spud in the head with his elbow as he moved past him.

"Ouch!" Spud whispered and rubbed the side of his head. I knew in my heart at that moment that Rusty Jackson might have escaped the witch in the woods, but I was going to get him someway somehow before the school year was over.

"I have my eye on you, *Elmo*, and I won't hesitate for one moment to call your father, who incidentally is a former student of mine. Do you understand?"

"Yes," he growled back at her in a disrespectful tone of voice.

Mrs. Martin gave Rusty a look that made Mama's evil eye pale in comparison. That look would have killed me instantly if she had ever turned it on me, sort of like in the story we had read about Medusa. "Yes *what?*" Mrs. Martin asked Rusty.

"Yes, *ma'am*," Rusty sputtered, looking like the words had just left a bad taste in his mouth.

"Then focus on our work and don't waste any more of our

class time by calling our attention to you and your poor behavior." Her usually gentle blue eyes seemed to have sparks of fire in them.

Ah, Rusty had finally met his match, a teacher who didn't care for one minute that his father was on the school board.

* * * *

"Sissie, you know The Preacher is coming to our house. You and Biddie straighten up this living room right now. Put the playing cards away." Mama was barking out orders like an army officer. "Here, hide 'em in the desk drawer."

"What about Daddy's Hawaiian hula dancer?" Biddie reminded her.

Mama's eyes suddenly became as big as saucers. "Oh, my Lord, I almost forgot about that thing." She quickly ran into their bedroom, grabbed the offending statue off the chest of drawers, and hid it in the closet.

Daddy watched Mama from the hallway. "How in the world would The Preacher see somethin' in our bedroom?"

Mama looked at him in disbelief. "Well, he might decide he needs to use the bathroom, and if he does, he will walk right past our bedroom door."

"Then, for heaven's sake, just close the door."

"I can't do that, Jeb. That would look like we're hiding something. Besides, if I close the door, he won't be able to see our new bedspread I just ordered from Sears."

Maybe I should explain about the hula dancer. When I was seven, Mama and Daddy took Biddie and me to a carnival in town. At one of the side shows, Daddy tried his luck at tossing small, colorful rubber balls into numbered cups. And since he managed to win some points, he got to choose a prize. He looked over all the possibilities, but his eyes lit up when he saw that Hawaiian hula dancer. Maybe the islands were calling to him, or maybe he was dreaming of ocean waves washing up on sandy beaches. I don't know, but he *had* to have that hula dancer.

Mama despised that statue. "What in the world are you gonna do with that gaudy thing?"

Daddy smiled proudly, like Mama had just paid him a real

compliment. "We can put her in the living room."

"Oh, no, we can't," Mama shot back, both hands on her hips and her feet firmly planted in the carnival sawdust.

The dancer stood almost two feet high, and her raised hands lifted in the air to her right made her look as if she were in motion. The colorful, painted-on flowers of her lei barely covered her naked breasts, and her grass skirt had frozen in time just at the moment her hips had swayed to the left. I thought she looked exotic, even if she was just made out of painted plaster of Paris.

Daddy carried that hula dancer back to our car the way someone would carry a sacred statue he had just discovered in a dusty Egyptian pyramid. Once she got to our house, she traveled from room to room before finally coming to rest on the chest of drawers in Mama and Daddy's room, not because Mama liked her there, but because it was next to the closet.

* * * *

Mama stayed up half the night cooking for twelve people. At least when she was cooking she wasn't cleaning, and Biddie and I were grateful for that. How many times can a person clean Venetian blinds and window panes and screens and live to tell about it? We had vacuumed under the sofa cushions and divided the coins we found there. We had moved the washing machine so we could mop underneath, and we had moved the refrigerator in search of elusive rolls of dust. We had cleaned in places where no one had looked for years and never would.

Meanwhile, fifteen minutes till high noon Mama lined us up and explained our duties before everyone else arrived, like a drill sergeant. She raised her right eyebrow and looked over at Daddy. "These are *your* people, so your job is to make sure everyone gets along. So if your Aunt Pearl starts ranting about some useless topic, change the subject."

"Sissie, one of your jobs is to set the table and make sure everyone has enough ice. If their tea gets low, ask them if they need more tea," she continued.

"Biddie, your job is to help me make sure all the food is on the table. Don't let me leave something in the refrigerator and forget to serve it. You know how hard it is to think when everybody's here. You need to help me in the kitchen, too."

"But, Mama, what about Sissie?" Biddie whined. "She's old enough to help in the kitchen, too."

"Yes, and she will, after dinner, but her main job is to keep an eye on Spud. Sissie, if he looks like he's headed for the bathroom, be ready to grab the toilet plunger."

"Oh, Mama, Spud's not that bad!"

"Don't 'Oh, Mama' me, Sissie. I don't have time to cook and serve food and be a plumber, too." She disappeared into the kitchen. I could hear her rummaging through the cabinets, and I figured she was looking for the bottle of aspirin.

At noon The Preacher and his wife Thelma arrived. She was as heavy as The Preacher was thin, and when she hugged me, I almost disappeared into her arms and bosom. "You are the sweetest girl. I know your Mama and Daddy are proud of you. Come 'ere, Biddie, and let me give you a hug. You, too, Spud."

She didn't come empty-hearted or empty-handed either, because The Preacher brought in a pound cake covered with thick, pink frosting.

Gemma brought her macaroni and cheese casserole and a colorful tray of her canned pears that not long before had been ripening on the pear tree in her backyard. Aunt Pearl brought squash casserole, homemade cucumber pickles, and a big dish of meringue-covered banana pudding right out of the oven. The slightly browned peaks of meringue reminded me of mountains on the maps in my geography book. I hated to admit it, but Aunt Pearl was a good cook. And nobody made banana pudding that tasted as good as hers, not even Gemma.

After The Preacher asked a short blessing, Grandpa carved the turkey and served a platter of the slices all around. For some reason, The Preacher didn't feel the need to say a long prayer. I guess he didn't want the food to get cold.

We helped ourselves to the many different types of casseroles, and I couldn't help but think that the first Thanksgiving meal probably didn't have a single thing in it that we were eating. Somehow I couldn't imagine the Pilgrims eating casseroles and banana pudding.

The table conversation was pleasant enough, except for two incidents. Aunt Pearl used the opportunity to make a comment about Spud's grades in front of everyone at the table, including The Preacher and Miss Thelma. "His grades have been fairly good this year, and I know that he can be smart if he wants to be, but I think he wastes far too much time running around outside with Sissie when he needs to be at home studying."

"More sweet potatoes, Aunt Pearl?" Daddy almost shoved the hot sweet potato casserole into her hands.

Rose spoke up quickly, like someone who had just sat on a cactus. "I disagree. I'm very pleased with Spud's grades. But I'm even more pleased by the fact that he is a good person, and that's more important to me than his grades."

Gemma spoke up as well. "Pearl, a lot of times when Spud and Sissie are at our house, they're working on homework together. I don't think Spud and Sissie are wasting time. They need to be children while they can. We were young once. Before they know it, they'll be old like us."

Grandpa cleared his throat. "Does anybody need more turkey?" He carved more slices, and when he had carved down to the turkey's breast bones, he reached in and took out the wishbone. "Who wants the pully bone?"

"I do!" Spud spoke up so fast that I hadn't even drawn in a breath to answer. Grandpa handed the wishbone to Spud.

"Here you go, Spud."

Spud turned to me. "Here, Sissie, make a wish." Spud and I each took hold of one end of the wishbone, closed our eyes, made a wish, and pulled. When the bone snapped in two, Spud held the longer end.

"Wow, you'll get your wish, Spud. What did you wish for?"

"Something. I don't wanna say. It might not come true if I tell."

"That's okay, Spud. You don't have to tell me." He really was acting peculiar. What was going on with him today? Aunt Pearl wasn't any more ornery today than she usually was.

"May I be excused from the table?" Spud suddenly asked. I

wasn't sure if he was going to use the bathroom or trying to escape Aunt Pearl.

Before Rose could answer her son, Aunt Pearl spoke up, "Yes, Spud, and remember what we told you about the toilet paper." He laid his napkin down beside his plate and silently left the room.

I excused myself and followed Spud according to Mama's directions, but Spud wasn't headed to our bathroom. He was headed instead outside to the steps of our front porch. We sat down beside each other on the top step, looking out toward the mountain.

"You know what I wished for, Sissie?"

"No, what?"

"I wished that Gemma was my grandmother."

CHAPTER 10

A Mostly Silent Night

"'Twas the night before Christmas, and all through the town
Not a creature was stirring, except the mouse in Aunt Pearl's gown."
— Sissie Stevenson (borrowing from Clement Clarke Moore)

The clock finally ticked away Thanksgiving Day and the few remaining days of November. My family was thankful all year long, not just one day of the year, but by the first day of December I think my family was mostly thankful to see the end of leftovers. Now it was time to tear off another page from the calendar and set our sights on its final page and on yet another holiday on which we could celebrate the many uneasy joys of kinfolks gathered together: *The Stevenson Family Christmas*.

On the Friday night three weeks before Christmas, Biddie and I were putting a jigsaw puzzle together on the dining room table. Mama and Daddy were sitting with us, drinking coffee, working a crossword puzzle together, and having one of their discussions.

"Jeb, I'm not sure if I can make it through another Christmas with your family. I haven't even gotten over Thanksgiving yet. I think we need to stay home and make our own family traditions."

"Honey, you know if we stay home, they'll all just come pilin' in here."

Mama suddenly got that same distant look on her face, the same expression that she was wearing for most of Thanksgiving week. Actually, it was more of a blank stare. The next sound we heard was Mama in the kitchen, rummaging through the cabinet, looking for the aspirin.

Every day at school during the next few weeks, everything seemed to be geared toward Christmas. In our classroom we cut out mimeographed Santa Claus faces and glued on cotton beards, some of which mysteriously became glued to the back of Spud's coat that was hanging on a peg in the back of the classroom. We colored paper plates to look like pieces of peppermint candy and hung them on string suspended from the ceiling around the classroom, and we even made glitter snow globes in baby food jars.

At home, Christmas music was everywhere – on the radio and on television. At night we watched every Christmas special we could find in the *TV Guide*. Almost all of them had lots of fake snow falling on the singers, and I could understand that because in Georgia we never had a white Christmas either.

The last day before our Christmas holidays began, all the fourth graders performed for the school's monthly assembly. The students, dressed to look like Christmas trees, with their costumes made of layered green crepe paper and real glass ornaments sewn right on them, stood on risers and sang song after song about Christmas. They ended with "The Twelve Days of Christmas," and by the time they had finished singing all of their numbers under the bright lights on the stage, most of them filed off the stage with sweaty green underarms.

Mrs. Martin gave each of her students our own box of twelve pencils with our names printed in gold. Joe Borders would have a hard time getting away with stealing those, but I wasn't taking any chances. Heeding Daddy's advice, I squirreled them away in my coat pocket.

I wanted to give Mrs. Martin a gift, so Gemma baked pecan brownies and put them in a Christmas tin. She also made a beautiful white apron and trimmed its pocket in tatted lace. I couldn't imagine Mrs. Martin in an apron, but after she had slowly peeled away the Christmas wrapping paper, she smiled a huge smile and hugged me. "I will wear this during the holidays when I'm cooking for my family, and I will think of you," she said. I felt good on the inside because I had done something special to make Mrs. Martin happy.

With school finally out of the way for two weeks, it was time for us to hunt a Christmas tree at the home place in the mountain. Of course, we all went along in three cars. With the four of us in our car, Daddy led the way, stopping at the crossroads before heading toward the mountain. Aunt Rose and Uncle Toolie came next in Uncle Toolie's truck, and Grandpa, Spud, and Gemma brought up the rear, grinding along after us in the old Mercury.

Mama looked in her side mirror. "Honey, you need to slow down. You know your father can't keep up."

Can't keep up? She obviously hadn't ever ridden with Grandpa. He might have moved slowly with his walking stick, but his driving was another thing. And those grinding gears might have sounded awful, but once he hit the right one, he was gone in a cloud of dust.

When we reached the home place, we walked up and down the slopes on each side of the branch, looking at trees, trying to find the perfect one. I was also trying to remember the location of the holly I had scouted out back in October. Suddenly there it was — a cedar tree just tall enough, but not too tall, for our living room.

Grandpa leaned on his walking stick. "There you go. That's a good one. Sissie, Biddie, Spud, why don't you take turns cutting down the tree?" Daddy was carrying Grandpa's axe, and he handed it over to Biddie. Slowly we worked at the stubborn trunk before the fragrant cedar finally gave in and became a Christmas tree.

Uncle Toolie and Rose had headed off in a different direction to find a tree that would please Aunt Pearl. Was that possible? Grandpa leaned on his walking stick and looked around, smiling and taking in the view of the woods he loved and knew so well.

"Your grandma wants a small one for our house, and I think I know exactly where I might find one," Grandpa said, heading back toward the branch.

Running to catch up with Grandpa I spoke without thinking. "I think so, too, Grandpa. It's near that stand of holly."

Spud coughed and cleared his throat.

"I haven't seen any holly," Daddy muttered, looking a little confused.

"Well, I'm sure there's some up here," Grandpa responded in a hurry, "and I'll bet there's a cedar tree growin' near it." Before Daddy could give that much thought, Grandpa called out. "*There's* a good one, and would you look at all that holly. It's full of berries."

Uncle Toolie called out from over near The Devil's Land. "Here's one for your grandma. She doesn't want a very big one either. This one'll do. Come help us, Spud."

Happy to be asked to do something to help his grandfather, Spud quickly made his way through the low-growing bushes, dodging fallen logs and roots on the way. "Watch for snakes, boy, this is a warm day for December," Uncle Toolie called out. "Them old snakes don't know it's Christmas."

With Uncle Toolie's truck now loaded with three cedar trees and plenty of holly to go around for everyone, we made our way back home in our little caravan to deliver the trees and begin decorating them. Spud rode back with us, and we all sang Christmas carols.

While we brought the tree into our living room and set it up in a metal stand, Mama went to the kitchen and made a big pot of hot chocolate. She put just enough powdered cocoa in the scalded milk, then added sugar and a little vanilla. The sweet fragrance drifted all through our house. Spud and Daddy brought down two cardboard boxes of decorations that had been stored in the attic.

"Spud, aren't you going to help Pearl and Rose decorate your tree?" Mama looked a little irritated, but I think she had finally come to realize that, like it or not, Spud was the son she had never had.

"No, ma'am," he answered politely. "Grandma wants to decorate it herself. She said she has definite ideas about how she wants it to look."

Apparently Aunt Pearl still hadn't realized that Spud wasn't a little kid anymore. He wasn't going to throw gobs of silver icicles on the tree or try to hang five ornaments on one branch. For Pete's sake, she was decorating a Christmas tree, not putting up wallpaper. I was ready to say something about Aunt Pearl, and it wasn't nice.

Daddy spoke up before I could. "Spud, I think I know what your grandmother's problem is." *Problem?* Shouldn't that word be plural?

"And what's that?" Spud asked. Maybe he was hoping that Daddy really had an answer to that question.

"She still remembers when you were two," Daddy laughed, as he started pulling tangled strings of Christmas tree lights out of the box.

Spud looked puzzled. "What d' you mean?"

"Well, that year she and Rose put up a small tree and decorated it, but while they were putting on the decorations, you were watching them like a hawk from your playpen."

"I remember that," Mama added, sipping her hot chocolate. "Rose laughed and laughed when she told us. She said that after they finished decorating the tree, every time you got a chance, no matter where you were in the house, you headed for the living room. You couldn't keep your hands off the ornaments and it was driving Pearl crazy."

"What happened then?" Spud asked, looking pleased. Was he glad he had driven Aunt Pearl crazy?

"Aunt Pearl finally gave up and put the Christmas tree in your playpen where you couldn't reach it. And then she fumed about her tree until after Christmas was over," Daddy laughed out loud.

At that moment, I happened to pick up an ornament that had gotten broken in the storage box, and the thin, razor sharp glass sliced a small cut in my finger, sort of like a large paper cut, that started bleeding everywhere. I had to take a break while Mama hunted up a bandage.

Biddie and Spud, who were still hanging ornaments, kept saying, "Ouch!" The cedar made a beautiful Christmas tree, but it got a little bit of revenge by reminding us all that its green branches could deliver sharp pricks, like tiny straight pins jabbing right into the ends of our fingers. Those jabs felt like they had gone all the way to the bone.

When the last ornament in the box was hung on the tree, Mama opened a small box and handed Daddy a beautiful angel to put on the top of the tree. Daddy was so tall that he didn't even need to use a ladder. Sipping our hot chocolate, we stood back ready to admire the final results of all our work. Then it happened – a true Christmas miracle: Daddy plugged in the lights and they all worked.

The Stevenson family's Christmas had officially begun. Now it was on to buying presents, which would certainly be interesting, since I had *no* money.

The next day Mama gave Biddie and me enough money to buy some small presents at the five and ten cent store. I couldn't decide what to get Mama. I almost bought her a giant bottle of aspirin, but I decided on a pink scarf and some pink pearl clip-on earbobs to match. Biddie and I put enough money together to buy Daddy a new billfold and some handkerchiefs with a fancy S embroidered on them.

When the last presents were wrapped and Biddie had curled the final strand of ribbon with a pair of scissors, we put our presents under the tree. Now all we could do was wait until early Christmas morning.

* * * *

Biddie got clothes and a pink leather diary, complete with its own key, and several books by Charles Dickens. How many did he write anyway? I thought she already had them all. She also got a record player and at least a dozen 45 rpm rock 'n roll records. Mama had made her some pink and blue checked ruffled pillows to put on her bed. I mostly got sweaters and homemade skirts, but I finally got a new watch. I had accidentally drowned my old watch when I stuck my hand into the creek while I was trying to catch some tadpoles.

To my complete surprise, I received a pinball game that operated with batteries. Somehow I had a feeling that Daddy would be playing that as much as I would. Mama remembered my love of reptiles and amphibians, so she and Daddy gave me a book that was full of colorful pictures on how to identify snakes of the United States and another one about identifying frogs, lizards, and turtles.

I gave Biddie a large pink, glittery plastic case that had a key, and inside it I put a new pink lipstick and some pink nail polish. I wrote a note and put it inside the case. "I know how much you love pink. This will be a good place to keep all of your hair curlers or to hide your chocolate from me."

Biddie's present to me was special. It was a journal, not a diary. When I opened it, she said, "I know how much you like to write, Sissie. You ought to write something interesting in there every day so you won't forget it. Use your fountain pen."

"Starting tonight," I promised. "I already know lots of stories that I can put in here." I held the journal in my hands, almost like it was a sacred book.

After we finished opening presents, it was time to head across the field to Gemma and Grandpa's house for Christmas morning breakfast. When we walked into the house, the heavenly smells of Gemma's homemade buttermilk biscuits, country ham, and red eye gravy met us at the front door.

The heat from the coal burning in the living room fireplace warmed up the entire room and sent dancing reflections on the ornaments on the cedar tree, which was standing in the corner, lit up with strings of bulbs in all different colors and covered with silver icicles. Christmas gifts wrapped in colorful wrapping and ribbons were stacked around and underneath the tree.

We made our way into the kitchen, where Gemma had set the table with all different patterns of plates and cups. Of course, The Napkin Holder was in the center, bulging with paper Christmas napkins.

In the midst of all the heavenly smells of Gemma's cooking, trouble was brewing. The phone rang a long and a short. Who would be calling on Christmas morning unless it was Aunt Pearl?

We could hear Gemma talking calmly on the phone in the living room. "I certainly understand, Pearl. You just get yourself together as soon as you can. Y'all can always open your presents later."

When Gemma walked into the kitchen, I couldn't read her expression at all. Was she sad, upset, mad? Was she going to cry or laugh out loud?

Grandpa looked at her. "Well, don't keep us in suspense. Who died?"

She gave Grandpa a playful poke in the ribs. "You're awful! Well, it's like this. Sometime during the night, Pearl was having what she thought was a bad dream, and she dreamed something was crawling on her. Turns out that somehow a mouse had got on their bed during the night and then slipped into her flannel night gown." Well, even mice have to keep warm.

Mama started making shuddering noises while Gemma continued the story. "Pearl screamed so loud Toolie woke up thinking someone was trying to kill her. Without thinking, she reached in her gown, grabbed the mouse, and threw it against the wall. It bounced off and got away, so they've all been awake most of the night. Pearl figures she made a complete fool of herself."

"Well, that ain't the first time that's happened," Grandpa added.

"What, Woodrow, having a mouse in her gown?" Gemma looked surprised.

"No, makin' a fool of herself." For that remark Grandpa earned another poke in his ribs.

After breakfast Aunt Pearl, Uncle Toolie, Rose, and Spud finally made it to Gemma and Grandpa's house. Aunt Pearl was still acting jittery, like she was afraid a mouse was going to run out from under the table at any second. She washed her hands at least four or five different times. "I just can't believe that we have three cats, and that mouse still got in my house."

Grandpa winked at me. "Now, Pearl, if you'd had a good rat snake nearby, that probably wouldn't have happened."

"*Rat snake?*" She gave Grandpa a look of disgust. Luckily she wasn't holding a hoe. "Have you lost your mind, Woodrow? They're chicken snakes. They eat chicken eggs. The only good snake is a dead snake." Exactly what I thought – Aunt Pearl was the snake killer. Hooray for the mouse that got away!

After breakfast we opened Gemma and Grandpa's gifts.

Biddie and I both received a pair of white flannel pajamas with red and blue snowflake designs on them. Biddie's pajamas were trimmed in blue, and mine were trimmed in red.

"Thank you, Gemma. Thank you, Grandpa," we both chimed in together.

Then I made the mistake of adding, "I can't wait to wear these tonight!"

"Now hold on, Sissie, remember what I've always told you," Daddy quickly reminded me. "You need to learn to put things away and save 'em for later." *Not another squirrel speech*. I didn't need flannel pajamas in June. I needed them *now*.

Spud gave me a special present, my very own thesaurus. "Now you can have your own book with your name in it and all. You can underline words you like or look up new ones for your poems." I gave Spud a big hug.

His present to me was much better than my present to him. I gave him a small brass compass and a whistle. I had written him a note, too. "Use this compass, Spud, and you can always find your way. But if you ever do get lost, just blow the whistle, and Grandpa and I will find you."

He put the whistle in his pocket, and he turned the compass over in his hand several times, looking at it. "Thank you, Sissie. This is real nice. I'll give it a special place on my chester drawers."

Laughter. It was Aunt Pearl. "Spud, you don't have chester drawers. You have a chest of drawers." Spud suddenly looked embarrassed, and his ears began to turn red. Sometimes I wondered if Aunt Pearl was secretly kin to Rusty Jackson.

The afternoon of Christmas Day all sorts of relatives started showing up at Gemma and Grandpa's house. Among the many visitors were Uncle Toolie's sister Eleanor and her husband Walter. That would have been all right except for the fact that their granddaughter Raedean came, too, which meant that her awful son Raleigh was with them as well.

Raleigh was two years younger than Spud and me, but he was every bit as big a bully as Rusty Jackson had ever dreamed of being. The only difference between the two of them was that Raleigh was even sneakier. He never spoke to his mother in a normal voice, just in a high-pitched whine that came more out of his nose than from his mouth.

After everyone had finished eating our Christmas meal, Aunt Pearl acted as if she had just noticed that there were children in the room and we were in her way. "You children go outside and play." Of course, it didn't matter to her that it was freezing cold outside. It also didn't seem to matter that we were in Gemma's kitchen, not hers.

"You children" were Raleigh, Spud, and me. Biddie didn't count because she was a teenager who had wisely hurried home to read one of the new books she had received for Christmas. That meant that Spud and I were stuck with Raleigh.

The three of us went out on the front porch and sat in the cold metal porch chairs. The smoke from the fireplace smelled inviting, and I longed to be sitting in the living room in front of the fire. Raleigh's nose was running, and he kept wiping it on his sleeve. His fingernails were too long, and they made him look even creepier than he usually looked.

For no reason at all, he looked at Spud and said, "You don't have very good sense, do you?" Spud was silent and looked as if he couldn't believe his ears.

I looked at Raleigh like he was a slimy worm, which he was. "You don't have any reason to talk to Spud like that!"

"Spud! What kind of silly name is that?" He kept on goading Spud.

I gave him the best evil eye I could muster, kind of a weaker version of Mama's. "Well, what kind of name is Raleigh? You don't look like the capital of North Carolina to me."

He couldn't stop staring at Spud. "I know something about you."

"And what's *that*?" Spud asked him.

"Your mama and daddy weren't married."

"What are you talking about?" I asked. I was ready to slap him halfway to Sunday. "Why would you say something like that?"

He looked back at Spud. "'Cause I heard my mama and daddy talkin' about you and your mama one day. They said you're *illiterate*."

What an idiot. "Well, your mama and daddy must not know what they're talking about, because Spud can read perfectly well. It's too cold to sit on this porch no matter what Aunt Pearl says. I'm going home. Come on, Spud." We left Raleigh sitting on the front porch. I glanced behind us once, and he was still sitting in the cold metal porch chair, staring at Spud and swiping his nose with his sleeve.

By the time we reached my house, I could tell that Spud was really upset. He wasn't crying or anything, but he wouldn't say a word. Even though we were both so cold our teeth were chattering, we went to the front porch steps and sat down, away from Raleigh's staring eyes.

"Are you all right?" I asked him as I bumped his shoulder softly with my shoulder. "Say something to me."

For a few moments he was silent, but he finally spoke to me. "I'm sorry, Sissie, but I don't know what to say. Except I've sorta always had a feeling about my daddy, like something wasn't right. Nobody ever talks about him."

"Dang, Spud, you don't know that what Raleigh said is the truth. That boy is an idiot."

"But what if it's true? If Mama didn't ever marry my daddy, I guess you know what that makes me. I'm a…"

"Spud, don't you dare call yourself that word. Even if what he said *is* true, you can't help how you came into this world. Nobody can. And it doesn't change a thing about what kind of person you are."

"You don't think so?"

"Of course not. And who does Raleigh Brown think he is anyway? He thinks he's so high and mighty because he lives in town and his street is paved. If I was gonna use that word you were just thinking, I would use it on Raleigh."

"Sissie, promise me that you won't tell anybody what Raleigh said, no matter what."

"That's a hard promise to make, Spud."

"Promise me, Sissie, please," he begged. "Promise me." He raised his eyebrows, and the look on his face demanded me to be honest.

"All right, Spud. I promise." I couldn't help myself – all the time I was promising him not to tell anybody, my right hand was behind my back, fingers crossed. I needed to have a serious talk with Grandpa and soon.

On Christmas night the air had turned so cold that it almost hurt to breathe it in, but I had to go somewhere quiet so that I could think. I knew just the place. I headed straight for the mimosa tree. My hands felt chilled and numb as I climbed up into the leafless tree, and I prayed that I wouldn't lose my hold on the cold limbs of the tree and slip and fall out on the ground. I managed to climb carefully and safely reached my favorite perch. There were no feathery green branches and soft pink flowers to shelter me, just the coldness of the smooth bark – but somehow that tree felt connected to my soul, almost as if an invisible cord held us together, heart to heart.

What was Raleigh saying to Spud today? Did he really know something bad about Spud? And if he did, why couldn't he have just kept it to himself? He didn't even really know us. We saw him only a time or two every year.

I made up my mind then and there that Raleigh Brown was wicked, and I did not care what he supposedly knew about Spud. A friend is a friend, no matter what. Spud was my friend, and Raleigh was not.

I looked up through the bare branches of the tree. Even in the bitter cold air, the mimosa tree stood tall and didn't give in to the weather. The black night sky was so clear that every star stood out, and I believed I could almost reach out and touch one. Which one was the star that had shone over Bethlehem? Which one was given that great honor?

From up on my perch I looked at the cedar tree sparkling beautifully in our living room window. I appreciated all the Christmas presents I had received, but at that moment I decided that, for me, Christmas was really about the cold, crisp December night air and the twinkling stars shining up in heaven, like gold paper stars tacked onto a gigantic bulletin board covered in black construction paper.

Were the stars actually singing? Were they telling me not to worry, that Jesus loved Spud, no matter whether or not his mother and father were married when he was born? I knew Jesus would certainly understand.

CHAPTER 11

The Burning of the Greens (Collards and Christmas Trees)

*"Never wash clothes on New Year's Day. If you do, you'll
wash away a family member."*
– An Old Superstition Kept Alive by Mama

I couldn't believe it was already New Year's Eve, but when
the volume went way up on the television set and Mama and
Daddy started dancing and singing along with Guy Lombardo in
the living room, I knew that the time on the kitchen wall clock
must be one minute past midnight. I was sitting with Biddie in
the dining room, where we were working on our list of New Year's
Resolutions.

Despite all the busy days at school and all the family gatherings
and all the holidays, in the new year I refused to lose sight of my
main goal: Some way, somehow, I was going to Florida. That was
the number one item on my list. Biddie's number one item was to
wear her hair like Jacqueline Kennedy. Mrs. Kennedy's husband
was running for President of the United States, and Biddie had
seen her picture in all the women's magazines.

"I wish I could be beautiful and glamorous like her. I want
my hair to be straight like hers and not have all these awful curls,"

Biddie said, running her fingers through her curly brown hair like she purely despised it. "I'm gonna try bigger curlers and use some Dippity-do." And don't let Mama give you a home permanent.

I didn't care about being beautiful and glamorous, and my hair was always curly and out of control anyway, so my second resolution was to look up ten words every day in my new thesaurus. I figured that way I could learn even more new words and write better stories and poems in Mrs. Martin's class.

Biddie resolved to keep her grades up and get into the Beta Club, not so much because she wanted to be a great student, but because she wanted to go to the state Beta Club convention in Atlanta in the tenth grade. "Everyone knows that you get to meet a lot of dreamy boys from all over Georgia. Elizabeth told me all about it. Her sister went last year." Elizabeth Long had become Biddie's best friend at high school, and they called each other all the time in the afternoon, except when Aunt Pearl was hogging our party line.

My third resolution was to find a way for Spud to learn the truth about his parents. Once I had a question in mind, there was no stopping me until I had the answer. And speaking of Spud, I resolved to find a way to make Rusty Jackson stop picking on him. I really wanted to write more resolutions, but Biddie stopped me. "Sissie, if you do the first three, you will have more than enough to keep you busy." Actually, I didn't tell Biddie about Spud's secret, just the part about Rusty Jackson picking on him.

This particular New Year's Eve was very special. At the stroke of midnight, we started not just a new year but a new decade: 1960. I didn't remember 1950 because I was a baby then, of course, but I knew I would remember this year. It was going to be so strange to write a new decade on my homework papers. Sissie Stevenson, January 2, 1960.

I was still working on my list in the dining room after breakfast on New Year's morning. Mama had already started cooking our good luck dinner of collards and black-eyed peas with hog jowl. The collards were bubbling away on the stove, and I was glad it was the dead of winter or green flies would probably have been hanging on for dear life on the backdoor screen, hoping for a chance to get into the kitchen and locate the source of that smell.

Mama had sat down at the table and was enjoying her second cup of coffee, and Biddie had started reading yet another book, when Daddy suddenly walked into the room and interrupted Mama's quiet coffee break. "Mama, I'm runnin' short on underwear. Are you gonna wash a load of clothes today?"

She looked at Daddy and her mouth dropped open. "Are you *crazy*, Jeb? It's New Year's Day. You know I can't wash anything today. It's bad luck. We'll wash away some member of the family. Somebody will *die*."

I didn't say anything, but I could think of at least one or two relatives that needed to be washed away somewhere. Could we wash a load of clothes and suggest a name or two? Besides, I figured that Mama probably loved that superstition just because it gave her a good excuse to take a real day off.

Daddy looked at me. "Sissie, haven't you finished that list yet? You've been working on it for two days."

"No, sir, I want to get it just right."

He sat down at the table. "I think I need to have a look at this list that you're making. It must be a doozy."

"Uh, well, Daddy, I can't show you my whole list, but I can show you the first two." I quickly folded down the paper so that Daddy could see only part of my sentences.

He read over them. "Hmm, go to Florida. Is that what you'd like to do?"

"Yes, sir, and I want to walk on a real beach, with real sand. I want to see the ocean and palm trees. Do you think it would ever be possible for us to go to Florida?"

Daddy rubbed his stubbly chin. "Well, it's possible. I don't know when or how. But you keep up your other resolutions and maybe this one will come true." He turned to Mama. "So I guess that's a *no* on washin' my underwear."

She gave him one of her looks. "Jeb, I am not washing away any of my family, not even so you can have clean underwear."

I looked at Daddy, a question forming in my mind. "Daddy, don't you make any New Year's resolutions?"

"Why, yes, I do, Sissie, just one big one. I resolve to never make New Year's resolutions. Besides, I have more things to do around here than I can shake a stick at." I couldn't help but notice the sidelong glance Mama gave him. She was about to make a comment when a scorchy smell started drifting into the dining room. Mama jumped up from the table.

"Oh, my goodness, I've burned my collards. That can't be a good sign." Well, no, it wasn't, because on New Year's Day collards represented our dollar bills and black-eyed peas were our coins for the year. We couldn't go burning up our money if we were going to go to Florida.

"Good news," Mama called from the kitchen. "They were just bubbling over a little on the stove eye. Our money is safe."

We had another lucky thing going for us. Aunt Pearl had insisted that it was bad luck if we didn't take down our Christmas trees before New Year's Day, and to make certain that we did just that, we had held a burning of the greens in Uncle Toolie's front pasture on New Year's Eve. It was the same pasture where that poor old rat snake had met his demise, so I wasn't sure it would be a very lucky place for a good luck bonfire.

We piled the three trees together, and Uncle Toolie made a little speech about the coming year. He ended it by saying, "I'd like to see all of our loved ones together again somehow. I hope that 1960 will be a good year for our family and that we'll all have good health and prosperity." Then he struck a match to a rolled up newspaper and set the cedar trees on fire. They went up in a great burst of hot flames, and we stood around watching as our Christmas trees became ashes and memories.

I wondered what he had meant about seeing all of our loved ones together again somehow. *Somehow?* Well, I decided to tack that question onto the list of questions I had already formed in the back of my mind. The time had not been exactly right just yet, but I was planning a heart-to-heart talk with Grandpa. I didn't care if I wasn't an adult – I wanted some answers to my questions about Spud's parents and about why Aunt Pearl could be so mean.

I returned to what I was writing and added one more item to my list. New Year's Resolution Number Four: Keep resolutions number two and three so we can all go to Florida.

CHAPTER 12

Destination Unknown

"There's only so much of her old-fashioned opinions
on life and religion I can stand."
– Mama (after being cooped up with Aunt Pearl)

After Christmas and New Years Day had come and gone and Mama had hung up the new insurance company calendar on the wall in the kitchen, I would have gladly ripped off the months of January and February and skipped straight ahead to March to welcome spring back again. But that didn't happen. Instead, January seemed to linger on forever, February was shivering somewhere off in the distance, and I couldn't remember how it felt to be hot in the summer.

The trees had no leaves on them at all, except for a few stubborn brown ones that hung on for dear life, never realizing that they were actually dead. Cold gusts of wind caught up some of the dried brown leaves on the ground and swirled them around in circles. Often it rained, and the cold, wet air chilled me straight to my bones.

Every Saturday in January I was stranded inside the house, cut off from the world of nature that I loved, while the sound of country-western steel guitars twanging from Daddy's television show reached every single corner of our house. Daddy and his country music singers were holding us all hostages.

One Saturday morning Biddie and I had braved the bitter cold to hang out the laundry. Later that afternoon, Mama called out to us, "Biddie, Sissie, would y'all please check to see if the clothes have dried?" We reluctantly gathered up the basket and headed for the clothes line in the back yard where we discovered that not only were the clothes still wet, they were frozen stiff.

The next day was cold, too, and Biddie and I were very slow about leaving our warm, snug beds to get ready for church. With any luck, one of the deacons had gone to Mount Olive early to light the gas heaters and warm the sanctuary before everybody else arrived.

But the worst days of all were the school day mornings. Catching the school bus was pure misery in the wintertime anyway, because girls were not allowed to wear jeans or pants. So all that next week, every morning, I put on two slips, a blouse, a wool skirt, a sweater, two pairs of socks, shoes, a coat, gloves, and earmuffs. But no matter how much I put on, I still had one problem: my bare legs. The icy wind whistled up my skirt, freezing my legs and thighs, and walking on the cold ground made my toes numb.

Biddie and I tried to watch for the bus from inside the house and to run out to catch it at the last minute. We just couldn't stand outside and wait. One Friday morning our school bus, loaded with half-frozen students, slowly started making its way into town to drop us off at school. Until then, the two of us huddled together on the cold green vinyl seat and tried to stay warm. "Look at that, Biddie," I said, pointing my gloved finger and tracing patterns formed by ice crystals that had frozen on the glass window beside our seat.

"Yeah, and look out there," Biddie pointed out the window. Rainwater puddles in the ditches had become miniature ice ponds. There had been a hard freeze during the night, and alongside the road, ice had spewed up from the frozen earth, leaving interesting crystal formations that looked like ice flowers.

When the bus brought us back home that afternoon, freezing rain had begun to fall. We hurried to reach the shelter of our front porch. Winter weather was holding us tight in its fist, and no relief was in sight. No relief, at least, until around midnight that cold, rainy Friday night in mid January when we heard the low whistle.

Standing over my bed, Biddie shook me by the arm, but I was already awake. "Do you hear the wind, Sissie? It sounds almost spooky." She jumped into my bed and covered up with the quilt as the low whistle became mournful gusts that howled and rattled the windows.

Strong winds were blowing in from the northwest. Rain had already been coming down most of late Friday morning as a mist, but had turned into a messy drizzle of freezing rain in the late afternoon before becoming a heavy rain that evening. There had even been a loud clap of thunder.

"It's a *sign*!" Aunt Pearl had warned Gemma. "We are surely in the end times."

Then when the wind began to whistle and howl its way through the rain, it moved across the valley and sealed our fate. We woke up on Saturday morning in a wintry wonderland, the likes of which Biddie and I had never seen.

I had to call Spud. If Aunt Pearl was on the phone, she would just have to stop talking and give him my message. Without even switching on the lights, I hurried to the phone in the living room, picked up the receiver, and started to dial Spud, but nothing happened. The phone was stone dead. I ran to look out the window again, but this time with a purpose. The telephone lines were down, touching the ground. That meant that the power was off, too. No wonder the house had felt so quiet.

Biddie came into the living room, shivering in her usual layers of flannel and chenille and wearing her pink fuzzy slippers. We were both peering out the living room window when someone started knocking on the front door loud enough to wake the dead, which was about how Daddy slept. It was Spud, standing on the front porch, bundled up in so many layers we hardly recognized him.

"Have you seen it, Sissie? It's beautiful. It's the most beautiful thing I think I've ever seen."

Biddie grabbed him by his coat collar. "Spud, get in here

before you freeze to death." Spud came in, tracking ice mixed with debris all over Mama's clean floor.

"What in the world is all the noise in here?" Daddy's scratchy, aggravated voice sounded from the doorway. Spud had awakened the dead on a Saturday morning.

"Look, Daddy, can you believe it?" I almost didn't believe it myself.

He looked out the window and did a double take. "Naw, I can't."

Mama came into the living room and looked out the window at the ice-covered paradise on the front lawn. "Oh, Lord, what are we going to do about breakfast?"

She really shouldn't have worried about breakfast. She should have worried about the whole week-end, because the power was off for three days. Lucky for us we had gas heaters or we would probably have frozen to death.

This time, it was Uncle Toolie and Aunt Pearl to the rescue. I guess. They had a gas stove, so everyone gathered at their house for meals. By the end of the second day, I overheard Mama talking to Daddy in our kitchen after we returned home from Sunday dinner.

"I appreciate everything your family has done, Jeb, I really do, but I think I've had just about a craw-full of Pearl. There's only so much of her old-fashioned opinions on life and religion I can stand."

"Yep, there's a gold crown full of stars waitin' on Toolie in heaven," Daddy added, nodding his head in agreement with his own comments.

Outside we heard the sound of a car pulling into our driveway and a horn blowing twice. "Who in the world is that in the driveway?" Mama asked, with the sound of panic rising in her voice.

Daddy peeked around the curtains. "It's The Preacher."

"Oh, Lord, I hope he doesn't come in! This house is a disaster. Go out and talk to him, Jeb," Mama gasped, the panic in her voice increasing. Daddy put on a coat and hurried outside before The Preacher had time to get out of his car.

I guess the house really was a disaster. Like the rest of us, Spud was doing his best to avoid being cooped up with Aunt Pearl, so he was spending practically every moment at our house, and everybody was beginning to go stark crazy piled practically on top of each other. We had huddled around the gas space heater in the living room, and board games were scattered everywhere. We hadn't been able to do much work around the house without lights and electricity.

A few minutes later Daddy walked into the living room, where we were all huddled around the heater trying to stay warm, and made an announcement. "The Preacher just stopped by for a minute. He says the roads are pretty clear. You girls up for an adventure?"

Mama looked at Daddy with a crazed look in her eyes. She had just walked back into the living room from an adventure of her own, having just finished unstopping the overflowing toilet, once again thanks to Spud and his fondness for lots of toilet paper.

I was ready for an adventure. "Yeah, Daddy, I am!"

Biddie chimed in. "Me, too!" I guess she needed an adventure, too, because she was tired of hearing Aunt Pearl lecture her on how she needed to work on her sewing and canning skills and how she needed to learn to use her right hand because left-handed people owed the Devil a debt.

Spud was quiet. For a moment, I think he felt like an outsider intruding on our family. When Daddy saw the look on his face, he added, "You, too, Spud, we've got plenty of room in the car, but you'll have to ask your mama first." A smile started at both corners of Spud's mouth and turned into a broad grin.

"Can Gemma and Grandpa go with us, Daddy?" I begged. "Please?"

"Well, why not. We'll drive through the yard and pick 'em up."

Mama's crazed look had gotten even wilder. "Y'all go, and I'll just stay here and straighten up this messy house. We can't all fit into one car anyway."

"Naw, Mama," Daddy nipped that idea immediately. "You get everybody ready for Destination Unknown. Y'all bundle up now. I'll go crank up the car and warm it up." Daddy wouldn't take no for an answer.

And so we all set off, jammed into our Plymouth, with only Daddy knowing what he had in mind. Carefully and slowly he steered the car down to the crossroads and headed for the mountain. I figured we must be going to the home place, but instead, he went further on up the road and headed for Dowdell's Knob, the highest point in the county.

Soon we were riding the blacktop highway across the mountain with Daddy being extra careful to avoid any icy patches on the pavement. As we turned off the main highway and onto the road leading up to the Knob, the sun was shining through icy fingers that had once been only brown branches of leafless trees.

Everywhere we looked, the forest around us seemed magical. I wouldn't have been the least bit surprised to see a unicorn appear at the edge of the woods. Even a fairy princess would have felt quite at home in the silvery wonderland of icicles.

When we reached the Knob, we all clambered out of the car and looked down on the ice-covered valley below. All down the mountainside and across the valley, houses with white frosty roofs were surrounded by trees bent in all directions by their heavy load of icicles. Daddy pointed into the distance. "Look, there's our house, and Spud's house, and Gemma and Grandpa's house."

As we stepped carefully on a short pathway to get a better look at the valley below us, we moved near an ice-covered barbecue pit made of flat rocks. Daddy reminded us, "You know, up here, this is the very place where President Franklin D. Roosevelt sometimes came to be alone and think during the war. He wouldn't recognize this place now, I bet." The president's barbecue pit, once used for cooking up presidential meals, was now standing silent, draped with icicles.

I could see why Mr. Roosevelt would have liked this place. It was high up, at least by our valley standards, and he could look out over a big world from this mountain. I guess it wasn't anything like the Rocky Mountains and the continental divide, but it was still a good place to get some things organized in his mind and find some answers to some of his questions.

"I'm freezing to death," Biddie complained, wrapping her arms around herself to get warm.

We *were* freezing, so we started back toward the car. Daddy stopped us. "Wait! Y'all come over here and look at this." He was standing under a small hardwood tree whose branches were covered in glittery crystals.

Just as we all gathered under the tree to see what Daddy had found, he reached up into the tree and shook several of the heavy branches. Icy, sparkling diamonds began to drop onto our heads and then into our upturned faces.

I looked up to see the laughter on Daddy's face, the shoulders of his jacket covered with ice crystals. Mama was brushing off pieces of ice and fussing about how Daddy was messing up her hair. Spud was dancing around, because some of the ice had managed to go down the back of his shirt collar. Biddie and I started singing "Walking in a Winter Wonderland," while Spud kept dancing.

Gemma and Grandpa knew Daddy far too well to fall into his trap, and they watched us from a safe distance, laughing at the scene that was playing out in front of them. I figured at that moment that God must have been looking down on us and thinking that we looked like a little family in a snow globe.

* * * *

School started back on Tuesday morning, and we walked into the classroom feeling like human icicles. The radiators hadn't had enough time to warm up the classrooms after three days of rest, and we were all blowing our breaths on our hands and fingers to help us warm up. When we settled in for class to begin, Mrs. Martin gave us a special assignment.

"To help us warm up," Mrs. Martin explained, "I would like for each of you to write a story about your favorite summer memory." We stapled our stories onto long sheets of hand-decorated construction paper and tacked them up on the walls of the classroom.

"This way, we can each read everyone else's story and see each other's art work as well," she added.

Lee Coleman chose blue construction paper, pasted his story in the middle of the sheet, and around the edges he glued on pictures of sea shells he had drawn on white paper. His story was entitled "My Summer Vacation in Flordia." Good Lord, Lee had been to Florida and he couldn't even spell the name of the state. How stupid was that? I bet he sure couldn't spell *peninsula* either.

I wrote about one of my favorite summer memories, and, of course, it included Grandpa and Gemma. I was kind of disappointed, though, because I would much rather have written about Destination Unknown.

CHAPTER 13

Miss Cold Germ 1960

"Sharing is a good thing, unless you're sharing your germs."
— Mrs. Clara Sue Martin

"Boys and girls, as you know, January is the month for the fifth grade to present a program for the whole school during the monthly assembly. Now I have in mind doing something that's clever and inventive. It will also benefit everyone, since it's wintertime." We all leaned forward in our desks to listen to Mrs. Martin's idea.

"Because so many people get sick this time of year, we are going to present a disease pageant, and each of you will be a contestant." Spud and I looked at each other in disbelief, but we trusted Mrs. Martin to come up with something new and different.

Mrs. Martin passed around a shoe box containing small folded pieces of paper.

"Now I want each one of you to draw a slip of paper out of this box. I have written the name of a disease on each slip, and you will represent that disease in our pageant on the last Friday of this month. You will explain how to recognize and prevent your disease."

"Will one of us win the pageant?" I could not believe that

Maudie Dinsmore had just asked that question.

"No, Maudie," Mrs. Martin patiently replied, as if that was just the most intelligent question she had ever been asked. "In fact, I believe we will all be winners. Maybe because of our pageant, we will help our audience learn how to be healthier."

I couldn't wait to get off the school bus after school, step into the cold January air, and hightail it for Gemma and Grandpa's house before my legs froze together, so I could tell them about the pageant.

That night I was lying on my bed, still thinking about the pageant. Then I looked over at the wall, and I started thinking about the road map of Florida that I had tacked up there. Outside, the wind was whistling around the corner of my house, and the temperature outside was below freezing. How cold was it in Florida? Did it ever snow there? If it did snow, what did the pink flamingos do to stay warm?

At that moment someone tapped on my open bedroom door. I looked up to see Mama smiling in at me.

"So, my daughter is going to be a disease."

"Yes, ma'am. You *will* come to the pageant, won't you, Mama?"

"Sissie, I'd love to be there, but the assembly is on a Friday, a workday." Mama had a look of sadness on her face.

"But, Mama, you *have* to come to the pageant. It's important."

"Honey, you know I have to work. I can't get off in the middle of the day to come to a play."

"It's not a play, Mama, it's a pageant. We even get to wear make-up."

"Oh, *really!*"

"Mama, please, it's very important."

"Sissie, I wish I could. You know I do. You just have to understand. Sometimes things are impossible, and this is one of those things."

That night Daddy gave me a whole roll of adding machine paper that he had found in his desk, and I carried it to school the next day to share with everyone. We worked during health class, using the roll of paper to create our pageant ribbons and listing disease facts on poster boards.

I kept thinking about one of the best parts of our pageant. Since we had to be on stage in the school auditorium, Mrs. Martin was allowing us to wear make-up for our performance. Prissie Swanson brought in a tube of her mother's lipstick and passed it around for all of us to see during afternoon recess.

"This is called *Ripe Cherry Red*," she explained to us, acting as if she sold cosmetics in the drugstore. "Isn't it a beautiful shade?"

"Ooh," all of us called out together, acting as if we had never seen a tube of lipstick in our lives.

"I'll bring it Friday morning, and we can all wear it for the pageant," Prissie promised.

I couldn't wait for Friday to arrive, but I was sad because no one in my family would see me perform in the disease pageant.

At last, Friday morning arrived, and the weather was bitter cold. I wanted to look good on stage, but I really hated the thoughts of wearing wool, because it always scratched my skin. Finally I settled on a white blouse with a pink sweater and a gray plaid skirt. I hoped ripe cherry red would match my sweater.

All of the students in our classroom had a terrible time trying to focus on school work. We simply could not concentrate. The pageant was set to begin at ten o'clock, and by half past nine, it was finally time to get ready. We closed our books and stashed them hurriedly in our desks. Then we all began to put on our ribbon banners. Taped across my chest from my left shoulder to the right side of my waist, my name sparkled in glittery letters: Miss Cold Germ 1960.

Yes, I was Miss Cold Germ. I thought I really should have been Miss Strep Throat, but Shirley Mallory had drawn that disease out of the shoe box first. Rusty had drawn a really appropriate disease. He was Mr. Twenty-Four Hour Virus.

"It's too bad that there was no slip of paper for Mr. Pain in the Butt," I whispered over to Spud.

"Or Mr. Diarrhea," he whispered back.

"But I reckon throwing up all day is good enough for him," I added.

Spud was Mr. Tetanus, and as part of his costume he wrapped his right foot in a bandage and limped. He had even painted orangey-red spots of mercurochrome on the bandage. Grandpa had suggested that idea.

"When I was your age, we lived way back in the mountain and we didn't go to the doctor if we stepped on a nail. My mama just made me pour turpentine on my foot." I didn't say anything. I just looked at Grandpa and wondered how in the world he had managed to live through being a child.

* * * *

And now the beginning of the pageant was moments away. In the classroom the excitement had grown so much that everyone was talking at the same time, creating a nervous buzz throughout the room. Spud was talking to Patsy, and I was leaning over my desk talking to Shirley, when suddenly from behind me I felt a gentle touch on my shoulder. I turned my head to see a soft, fuzzy pastel blue coat. *Mama.*

I looked up and saw that she was standing by my desk, smiling down on me. "You didn't think I was gonna make it, did you?"

"No, ma'am, but I sure was hoping you would be here somehow."

"Well, it's not every day that your daughter is Miss Cold Germ. I got off work long enough to see your play. I'll go back to work after lunch. Gemma and Grandpa are here, too. They're saving me a seat." She put her arms around me and hugged me, and I hugged her back.

"Thank you, Mama. I love you."

"I love you, too, Sissie," she said, smiling and waving a small good-bye.

We were interrupted by the sound of Mrs. Martin's voice. "Boys and girls, it's time to go to the auditorium for the program. Please line up."

"I have to go find my seat now," Mama said, and she hurriedly left the room.

We filed out of the classroom, everyone wearing a ribbon banner declaring the name of our disease and carrying our poster on which we had described our disease and its symptoms. We headed straight for the auditorium, where The Disease Pageant was about to begin. An air of excitement and germs was in the air as we peeked out at the audience from backstage.

Mrs. Martin walked out on the stage and addressed the audience. "Ladies and gentlemen, welcome to our first annual Slippery Branch Elementary School Disease Pageant. In this cold winter month, my students would like to call your attention to diseases and how they are spread. They will each explain to you how perhaps we can all prevent ourselves from getting sick."

Each of the pageant contestants had lined up back stage. Prissie Swanson, Miss Chicken Pox, did a quick make-up correction on Vickie Perkins, Miss Mumps, whose ripe cherry red lips now had a streak running astray toward her cheek.

The line backstage was orderly at first, but suddenly there was slight push from behind, and the entire line of contestants almost tumbled forward. A sudden confrontation was going on at the back of the line between Rusty Jackson and Vickie Perkins. I lost my balance and almost knocked over Miss Influenza.

"Rusty Jackson, you'd better put that hat pin away," Vickie hissed. "If you stick me with that thing, I swear I'll slap you so hard your own mama won't recognize your ugly face."

The once orderly line had now become a circle, as all the diseases gathered around to watch Miss Mumps take on Mr. Twenty-Four Hour Virus.

"Ahwoooh, I'm *telling!*" Belinda Jackson informed Rusty and Vickie, and then clamped her hand over her mouth as if she had just witnessed something juicy to report to Mrs. Martin. Nobody paid any attention to Belinda, though, because she tattled so much that sometimes she forgot and tattled on herself. And Mrs. Martin, unlike Miss Maude Jones, was not impressed by Belinda and her silly questions in class.

Suddenly, Mrs. Martin appeared backstage. "Children, what's going on back here? It's time for you to be introduced to the audience. Line up in correct order immediately. Have your information posters with you as you come out on the stage. Belinda, your whooping cough poster is upside down. Concentrate on what you're supposed to be doing and not on what everyone else is doing."

As we once again took our places in line, Rusty blurted out a low insult at Vickie, and Vickie looked around at him with fire in her eyes. "You must have me confused with your mama."

Before Rusty could respond, Mrs. Martin caught him by the collar and pulled him out of line. "Young man, if you wish to participate in this event, you will stay in line and focus on your disease. Otherwise I have lots of things you can clean in my room during recess for the next week."

He reluctantly got back into the line and sneered at Mrs. Martin's back as she went back out on the stage. The look he gave Mrs. Martin was enough to make me despise him even more.

Then Susan Porter, Miss Measles, leaned forward and whispered in my ear, "Did you hear what Rusty just said to Vickie. He called Mrs. Martin an old bench. Why would he say something like that?"

Poor Susan. Her parents never told her anything. I knew exactly what Rusty had really called Mrs. Martin. Just because I never used that word didn't mean I didn't know what it was.

Behind Susan in the line, Patsy Stephens, Miss Rubella, offered us advice. "Don't y'all worry one bit about Rusty Jackson. If that boy don't change his ways he is going straight to 7734 upside down." Oh, Lord, Patsy had stopped spelling and switched to using numbers.

Later when Mrs. Martin released us for our afternoon recess, the girls hurried down to the playground and went behind the gym, where we all freshened up our lipstick, thinking that maybe Mrs. Martin wouldn't realize that we weren't wearing the same lipstick we had smeared on before the pageant.

Somehow, despite our hard work on the morning's pageant, we had all failed to learn a major lesson about spreading diseases as we passed Ripe Cherry Red from one girl to another: Our desire to be beautiful had triumphed over common sense.

CHAPTER 14

The Great Poetry Writing Contest

"Why in the world would a girl write a poem about a snake?
I never heard of such."
– Miss Maude Jones

The month of January at last blew away and we peeled its page off our calendar. "I declare, this has been the coldest winter I have *ever* seen," Rose complained to Gemma. "I've had to wear a coat and a sweater every day."

We were huddled in Gemma's kitchen around the table, finishing Sunday dinner and trying to stay warm.

"It's not the coldest one *I've* ever seen," Aunt Pearl chimed in. "I remember back in the forties. We had a winter so cold that the chickens froze solid in the henhouse."

Grandpa looked at me and winked. In a low voice he said, "Why is she complainin'? All she had to do was pick 'em up and cook 'em. They'd already been in the freezer."

"What was that?" Aunt Pearl had heard Grandpa whispering to me.

"Oh, nothin', how 'bout passin' me some more of that blueberry pie, Pearl."

The first day of February didn't start off too kind to us either. Cold blasts of air hit us from all directions as Biddie and I ran out the front door and hurried to the school bus. And just as strangely, on the following day the weather turned so mild that we didn't even need a sweater during the afternoon.

Once the sun went down, though, the cold chill in the air reminded us that it was still winter. Surely spring couldn't be too far away, because at last the long stretch after Christmas was almost over and Valentine's Day was hovering close by on Cupid's wings.

As part of the festivities leading up to Valentine's Day, Mrs. Williams announced a school wide poetry contest. A group of teachers would choose one poem from all the entries as the winner for each grade level from the fifth through eighth grades. Then the grand prize winning poem would be judged by the editor of the local newspaper, *The Valley Voice*. Every student had to enter the contest.

Spud and I got off the school bus and headed straight for Gemma's house.

As we walked into the kitchen, a heavenly aroma wrapped us up in a warm cloud. She was taking some fresh buttermilk biscuits from the oven, and she had placed a jar of her homemade pear preserves on the kitchen table.

"Gemma, we're having a writing contest. We have to write a poem about something we love." I could barely breathe with the excitement.

Spud threw down his books in a chair by the back door and pulled out a sheet of paper and a pencil from his notebook. He sat down at the table and stared at the blank blue lines on the page.

"What in the world am I gonna write about, Sissie? I don't have a girl friend."

"Miz Martin didn't say that your poem has to be about being in love with someone. You just have to write about *something* you love."

He looked puzzled. "Well, that still doesn't help. I love a lot of things."

"Well," I grinned, "you can't write a poem about mashed potatoes and gravy. That doesn't fit Valentine's Day very well."

"Hmm, that's not a bad idea. I can write about how I love

food."

He started writing a few lines, and then he stopped and looked over at Gemma's insurance company calendar that was hanging on the wall near the sink. Every month featured a picture of a tropical scene. "Or maybe not."

I thought for a few minutes, and then I remembered that poor old rat snake that Grandpa and I had seen on Uncle Toolie's barbed wire fence. I started writing. Every now and then I would look up and see Spud hard at work. I knew he was thinking really hard, because his mouth was slightly open, and I could see his tongue pressed hard against the outside left corner of his mouth. He had a look of complete determination.

We must have worked for nearly two hours. Gemma was humming softly as she fixed chicken and dumplings, Grandpa's favorite dish. Every now and then she would stop and look over what we were writing. Sometimes the steam from the dumplings had fogged up her glasses, and she wiped them off with her apron.

After eating four biscuits covered with pear preserves, Spud put down his sticky pencil. "Finished."

"Me, too. What did you write about?"

"I wrote about the ocean."

"Shoot, why didn't I think about that? But Spud, you've never even seen the ocean."

"Yeah, but I would really love to see it. And I love pictures of it, like that one on the calendar. What did you write about, Sissie?"

"Well," I hesitated. "Promise you won't laugh."

"I promise."

"I wrote about a rat snake."

Spud burst into laughter. "A rat snake? You love a rat snake? Now that's some poem for Valentine's Day. Will he give you a hug? I guess not, since he doesn't have any arms. *Sissie's in love with Mr. No Shoulders.*"

"You promised you wouldn't laugh," I fussed.

"Yeah, but I had my fingers crossed under the table."

I tapped my pencil eraser on Spud's sheet of paper. "Your poem isn't about Valentine's Day either."

"I know, I know. Read me your poem."

"Not just yet. It has to be written in ink first," I explained. "That way it will officially be a poem."

Gemma shook her head. "You know, Sissie, I have to agree with Spud about your poem. I *do not* love rat snakes. In fact, I hate rat snakes. Someday I'll tell you why." I already knew why, because Grandpa had told me that story lots of times.

"Tell me later, Gemma. I'd really like to hear that story." I wanted to hear her version of what happened, but it was beginning to get dark, and we both had to head home.

After gathering up all our books and papers, Spud and I headed out the back door and into the cold evening air.

"Call me after while and read me your poem, Sissie."

"I will, Spud, if Aunt Pearl isn't on the phone with one of her friends."

I hurried down the path across the field and into my house. Mama and Biddie were in the kitchen cooking supper, and Daddy was sitting at the dining room table reading the newspaper.

Mama fussed, "I was getting ready to call you. Did you forget your way home? You should've been home an hour ago."

"Yeah," Biddie complained, "and it's your turn to clean up the dishes tonight."

After supper was finished and all the dishes were washed and put away, Mama and Daddy headed into the living room to watch *Maverick*. Biddie sat down at the dining room table to do her homework.

I went to my room to look for my bottle of black ink, a sheet of crisp, white paper, and my pink and gold fountain pen. Mama had bought it for me last year when we were learning proper penmanship. I loved the feel of ink flowing on paper, not scratchy pencil points.

I carried my writing supplies into the dining room and took a seat at the table with Biddie. I unscrewed the cap on the ink bottle, put the point of the pen into the ink, slowly pulled down the tiny gold lever on the side of the pen, and gently pushed it back up again. My ink pen was full, and I was ready to write.

The Rat Snake

I am the rat snake — let me live.
For I have many gifts to give.
Though I am dark and very long,
That does not mean that I am wrong.

I do things that are very nice,
Like eating rodents, such as mice.
Though I was made without arm or leg,
I do not whimper, complain, or beg.

I crawl around upon my belly,
As smooth as a ribbon of blackberry jelly
Looking for things that I might eat:
Frogs and mice — but not your feet!

Because I live upon this earth,
My God in heaven gave me worth.
I am the rat snake — let me give!
For, just like you, I want to live.

And if you see me in the grass,
Just step aside and let me pass.
For just like every one of you,
God has given me things to do.

I serve Him in my special way,
As I live out my life each day.
Remember that God created snakes,
And God just doesn't make mistakes.

You do your job and I'll do mine,
We'll get along together just fine.
I am the rat snake — let me live.
For I have many gifts to give.

We all serve the same God on high.
We all have gifts – both you and I.
Let all creatures praise our God above.
And share His greatest gift – His love.

Sissie Stevenson

"Sissie, what are you doing?" Mama was standing behind my chair, reading over my shoulder. I hadn't even heard her come into the room.

"I'm writing a poem for the poetry contest at school. Do you want to read it?" I asked, hoping she would read it and like what I had written.

"I just did. It's very good. Although I can't say I care too much for rat snakes. Besides, snakes all look the same to me. I'm going to bed. 'Night."

"'Night, Mama." As she headed off to bed, I couldn't help but think about what she had just said about snakes. It never ceased to amaze me that most people couldn't tell one kind of snake from another. Why, all anybody had to do was look at the pattern on a snake's back. Somehow I didn't think Mama would want to get that close.

* * * *

My parents never criticized a teacher in front of Biddie and me, nor did they allow us to say anything bad about a teacher in front of them. The teacher was always right, no matter what. That rule was sorely tested two days after I submitted my poem for the contest. In fact, if Miss Maude Jones and Mama had been face to face instead of on the telephone, I'm sure Miss Jones would have been the recipient of the full effects of Mama's evil eye.

Biddie and I were in our usual places in the dining room doing homework. She was drawing pictures of the inside of a human cell for her science class, and then coloring them with her colored pencils. I was hard at work on my arithmetic homework, and later Daddy was going to help me recite the states and their capitals.

The phone in the hallway rang a long and two shorts, and

Mama answered it.

"Yes, this is her mother." Then a long pause.

"*I beg your pardon*, Miss Jones." Mother's voice became louder. "Why, my daughter writes poems all the time at home. She certainly is capable of writing that poem." Another pause.

"Yes, I'm certain. I watched her write it in our dining room. And I might add, for your information, that my children don't cheat. We are Christians. And besides, they make excellent grades. They don't need to cheat."

By this time I had left my unfinished arithmetic homework on the table and headed to the hallway so I could listen to Mama. What an experience, hearing Mama tear into Miss Jones. At that point Mama resembled a mad bantam hen defending her chicks against an intruding weasel. If Mama had had feathers, they would have ruffled her up to twice her size.

"Well, I'm sure you're looking out for the best interest of all the students, but my daughter wrote her poem, and she can write about snakes if she wants to write about snakes." The conversation went further downhill from there, with Mama ending up putting the receiver back on the phone a lot more firmly than usual.

"That was Miss Jones. She accused you of copying your poem."

"Mama, you know that's not true," I insisted. "I don't ever copy off anybody."

"She said she didn't think you were capable of writing that poem. Did you copy the poem in any way, Sissie?"

"Of course not, Mama. Besides, where in the world would I find a poem about a rat snake?" I didn't say it, but I thought it: Not only was Miss Maude Jones a terrible teacher, she was an idiot.

"Do you know what she asked me? She asked, *'Why in the world would a girl write a poem about a snake? I never heard of such.'* I can't believe that woman. I'm a good mind to talk to the principal." Which she did the very next day.

The following Monday the winning poems were chosen, and my rat snake poem was chosen to represent the fifth grade. And what's more, Mr. Grady Starr, editor of *The Valley Voice*, chose my poem as the grand prize winner. When he shook my hand, he told me, "This is an unusual love poem. I can't remember ever reading a poem about loving a snake." I received ten dollars and a blue ribbon.

I almost floated off the school bus that afternoon. I ran into the house with my poem, prize money, and blue ribbon in hand. I laid them on the dining room table.

When Mama and Daddy came home from work and saw my blue ribbon, Mama proudly said, "Here now, we've got to do something special for Sissie for being an award winning poet." She took out a roll of Scotch tape from the cabinet drawer and put my poem on the front of the refrigerator, along with my blue ribbon.

That night for supper, she made a small chocolate cake with vanilla frosting to celebrate my award. Spud went home and came back with a long string of licorice and coiled it on top of the cake. Gemma and Grandpa ate with us, too. She looked really happy, but, I declare, Grandpa's eyes were almost twinkling as he smiled at me over his piece of cake.

"Sissie, I'm real proud of you. You won a prize for tellin' people to love rat snakes. I guess that old snake on the fence didn't die in vain."

But two other wonderful things had already happened to me that day. Mrs. Martin gave me a hug, and the words she spoke to me were magical. "I'm proud of you. You have the ability to be a writer someday, so keep writing. In fact, I think you are capable of doing anything you dream of doing."

The other wonderful thing was that Miss Maude Jones apologized to me. What an experience to watch her tell me she was sorry for her mistake, when I could tell from the expression on her face that apologizing was the last thing in the world she wanted to do. If fact, I didn't even know she was capable.

CHAPTER 15

A Curious Visitor

"You don't laugh at people because they're afraid of something."
— Grandpa

I understood very well why Gemma didn't like snakes. She was afraid of them. In fact, she was terrified of them. She always promised to tell me someday why she didn't like snakes, but she never did. That didn't matter, because I already knew why, thanks to Grandpa.

"At the home place, we never gave much thought to indoor plumbin', because we never had it to begin with, so we didn't miss it. If your grandma or me or your daddy needed to take a bath, we pulled out the wash tub, put it in near the fireplace, drew up several buckets of water from the well, and heated the water on the wood stove. Then the tub was ready for a nice hot bath."

"You mean you didn't even have running water?" I was amazed.

"Nope. Every bit of water we used, we had to draw it up out of our well. We did have the branch, though, so we could use that water sometimes, too, like for waterin' the garden or washin' off the car. If we wanted a watermelon to be nice and cold, we just picked one out of the garden in the mornin' and put it down in the branch all day, and by afternoon it was mighty good."

"You mean you didn't have a refrigerator either?" I couldn't imagine not being able to look in our refrigerator for a cold drink of water or an afternoon snack. And I had to have ice in my sweet tea.

"No refrigerator either. In fact, we didn't have electricity. So your daddy had to do his school lessons as soon as he got finished with his afternoon chores. And if it got dark before he finished studyin', he had to do his homework by the light of a kerosene lamp." Listening to Grandpa, I could've easily thought that Daddy had grown up in the 1800's, instead of the 1920's.

"Back then everybody we knew had an outhouse, and we weren't any different. That was just a part of everyday life. People visited their outhouse durin' the day and they kept a chamber pot under the bed to use at night."

"On the inside of the outhouse, the seat was like an enclosed wood bench with a diamond-shaped hole cut in the top. Beneath the hole was a deep pit that your Uncle Toolie had helped me dig out first before we built the outhouse over it. The worst problem we'd ever had was an occasional wasp that tried to build a nest in one of the inside corners of the outhouse roof, but nothin' worse." A wasp nest in the outhouse sounded pretty bad to me.

"I always made double sure to keep the area around the outhouse clean and free of weeds, and I made sure the path to it was clear, too, 'cause if we needed to get there in a hurry, we didn't need to trip and fall. But no matter how hard I had worked to make everything just right, something happened to your grandma one hot summer afternoon."

"What happened, Grandpa?" I knew very well what had happened, because he had already told me this story so many times.

"That afternoon your grandma was working hard in the garden, and she headed to the outhouse for some serious business. Just as she sat down on the seat and got all settled in, she suddenly looked up for some reason and discovered a huge rat snake hanging down from the rafter above her, lookin' right at her, flickin' his tongue. She screamed bloody murder, and I came runnin' with a shovel. I thought somebody was tryin' to kill her."

"What happened next, Grandpa?"

"When I got there, she was just outside the door of the outhouse, jumpin' around and screamin' at the same time, with her underpants around her ankles." I had a hard time imagining Gemma doing that, but if Grandpa said it was true, it was true.

"You know, rat snakes are good climbers, so I used the handle of my shovel to nudge that old rat snake and make him decide to come down off the rafter, and he got away so fast that I think he was a lot more scared than your grandma was." Grandpa chuckled and slapped his knee.

"I'll bet she *was* scared, Grandpa, because Gemma never has learned to tell the difference between venomous and nonvenomous snakes," I reasoned.

"I reckon even if you did know the difference, it would still kinda startle you, to sit down in an outhouse, look up, and see a snake hangin' over your head like that, especially when you're not expectin' it."

Maybe. "And then what happened?"

"When I first got to the outhouse and found out what was goin' on, I wanted to laugh so bad, but I knew better. You don't laugh at people because they're afraid of something. After that snake got away and your grandma calmed down a bit, I had to make three trips around the smokehouse to try and walk off the urge to laugh."

I thought a lot about that snake. He had found a dark place to get out of the heat. He probably was pretty curious, too, and he just wanted to check out the lady in the outhouse. After all, he got there first. So I guess Gemma had her own good reasons for not liking rat snakes, but unlike her sister Pearl, at least she didn't beat them to death with a hoe.

CHAPTER 16

The Old Clock

"A lot of folks are afraid of what they don't understand. That's why we have so many superstitions."
– Grandpa

Spring was still about a month away, and the constant cold days meant staying inside, looking out at bleak, empty trees and gray skies. Valentine's Day had come and gone, and Easter was still weeks away, so there was no big event to pull our attention away from the wintry weather. Staying inside all the time made us get antsy and bored. It became easier and easier to get on each other's nerves. Grandpa called it "cabin fever."

A warm coal fire was glowing in the living room fireplace, and Grandpa was dozing in his rocking chair. Even though it was only late afternoon, the gray skies made it seem much later. I was sitting forward on the couch, almost in a daze, staring at the fire, fidgeting with my hair, and feeling completely miserable.

An early March wind was whistling around the corner of the house, and branches of the oak trees by the house were making scratching sounds in the wind, as if they were rubbing together to stay warm. A few daffodils in Gemma's front yard had popped out early and were probably regretting their decision. As for me, I was dreading the short walk home.

"Gemma, I guess I'd better run on home. I've gotta help Biddie start supper," I spoke up with such a disgusted tone in my voice that I surprised even myself.

"Do you feel all right, Sissie?" She looked concerned.

"Yes, ma'am, I'm just tired of being cold. I think I'm 'bout ready for spring."

Her face brightened. "I know just the remedy. Since tomorrow is Saturday, would you come help Grandpa and me do some early spring cleaning?"

That woke up Grandpa in a hurry. "Huh? What?"

"But, it's cold. Are you gonna open all the windows and doors and air out your house like you usually do?" I asked.

"No, not yet. Actually, what I had in mind was cleaning out the loft." The loft, as Gemma called it, was their tiny dark attic, and the only way up there was to climb a ladder and slide through a small square hole in the hall ceiling. "There's stuff up there that's been there for at least thirty years. I don't even remember the last time we cleaned up there."

Grandpa spoke up. "If you have stuff that's been in the loft for thirty years, then you haven't needed it. Just let it stay up there."

"Don't pay any attention to him, Sissie. We can start cleaning as soon as you get here in the morning," Gemma said, and she hurried to add, "We'll eat breakfast first. Country ham and biscuits."

I swear I would have cleaned the attic all by myself twice in exchange for my grandma's buttermilk biscuits stuffed with salty ham and homemade pear preserves. "I'll be here just as soon as I can." In my mind I could already picture her rolling those biscuits in her dough tray.

She smiled at me. "Wear old clothes, because I'm sure it's mighty dirty up there."

I hastened to ask, "Can Spud help, too?"

"Of course. I'll have plenty of breakfast for him, too."

"I'll try to call him tonight and tell him what time to be here. If Aunt Pearl isn't on the phone," I added, this time with a hint of sarcasm in my voice.

"You let me do it, Sissie. I'll just interrupt her if she's on the line. I guess you'd probably never do that."

I smiled politely.

After we all were settled in bed Friday night, the wind continued to blow so hard that the cold air outside found its way under both the front and back doors of our house. Mama laid a folded towel in front of each door, but I could still feel the cold blowing in my bedroom window even though it appeared to be closed tight. There was no thunder or lightning, but I prayed anyway that there was no tornado forming somewhere. Finally I dropped off to sleep.

I heard Mama's soft voice in my room during the night. "It's okay, Sissie, go back to sleep. I'm just checking on you and Biddie to make sure you're all right."

* * * *

Saturday morning arrived too soon, and before I knew it, I had to crawl out of my warm bed to help Gemma with her early spring cleaning. "I must be crazy," I grumbled to myself. "I'm gonna miss all of my favorite Saturday morning TV shows." But I dressed as quickly and as warmly as I could anyway, because a promise was a promise.

Mama and Daddy were already sitting at the dining room table having their morning coffee and reading the newspaper. "Put on your coat, Sissie, it's very cold outside this morning."

The phone rang a long and a short ring. "I bet that's Aunt Pearl calling Gemma. I hope she doesn't get into a long conversation with her, because we've got work to do," I said, as I retied my shoe and slipped on my coat.

"Be careful out there poking around up in that old loft. There's probably spiders and scorpions lurking up there," Daddy warned me.

I didn't have any problems with the spiders, but somehow I had never been able to make friends with scorpions. The stinger on a scorpion's tail could whip up and down so fast that its unlucky victim could be stung several times before he even realized what was happening to him. Spud always said, "A scorpion is a spider's cousin with a bad temper." Gemma had been stung by one before, and so had Daddy. I suddenly had a major case of the willies, but nobody noticed because I was wearing my coat.

I tried to shake off the thought of lurking scorpions as I crossed the field and headed next door. Just as she had promised, Gemma had made a big pan of buttermilk biscuits. She had already fried the country ham and was in the process of cooking grits and red eye gravy when I came through the back door. Leaving the cold March air and walking into her kitchen, warm and fragrant from the biscuits and ham, was always like walking into a big hug.

"Mornin', Grandpa. Mornin', Gemma," I yawned, still not completely awake.

"Mornin', Sissie," they both replied at the same time. Grandpa was sitting in his place at the table, dressed in his overalls, a blue plaid flannel shirt, and laced-up leather shoes. He was more than halfway finished with his first biscuit, and I could see a fat piece of meat had been stuffed into the bread. "It's a good thing you came in when you did. I was just about to eat your piece of ham."

"Grandpa, don't you dare," I fussed.

He laughed, because we both always loved to pretend that we were arguing over our food. We argued over who was going to get the first piece of blueberry pie, who was going to get the last piece of apple pie, or who was going to get the first bowl of homemade ice cream when he took the top off the churn.

Grandpa had his usual cup, saucer, and plate before him on the table. None of Gemma's plates matched anyway, but no one ever ate out of the gold-trimmed plate with the wheat design on it, because that was Grandpa's plate. His favorite blue cup was his alone, too, even though it had two chips in the rim. The chips didn't matter to Grandpa, because he had used that cup so many times for his strong black coffee that the chips were dark and worn smooth from use.

The backdoor opened again with a blast of cold air. It was Spud, and his cheeks were red from making his way through the frigid March wind. "Mornin', everybody. Here, Gemma, Grandma sent you this jar of peach preserves. And this." He searched around in his pants' pocket and hesitantly pulled out a rabbit's foot.

"What in the world?" Grandpa asked.

"She said we might need some good luck this morning crawling around in the loft going through old things." He actually looked embarrassed to have to give us the rabbit's foot and Aunt Pearl's message.

"It's all right, Spud, I've already talked to Pearl this morning," Gemma told him, "so you can wash up in the kitchen sink and come eat breakfast." Spud laid the rabbit's foot on the chair by the back door and gave it a look like he wished it would hop on out of the house. Gemma gave Grandpa a sidelong look, and it was a telling look. I wondered what else Aunt Pearl had said to her in that morning phone call.

I sat down at the table and looked over at the rabbit's foot. I couldn't help myself. I had to speak up. "You know, I have always wondered why people consider a rabbit's foot good luck. How in the world can an animal's foot be good luck? It sure didn't bring that poor old dead rabbit any good luck, and he had four of 'em."

"Sissie, pass me that jar of peach preserves. Let's see how they taste on my biscuit and ham," Grandpa interrupted, changing the subject.

"Here you go, Grandpa." I passed the jar over to him.

"Much obliged," he said as he proceeded to wrestle with the tight lid that Aunt Pearl had used to seal the jar. When he finally succeeded in opening the stubborn jar lid, he used his bone-handled knife to scoop out some of the amber-colored preserves and smear them on top of his biscuit.

"Umm, this is good, Spud. You tell your grandma that she did a real good job on these peaches."

"Yes, sir. I will," Spud answered, taking a seat and accepting a warm ham biscuit from Gemma.

"Cooking is one of the things that your grandma does right." That was a kind thing for Grandpa to say to Spud. That way he didn't have to tell Spud all the things that Aunt Pearl did wrong.

Breakfast finished, it was time to climb up into the loft and get to work. Spud and I braved the cold outside to bring in a ladder from Grandpa's shed. We set it up in the hallway underneath the square loft door. Gemma put an old scarf over her head and tied it into a knot on the back of her neck.

"You know I'm a good climber, Gemma, so I'll climb up there and open the door. Are you going to be all right climbing up this ladder?"

"I will if Spud and your grandpa hold the ladder while you help me up. Once I get up there I'm not coming down again until we're finished," she vowed, turning to Grandpa. "You hold the ladder steady now, you hear?"

"I will. Don't you worry none. I can't climb up there with you, but I'll be right here to catch you if you fall," Grandpa laughed.

"Then I'd better not fall," she answered right back.

I climbed the ladder first and lifted the door that covered the entrance into the loft. Dust filtered down on my head, and I sneezed twice before I climbed through the door and stood up on the dusty floor. I called down, "Put on a coat. It's mighty cold up here. And we're gonna need some flashlights."

A few minutes later Gemma's head appeared in the entry way as she made her way up the ladder with two flashlights in her coat pockets. Then followed Spud, who was holding on to a broom and a dust pan as he climbed. I held out my hand and helped Gemma up into the cold, dark space.

"Here, Sissie, you take this flashlight." She turned hers on and slowly moved its beams across dusty old trunks, cardboard boxes with their lids tucked and folded together, a tiny wooden baby crib, and an old oval dresser mirror with dark spots on it where the silver on the back had peeled off. Scattered among the boxes and trunks were lots of household items that had simply been carried up in into the dusty space and set down somewhere to get them out of the way, discarded and forgotten.

A heavy layer of dust was everywhere, and so were the dirt dauber nests. The tireless little wasps had found ways to get into the loft and build their long mud houses in little cylinders they had attached to everything – the walls, the boxes, the trunks, everywhere. How many generations of dirt daubers had been hatched in this little room? How many insects had they eaten in thirty years?

Gemma opened a trunk and turned her flashlight's beam

so she could have a good look inside. Quilts were neatly stacked in the trunk. "I really should bring these down. Your great-grandmother made these."

As she lifted the quilts carefully from the trunk, my light revealed a wooden box of letters, neatly stacked and tied with faded ribbons. The letters had been tucked safely away in the bottom of the trunk. "Love letters. Someday when Grandpa and I are dead and gone, you children can read them. Grandpa was pretty romantic in his day, believe it or not. And so was I." Somehow I had never thought much about Grandpa and Gemma being young and in love. They were always my grandparents. "Here, take this when we go back down," she said, handing me the wooden box.

I turned my flashlight toward the entry door and walked over to put the box where I wouldn't forget it. Light was filtering up from the hallway, and Grandpa was still standing there faithfully, one hand on the ladder and his other hand on his walking stick.

"Found any monsters up there yet?" he called up.

"Nope, Grandpa, just some of your old love letters."

"Oh, mercy, child, don't you be readin' any of those letters. There's no tellin' what I wrote in those things," he called back, laughing.

I turned around to help Gemma, but she had started trying to sweep. Spud had pulled his shirt over his face to keep from breathing the dust that was swirling up from her broom, and he was holding her flashlight so that she could see where to sweep. My foot bumped into something, and I turned my flashlight to see what it was. "What's this, Gemma?"

She looked in the direction of my beam of light. "Oh, that's an old clock that belonged to someone in your grandpa's family. Some aunt, I think."

"Can I bring it down and have a look at it?"

"Of course, but it's covered in dirt dauber nests. Looks like the pendulum's fallen out of it, too. Isn't that it lying on the floor beside it?"

"Yes, ma'am." I moved the clock and its pendulum over beside the box of love letters. Spud started sneezing, and Gemma started a fit of coughing. She looked around at all the dust and dirt dauber nests. "I think we need to go back downstairs. I should've begun this project twenty years ago. It's much bigger than we are. Let's go."

We began our climb down from the loft. It was harder coming down because we were bringing more things with us than we had taken up. Gemma handed down the quilts to Spud on the ladder. We passed the other items down, too, and Grandpa set them on the floor in the hallway.

The last items to come down were the old clock and its disconnected pendulum. Coughing and sneezing, I climbed down slowly with my treasure into the hallway where Grandpa, Gemma, and Spud were waiting for me. I carried the old clock into the living room and set it on the floor where we could all get a better look at it.

The clock was barely recognizable. Its face was covered in dust and dried dirt dauber mud, but I could tell that it had once been a clock face set in beautiful carved wood. I figured that someone had probably set it on a mantel or a dresser. I laid the pendulum down beside the clock.

Gemma looked over at Grandpa. "Where did we get that clock? Whose was it? I've forgotten."

"You remember. It was my grandmother's clock. It was in her bedroom, the room where she died. But it stopped workin'. When we emptied her house to sell it, I didn't have the heart to throw her clock away, so I stuck it up in the loft. It's been up there for more than thirty years, I reckon."

At that very moment we heard a sound so strange that we looked at each other in disbelief. The old clock had started chiming, and it didn't chime just once or twice. It chimed ten times and then stopped just as suddenly as it had started. Ten strong chimes in a pattern, not just randomly, but like a regular working clock.

Nobody breathed. As the hours on the clock sounded, Spud's eyes became big and he swallowed hard. Gemma just looked at Grandpa. Finally she rubbed the back of her neck and spoke softly, "Good gracious, the hairs on the back of my neck are standing up."

"Don't anybody tell Pearl about this. Not a word," Grandpa cautioned us. "She will swear this was some kind of bad omen. A sign."

"I think I'll just put this back up in the loft," I offered. I could tell that Spud and Gemma were upset.

"There's no call for you to do that, Sissie," Grandpa disagreed. "Grandma Bess was a wonderful, sweet, godly lady, and this old clock is just that, an old clock. I should've gotten rid of this thing years ago, but I couldn't, because I always remembered seein' it in her bedroom. When I was a child, we used to sit in her bedroom in rockin' chairs in front of the fireplace, and she'd tell me stories."

"Sort of like you and me, Grandpa?"

"Just like you and me, Sissie," he answered, smiling at me. "People in the country didn't have livin' rooms much back then, so people kept rockin' chairs in their bedroom and visited with their relatives or company in front of the fireplace. The children sometimes hid under the bed so they could listen in. Sort of like you, Sissie."

"Just like me, Grandpa," I agreed.

I knew I didn't have to do it, but I carried the old clock and its pendulum up the ladder and put it exactly where I had found it. I hadn't really felt afraid when that clock started chiming. I just figured it had been up in the loft, silent and unnoticed all those years, and it had something it really wanted to say.

CHAPTER 17

Chickens and Dickens

"Never name a farm animal. You don't want to know its name
when you're eating it."
— Aunt Pearl

The entire week before Easter it felt like the sky had opened up, and rain poured down in bucketfuls. Grandpa called it a "frog strangler," and I hoped that wasn't really true. Those poor frogs! I was looking out the living room window onto the front yard, and my private mud puddle beach was ankle deep in water. "I declare, Spud, I think I'm going to start sloshing when I walk."

"Well, I keep on walking around, because I'm afraid if I sit still too long I might have mold growin' on me," Spud lamented. "This rain is awful."

"If this rain keeps up," I sighed, "there won't be an egg hunt at the church. And the Preacher said he was putting a five dollar bill in the gold egg this year."

"Well," Spud thought for a moment, "I guess that means we'll just have to pray for better weather."

By Tuesday afternoon Spud's prayers hadn't been answered yet, and our school bus driver, Mr. Tom Welch, steered our bus through torrential rains accompanied by flashes of lightning. When Biddie, Spud, and I stepped off the school bus, the rain had mercifully let up for a few minutes.

"Looks like the rain has slacked off," Mr. Tom said, before he closed the bus door behind us and pulled away down the muddy road.

Spud hurried across the puddles and mud to his house, while Biddie and I raced to our front porch. A flash of bright light and a loud boom of thunder let us know that the storm hadn't given up just yet.

Biddie was carrying her usual books – French I, Algebra I, and English literature – stacked neatly on her notebook. She had two other classes, but she always managed to finish her homework for those classes during study hall. I don't know how, because study hall was a good time for Biddie to sit with Elizabeth and pass notes every time the teacher wasn't looking.

"She never looks at us," Biddie explained. "We don't make any noise, and besides, she's always sitting at her desk reading a magazine." And speaking of magazines, Biddie was balancing a large brown paper grocery bag on top of her school books. Whatever was in the bag made the load she was carrying look extra heavy.

As soon as we got inside, Biddie headed straight into the living room and dropped her stack of books and the grocery bag onto the couch.

"What is *that*?" I asked, pointing at the bulging sack.

She turned the bag upside down and dumped out its contents for me to see. At least two dozen magazines tumbled onto the couch, and any movie star who was anybody in 1960 smiled back at us. "Elizabeth gave these to me." We both grabbed several magazines and hopped onto the couch where we began leafing through them, each pulpy page full of juicy details about the fancy life styles of the famous men and women we saw when we went to the movies. We were so busy looking and reading that we hadn't heard Mama come in the back door. Was it time for her to be home from work already? We hadn't even started supper.

Biddie and I both looked up at the same time to see Mama standing in the living room doorway, staring down at us. The look on her face said it all. It was not the evil eye or the stern look – it was *the guilt look.*

"How would you feel if Jesus came to visit and saw all these movie magazines lying around the house?" The guilt hanging in her voice was as heavy as the ripe scuppernongs on the vines in Grandpa's vineyard in the fall. We gathered up the offending magazines, put them back into the bag, and slinked out of the living room like scolded dogs.

The next afternoon when she came home from work, the magazines were all gone, the living room was neat, and supper was well underway. She smiled at us, so pleased with herself for what she had accomplished: She had made us get rid of our offensive reading material. What she didn't know was that Biddie and I had stacked them all, in chronological order I might add, in a cardboard box safely hidden in the back of Biddie's closet.

By Good Friday morning the last of the rain storms finally blew east. And later that afternoon as we drove into town for some last minute errands, the sun was finally showing its face through the remaining clouds that were scudding across the sky trying to catch up with their easterly friends.

Mama had a few more purchases to make for our Easter outfits, and I couldn't bear to think about what torture she had in mind for me. My guess was probably a little ruffled dress made out of some scratchy fabric, lace socks, and a white patent leather purse complete with white gloves.

As we got out of the car, Mama said, "I'm going into McKenna's Department Store. Daddy, you're going to the five and ten cent store. Right?" No answer. "*Right?*"

"Uh, right," he suddenly remembered.

"You're going to pick up some merchandise and put it in the trunk of the car while we're shopping. *Right?*" she hastened to add.

"Uh, right, Mama." Daddy agreed. Did Mama really think that we didn't know she was talking about Easter baskets?

She looked at me. "Come on, Sissie, we need to buy you a new dress and a pair of white gloves. Your old pair is stained."

"That's because she hasn't learned that you take your gloves off when you are rescuing lizards from mud puddles," Biddie smirked. When Mama turned her back, I crossed my eyes and gave Biddie a dirty look.

"What if your face froze that way?" Biddie warned.

"You've been listening to Aunt Pearl too much," I countered.

Biddie slowed to a stop on the sidewalk. "Uh, Mama, I don't really need anything from McKenna's, so you and Sissie go ahead." Biddie then added, "Do you mind if I go into another store? I'll meet you back here in a few minutes."

"I want to go with Biddie, Mama. You can pick out my dress and gloves for me. I don't care." Of course, I didn't care. She always picked out the dresses she liked for me anyway, and I hated gloves. If she bought the wrong sizes, maybe I wouldn't have to wear them.

"All right, but don't dawdle, because the stores close in an hour." Mama was too distracted to realize what I already knew. Biddie was on her way to the feed and seed store for her annual mission: She was going to rescue some baby chicks. And I was going with her to help.

Every year, as regular as the days of the week line up on the calendar, baby chicks arrived at the feed and seed store in time for Easter. And they arrived in dyed pastel Easter colors, their soft fuzzy down tinted with pinks, blues, and greens. First of all, why would somebody put color on a baby chicken? What was wrong with natural yellow? And then, why would somebody buy only one chick? What was that baby chick going to do all by itself on Easter Sunday? Perform tricks? Sing a song? It was a chicken, a farm animal.

Biddie was thinking further ahead than that. She was terrified that the chicks might be purchased by some doting mothers who would turn them over to the mercy of horrible, cruel children like Rusty or Raleigh, who might in turn hurt them somehow or let them starve to death.

When we entered the store, there they were at the front near the door. Downy prisoners crowded into a wire cage, making frantic peeping sounds, and colored like walking Easter eggs. Sissie placed both her hands on the top of the cage and looked down on the peeping chicks, like a mother who wanted desperately to scoop up all of her children and take them to safety.

"I can't save 'em all, Sissie, but I have enough money for one. Just not enough for two." Her eyes were filling with tears.

I reached into my jeans pocket and pulled out my new Davy Crockett billfold. I still had a half dollar left from my birthday presents. "Here, will this be enough?"

Biddie's eyes brightened. "Come on, Sissie, you pick out one and I'll pick out one." As we walked out of the store, Biddie was carrying a brown paper sack that was making peeping noises, and we left behind us a cage with two less prisoners.

We headed back to meet Mama. With any luck maybe McKenna's had sold out of gloves and Easter dresses. We arrived at the store just as Mama was coming out of the door with a large paper bag filled with purchases. Her face was beaming, so I knew she had completed her mission successfully. "I found you a pair, Sissie. They're white stretch lace. And the dress is perfect. I even found you a white patent leather purse."

At the sound of her voice, the baby chicks seemed to pick up a signal that it was time to start peeping really loud so they would be sure to get Mama's attention, which they did. "Biddie, what in the world do you have in that bag? Not baby chicks, I hope."

"Well, Mama, I had to. I just had to." she answered.

"We both just had to," I added.

"You just had to *what*?" Mama asked, knowing full well what Biddie was going to say.

"I had to rescue them," Biddie explained hurriedly.

"Biddie, you can't save the baby chicks of the world. What do you plan on doing with them?" Mama looked aggravated, but not surprised.

"I'm gonna feed 'em and take care of 'em," Biddie defended herself.

"Biddie, they're not puppies. They'd be a lot better off at Gemma's house with her chickens."

"No, not yet, Mama, they're too little. And the other chickens won't like 'em. They're pink and blue." She opened the bag for Mama to see the babies.

Mama rolled her eyes. "Oh, Lord, here we go again."

I looked in at the innocent chicks, which were little eating machines that would turn into bigger eating machines leaving little messy droppings everywhere so that everyone walking in the yard would have to watch where they stepped. "Biddie is right, Mama. Do we have a place they can stay in the house for just a little while?"

"Oh, all right, for just a few days. And then they're off to Gemma's chicken yard." The chicks gratefully peeped all the way home in the car.

Mama brought in a cardboard box. "They can stay in here today and tonight only. Make sure they stay in this box. You can get some feed from Gemma. Come on, hurry, we're eating supper with your grandparents." I took the box and set it on the living room floor, and Biddie lovingly set the two little peeping wonders inside.

"Here you go, Pip," she said to the pink chick. "And you, too, Copper." She looked up at me, smiling. "I hope you don't mind. I named yours, too." Baby chickens and Charles Dickens – what a combination.

The Good Friday sun was beginning to set as we walked across the field to Gemma and Grandpa's house. After all the rainy days, today had really felt like Easter. Even the dogwood trees had timed the blooming of their cross-shaped white blossoms to remind us of the importance of Easter Sunday.

After supper, everyone sat around the table talking while the adults finished their coffee and pound cake. Biddie spoke up, "We need to go check on my chicks. I know they're hungry. Come see 'em, Spud." We all headed home, with Biddie hurrying ahead of us. When we walked in the back door we heard a cry of surprise coming from the living room, so we hurried in to see what was wrong.

"Biddie, what's the matter?" Mama asked with an alarmed look.

"They're gone. They're not here. What could have happened to them?"

Spud and I looked into the cardboard box. I couldn't say that they had vanished without a trace, because they had left droppings all over the bottom of the box and a few on the living room floor, but Pip and Copper were definitely gone.

"Oh, my Lord, those chickens are in my house on the loose," Mama cried with a frantic voice. "*Everybody start looking!*"

The five of us started a chicken scavenger hunt. We looked in every room, under the beds, under the couch, in every possible corner, but there were no baby chickens to be found.

We all assembled back in the living room. Mama collapsed on the couch, and Daddy plopped down beside her, scratching his head. "I can't figure it out, Mama," he said with a puzzled look. "Nobody would have broken into our house and stole two chickens. Where'd they go?"

"Well, they couldn't have vanished into thin air," Mama fussed. The exact second that Mama finished her sentence, we heard a soft peep, so soft that we couldn't tell where it was coming from. Then two more faint peeps.

"Where is it?" I asked.

Spud looked at Biddie and me. "Shh! Everybody be quiet." For a few moments, we heard only silence. Then a faint peeping sound started again. "It's coming from over there!" Spud pointed to our old upright piano in the corner of the living room.

Mama sprang into action. "Jeb, go get a flashlight. Quick!" She started ringing her hands. "How in the world will we be able to get to them? That piano weighs a ton."

Daddy shined the light behind the piano, and there they were, a pink and a blue chick, sitting on a wooden brace in the back of the piano. Despite being inside the house, the chicks had somehow known it was sundown, and they had gone to roost for the night.

Biddie spoke up. "I'm sorry, Mama, I thought they would stay in the box, but I guess they escaped."

Spud looked at Biddie. "I believe those chicks had bigger and better places in mind than that box."

"That may be true," Mama said, "but they can't stay inside. They're going on the front porch. We'll fix the box so they can't escape again."

"Mama, no, let 'em stay inside just tonight, please," Biddie begged.

It took all five of us tugging and pushing on the old piano to move it out from the wall, and Biddie collected her chicks from their roost and put them gently into the box. Spud went home and found an old piece of screen wire in Uncle Toolie's workshop and put it over the top of the box to prevent future escapes. At least that much of our problem was settled. But even though the wire kept their little downy bodies from escaping from their cardboard cage, it didn't keep the chicks from peeping all night long so loudly that their little voices seemed to fill every corner of our house.

By the next morning, everybody, including Biddie, was ready to put the chicks outside. Daddy hammered together a little wooden and wire pen in the backyard to put them in. Well, actually, he repaired the same pen Biddie had used the past five years for her rescued chicks. Now it was time to think about Easter Sunday.

* * * *

Sunrise service would start well before the sun actually came up, so that we could sing a few Easter hymns and The Preacher could read some Bible verses and give a short sermon about the Resurrection as the sun slowly rose in the east. I didn't mind, because since he was outside and not standing in the pulpit, he talked like a normal person. I don't think he yelled too well when he was cold either.

But the early service meant that we had to get up before five o'clock to get ready. I didn't really mind getting up early on Easter, but I wanted to wear warm clothes. It was always cold, standing outside the church and looking off into the east, singing joyful songs about the Resurrection, and watching the Easter morning sun rise in soft pearl pink and gray clouds. But I sure didn't want to wear some ridiculous frilly outfit that would scratch me and freeze me to death at the same time.

Mama was in the bathroom putting on her make-up. I walked to the open door and watched her dabbing on face powder. "Mama, what should I wear to the sunrise service?" I asked sweetly, pulling my fuzzy yellow bathrobe around my neck and shivering like I was freezing.

"Don't put on any of your new clothes for the sunrise service, Sissie. I want your Easter outfit to look fresh and clean for the Easter worship service." It was a warning.

What was she thinking? Did she honestly believe I would voluntarily put on a single item of my Easter outfit? "Wear something warm like a skirt and sweater," she continued, almost as if it had just occurred to her that it was chilly outside.

"Yes, ma'am, I'll do just that." But I was one step ahead of her. Underneath my fuzzy robe, I was already dressed in my favorite blue corduroy jumper and white turtle neck shirt. I was ready to go, except for picking off all the yellow fuzz on my jumper.

For once Easter sunrise service went perfectly. There was no rain, and no overcast sky prevented us from seeing the sun rising in all its glory. Our small group of church members who had assembled so early in the morning and braved the chilly air for the service huddled close together and sang three verses of "He Arose." Then we turned toward the east and let the rays of the rising sun warm our hearts as well as our faces.

After we returned home from the sunrise service, something special was waiting for Biddie and me on the front porch. I guess while we were at church, Grandpa had been the Easter Bunny. There was an Easter basket for me. And since Biddie was a teenager, she received a beautiful pink glass basket filled with chocolates wrapped in colorful foil. My straw basket was covered in sheets of overlapped purple cellophane topped by a big pink bow, and it contained all kinds of candy. It was a like finding a treasure chest of pure sugar.

"Now you girls can't eat any of that candy before we go to church. Sissie, you don't need all those jelly beans and candy eggs. Wait till after dinner." Who was Mama kidding?

As a small child I had mastered the fine art of locating the elusive seam where the purple cellophane overlapped itself so that I could slide my hand through the seam to reach the jellybeans without damaging the cellophane. Before we left for Sunday school, I had already eaten a dozen jelly beans, three chocolate marshmallow bunnies, and a candy egg that was filled with grainy sugar cream covered in a sugary pink shell. But the contents of my basket looked practically untouched and undisturbed. Biddie, meanwhile, had put the empty glass basket on her dresser, surrounded it with her favorite white rocks from the home place and, as usual, had hidden her chocolate candy from me.

* * * *

Most every woman has her own notion about what is beautiful and what is not beautiful, what is worth suffering for and what is not worth suffering for. What Mama considered beautiful was torture to me, and quite frankly, it wasn't worth suffering for. "Hurry and get dressed, girls. You know the church will be crowded today. All those people who come to church only one time a year will be there this morning." Hey, was Grandpa going? I thought he only went on Reunion Sunday.

Mama had laid out my Easter clothes the night before, and I had tried not to think about them as I had drifted off to sleep. Why did she go to so much trouble to try to make me look like a lady? And why did being a lady have to hurt so much? Everything Mama bought for me to wear to church either scratched, itched, pinched, or rubbed blisters. I had tried to get some answers to my questions the night before.

"Mama, what does wearing new clothes have to do with Easter? It's not in the Bible," I complained. "I can't find it anywhere in there."

"Yes, it is. Honor your father and your mother that your days may be long upon the earth," Mama shot back with an irritated tone in her voice.

Some of those days seemed a lot longer than others, and today was going to be one of them. A lot of my friends in my Sunday school class didn't understand the meaning of the word *eternity*. I understood eternity very well. It was sitting through Sunday School and the worship service at Mount Olive Baptist Church in a starched or lacy dress that was supposed to make me look feminine, but instead reduced me to a scratching, itching, and miserable mess. I realized that Mama was determined to make me a lady, even if it killed me.

"But, Mama, everything I'm s'posed to wear is either tight or scratchy," I protested. I avoided looking her straight in the eye in case she gave me one of her looks.

"That's all in your imagination. Besides, you don't know the meaning of the word *tight*," she fussed. "You just wait, Sissie. In a few years you'll be wearing a girdle. Then you'll know what tight is."

"A *girdle*? Why in the world would I wear a girdle?" I couldn't believe what I was hearing.

"Because no Southern woman who calls herself a lady is properly dressed unless she's wearing a girdle," she answered. Well, that idea sure made me look forward to growing up to be a Southern lady.

So on Easter Sunday morning, after the simple beauty of the sunrise service, I took off my soft corduroy jumper and dressed for church in my new frilly, yellow nylon dress, its fabric dotted with little white scratchy daisies, topped with a stiff lace collar that left red marks around my neck.

I suffered through the service, constantly running my fingers around the inside of my collar to keep it from rubbing my neck so much and choking me half to death, but I didn't suffer for beauty. I suffered for two important reasons: I wanted to honor my father and my mother, of course, but, mainly, the children at Mount Olive always had an Easter egg hunt right after church. If I kept out of trouble with Mama, I might have a shot at finding that elusive gold egg with the five dollar bill tucked inside.

CHAPTER 18

Joad's Adventure

"If you ever get in trouble at school, you will be in double trouble
when you get home."
– Mama

April slipped away quietly and May stepped right into its place. The sun felt warmer, and I felt as if the world was finally coming back to life again. May was the best page on the calendar, and now I had arrived at the best part of May, the icing on the cake, so to speak. It was Friday, the school year was almost over, and summer vacation was only a week away.

Even riding on the bus was more pleasant, because we could let the windows down halfway and breathe in the fragrant late spring air. Beautiful pink rose mallows were blooming in masses alongside the highway in the muddy red ditches and on the shoulders of the road, and they stood out against the wild grass that had turned green but hadn't yet grown very high. The flowery heads of the mallows danced in the breeze as our bus roared past them. Wild roses spilled over harsh barbed-wire fences along the roadway, their many vines heavy with crowds of tiny pink clusters of blossoms. Someone had been cutting grass somewhere, because the scent of wild onions drifted in my open bus window.

When I got to school Mrs. Martin was absent for some

unexplained reason, and we had a substitute teacher, Miss Susan Clearstone. She was a cross between Miss Emily Dew and Miss Maude Jones – she looked pretty and sweet, but she had a wicked disposition. Mrs. Martin had left us lots of work to do, and Miss Clearstone would not allow us to say a single word. We were in prison.

But this day felt special, like something important was about to happen. All day I walked around with a spring in my step as if deep inside me my soul was humming a happy tune. The day was so bright and promising it could have been my birthday, but it wasn't.

When it was time for afternoon recess, our class lined up at the classroom door and headed down the hallway for a few minutes of well-deserved freedom in the beautiful weather outside. At last, we marched down the steps and then ran for the playground, leaving Miss Clearstone inside with two students who had dared to whisper to each other during class. I didn't really care about swings or slides. Spud and I had our sights set on a shady spot on a rock wall under a water oak tree at the edge of the playground.

Davey Morris and Chester Smith were squatting down in the sand on the other side of the playground. They had drawn a circle and were busy shooting marbles. I noticed Rusty Jackson and two of his friends as they slowly walked over to Davey and Chester. I hated to see Rusty picking on Davey, but at least that meant that he would leave Spud alone.

I figured Rusty would kick dirt on their marble game, but for some odd reason, he and Davey walked away and began to talk. Davey was nodding at Rusty, but they were too far away for me to hear what they were saying. I figured it didn't involve us, so Spud and I kept talking to each other about what we were going to do when school was out.

I looked up to see Davey walking across the playground, his right hand behind his back. He called to me nervously, "C-could you c-come here a minute? I, I j-just w-want t-to ask you a q-question." I could understand that, because I always had a question or two that needed a good answer.

I stood up, dusted off the back of my skirt, and started

walking toward Davey. Suddenly from behind me Rusty ran up and grabbed the neck of my blouse, stopping me in my tracks. "Oh, look, it's S-S-Sissie S-S-Stevenson, the s-s-snake lover," he hissed, making fun of me and Davey at the same time.

Suddenly he put his other hand on the front of my collar and pulled it hard while Davey dropped a toad down inside the front of my blouse. Rusty's friends, like circling buzzards, hurried over to see what was happening.

Rusty bent over double in laughter. He just knew I was going to scream, dance around, and generally act ridiculous.

But this would be the day he would always remember as the one on which he chose the wrong person to bully.

He turned his back on me and started to walk away, laughing and patting his friends on the shoulder.

"Looka there, boys, we just fed a frawg to a snake," he bragged.

But before Rusty knew what was happening behind him, I used my perfected Easter basket technique, reached inside the front of my blouse between two buttons, and caught the toad. Then I ran up behind Rusty and grabbed the collar of *his* shirt. That toad and I were working as a team. Just as I was about to drop him down the back of Rusty's shirt, the toad peed all over Rusty's neck.

And as my newest cold amphibian friend dropped down Rusty's shirt and started wiggling and scratching frantically, Rusty screamed like a girl, danced around crazily, and wet his pants. Everybody on the playground started laughing and pointing at him as he ran from the playground, crying like a baby, his pants soaking wet in front and in back and all the way down both his legs. It hadn't been a good day for Rusty to wear khaki trousers.

Suddenly I found myself in the principal's office for the first time in my life. Mama was going to kill me. She had already warned me, "Sissie, if you ever get in trouble at school, you will be in double trouble when you get home. We do not send you to school to misbehave." And that was the speech I got the one time I had brought home an A- in conduct on my report card. What in the world would she say about me putting a toad down Rusty

Jackson's shirt and being sent to the principal's office?

The next thing I knew, I was seated in a hard wooden chair in front of Mrs. Williams' desk. I attempted to plead my defense. "It was Davey and Rusty's fault, Miz Williams. They put the toad down the front of my blouse." I tried to read the expression on her face, but I couldn't. One thing was for sure – Mrs. Williams was not smiling. In fact, I had never seen her smile.

"Well, that's not the story Elmo told me. He said you came up for no reason and attacked him with one of your frogs," Mrs. Williams snipped, her eyes boring into me with a look I'd never seen even on Mama's face.

I was scared senseless and my mouth felt bone dry. But not so dry that I didn't blurt out an argument without thinking.

"It wasn't a frog, Miz Williams. It was a common Southern toad." I had to make sure that she had her facts correct. "And besides, I would never bring a toad to school, unless it was for a science class. Toads do not belong at school."

Double trouble. Not only had I made Rusty Jackson wet his pants, but I had just sassed the principal.

Mrs. Williams raised her right eyebrow, and I could tell from the deep breath that she was taking in through her teeth that she was about to punish me but good, partially because of the Rusty incident and partially because I had corrected her understanding of frogs and toads. She was interrupted in mid-breath by the sound of a soft knock on her closed door.

"Miz Williams," Spud's soft voice called out as the office door slowly squeaked open. Davey and Spud were both standing there, looking very serious.

"What is it, boys?" she fussed. "I'm busy right now. Don't interrupt."

Davey found his voice. "It w-wasn't her fault. It w-was m-me and R-Rusty. R-Rusty's friend J-Jeff found the t-toad on the p-playground. R-Rusty p-promised m-me a q-quarter if I w-would c-catch Sissie for him. Then he p-pulled her c-collar out, and I p-put the t-toad down the front of her b-blouse."

Davey had to muster up a lot of courage to say that much to Mrs. Williams. I was proud of him.

"This is serious, Davey," Mrs. Williams responded at once, looking at him sternly and then shaking her head. "Very serious business indeed."

"Please don't paddle Davey, Miz Williams. He's not telling you the whole truth," Spud pleaded and then looked over at Davey uncertainly before plowing ahead with his explanation. "Rusty didn't really promise Davey a quarter. He was black-mailin' him."

"*Black-mailing him*? What on earth for?" Mrs. Williams' stern look had turned to pure puzzlement.

"Well…," Spud hesitated and looked over at Davey again, but Davey didn't look up. He just kept staring down at his shoes. "Well…"

"Speak up, Homer," Mrs. Williams said impatiently.

He looked over at me and then looked down at *his* shoes. "Well, you see, Rusty already makes fun of Davey all the time as it is…and…and…uh…well." Then I reckon Spud must have found his courage in his shoes, because he gulped before finally looking straight at Mrs. Williams. "And somehow Rusty found out that Davey likes to dress up his sister's dolls," Spud blurted out all at once, his face turning three shades of red. "He threatened to tell everybody at school if Davey didn't help him with the toad."

"Oh, I see," she said, her voice softening. "Well, Davey, that's really nobody's business but yours. I'll take care of Mr. Jackson and shut down his little blackmailing operation. You three go back outside and play. I'm allowing each of you fifteen extra minutes of recess."

True to her words, Mrs. Williams shut down Rusty's blackmailing operation. In addition to being humiliated in front of everyone on the playground, Rusty couldn't come back to school for a week, which was the rest of the school year. And I could have sworn as Davey, Spud, and I left the principal's office that day, I heard Mrs. Williams laugh.

CHAPTER 19

The Wild Plum Bush

*"Some of the best lessons in life can be learned in a
little house on a dirt road."*
– Grandpa

Springtime had finished working its magic, painting its glorious colors of new life on the leafless trees and bushes. Then summer arrived to add its own special touches. Pink flowers that had bloomed earlier on the June apple trees were now becoming tiny green fruit. Soon they would ripen into sweet red apples, and Gemma and I would have to hurry to pick some before the birds pecked them.

And even if the birds didn't get to them first, the ripened fruit might drop to the ground, become bruised, start fermenting, and attract dozens of hungry yellow jackets with the fallen apples' vinegary scent.

I couldn't wait to taste one of Gemma's apple cobblers, filled with dumplings and sweetened with sugar and cinnamon, but I didn't want to step around in swarms of angry yellow jackets that were defending their food.

The days had become longer and warmer, and seemingly endless time stretched before me as my summer vacation finally released me from days spent inside a stuffy classroom. Morning glory vines bearing bright blue trumpets were weaving around the mailbox in front of Grandpa and Gemma's house. The morning glory seeds I had planted at our mailbox got a later start, because they were from a packet that Mama bought at the hardware store.

Gemma said, "Don't worry, Sissie. Your flowers will be up and blooming soon. Mine are already blooming because they're volunteers. They came up from seeds dropped by last year's flowers." I couldn't imagine a plant volunteering for anything.

The sunflowers she had planted out by the smokehouse were already taller than me. The birds were going to be really happy this summer, pecking away at those seeds. Grandpa put a small birdbath in the middle of the sunflowers. "The birds might need a little drink of water to wash down those seeds, don't you reckon?" he asked me.

I was worried about Grandpa. He didn't seem to smile as much anymore.

Some days he was perfectly fine, but other days he moved much more slowly. Lately, despite the June heat, he had taken to getting up, dressing in a long-sleeve shirt and overalls, putting on his heavy shoes, and sitting in the front porch swing. He sat there most of the day, just watching cars drive by and thinking, not swinging at all.

He still seemed to enjoy my company, and I tried to sit and talk to him as much as I could. I even tried to think of things I could do while still managing to be near Grandpa.

I always had to be in motion, so I took a seat in the metal glider on the porch while Grandpa sat in the swing. Mr. Herschel Lindsey, the mail man, pulled up to the mail box and left the morning mail. A few moments later Mr. Earl Bunch and his wife, Miss Rita, drove past in a cloud of red dust. Mr. Earl was a deacon, and he always made sure that Mount Olive's church yard was neat. They waved and Mr. Earl blew the horn. My glider moved back and forth making squeaking and tapping noises like a rusty little musical performance.

Grandpa didn't seem to have a thing to say, and that was all right, because sometimes just sitting and being quiet was a good thing. I had time to think, too.

"I'll go get the mail, Grandpa." As I started walking toward the mailbox, I heard a mockingbird fussing, and I looked out across the yard in her direction. In the very edge of the woods, a bush with something small and bright orange in it caught my eye. It was growing among some other low bushes, almost unnoticed. When I went to see what it was, I discovered that it was a wild plum bush, loaded with plums, most of which were still completely green. But two plums had already turned orange, which meant they were ready to pick. Carefully watching my step to avoid snakes and poison ivy, I plucked the plums off the bush, put them into my jeans' pocket, and headed back to the porch.

"Grandpa, would you like a plum?"

"I believe I would," he said, and stretched out his open hand.

I reached into my pocket and pulled out the two plums. One of them was bigger than the other one, and I'm ashamed to say that I laid the smaller plum in Grandpa's outstretched hand and kept the bigger one for myself.

"Much obliged." He took the offered plum, rubbed it on his sleeve to make it all shiny, took a taste of it, and then popped the whole thing into his mouth. I did exactly the same thing, except when I bit into my plum, it was crunchy and bitter.

Grandpa spit the plum seed into the palm of his hand and tossed it off the porch into the azalea bushes. "Um, that was really good."

"Well, mine wasn't. It was bitter."

He studied me for just a moment, and then he smiled and said, "That's what happens when you keep the bigger one for yourself and give the smaller one to someone else. My plum was sweet." I never did know for sure if Grandpa's plum really was sweet, but he sure taught me a good lesson about proper sharing.

I told Spud all about Grandpa and the two plums, and how I had learned my lesson. Spud said, "I would've learned my lesson, too, Sissie. Next time, just put both plums in your pocket and eat 'em when you get home."

CHAPTER 20

The Garden of Miss Information

"If you'll be really quiet, sometimes adults will forget about you
and tell something you're not supposed to hear."
— *Mama*

That night after I had shared wild plums with Grandpa, I lay awake for a long time listening to the night sounds. Through the open window of my bedroom the delicate, sweet smell of honeysuckle drifted in on the night air. Then slowly began the distant sound of a screech owl.

Now the call of a screech owl always made the hair on the back of Gemma's neck stand up, because she said that it was a sign that someone was going to die. I didn't put much stock into that idea, because I figured that a screech owl is just one more of God's creatures expressing his opinion the only way he knows how.

The next day we went to church at Mount Olive and then Mama, Daddy, Biddie, and I ate Sunday dinner with Gemma and Grandpa. Afterward, Biddie and I needed to help Mama with some housework. We had promised her.

"Don't worry about these dishes," Gemma said, as she shooed us all out of the house. "I don't have anything else to do all afternoon."

When I had finished my work, I went outside into the edge

of the woods and located the source of the wonderful fragrance. A huge honeysuckle vine with creamy yellow blossoms was draped over the branches of a low wild shrub. I broke off a little strand of the flowery vine and carried it to Gemma's house. It wasn't beautiful and it didn't really seem to fit into a vase, but in her warm kitchen the fragrance of the honeysuckle mingled with the aroma of Sunday dinner that was still lingering everywhere in the air. Fried chicken, mashed potatoes, green beans cooked with a little fat back, steamed cabbage, buttermilk biscuits, and two different dishes of juicy red, ripe tomatoes (one sprinkled with sugar for Grandpa and me and one without sugar for everyone else.)

Gemma still hadn't finished washing all the dishes. "I've had company since you were here."

"I can help you wash these, Gemma." We had washed and dried the dishes and were just about to wash the pots and pans when someone opened and closed the front screen door. A voice called out, "*Hello!*" Aunt Pearl had dropped in for a visit.

"Uh, Gemma, may I stop helping you for awhile and go sit with Grandpa on the porch?"

"Go ahead, Sissie. I'll finish these."

It was starting to get dark, so I switched on the porch light, quickly opened the screen door, and headed out to the refuge of the back porch to sit in the swing with Grandpa, just seconds before Aunt Pearl made her appearance in the kitchen. "My goodness, let me pitch in and help you with those supper dishes. Do I smell coffee?" From our swinging perch Grandpa and I could see and hear a lot.

"These aren't my supper dishes, Pearl. These are still my dinner dishes. I had company all afternoon." She reached in the cupboard and pulled out one of her old coffee cups decorated with roses and edged in gold.

"Who was it?" Aunt Pearl asked almost too sweetly, taking the cup from Gemma.

"Eleanor and Walter."

"I thought I saw their car in your driveway. I wonder why they didn't come over to see *us*? Did they bring Raedean and little Raleigh with them?"

"No, not this time," Gemma answered.

"Praise God," I whispered to Grandpa.

"Just their two little worrisome dogs," Gemma said. Two little worrisome dogs were a whole lot better than one little worrisome Raleigh.

Gemma continued washing the pans and then she started wiping down the stove and cabinets. Aunt Pearl was quietly drying the wet pans. I figured she was probably eavesdropping, waiting to hear anything Grandpa and I said, because we were doing the same thing, sitting on the porch eavesdropping on them.

All kinds of bugs had started buzzing around the yellow light bulb that cast a glaring light on the back porch and bathed the swing and its two occupants with its strange color.

Candleflies and a few larger moths were clinging to the screen door, caught between heaven and hell. If they were smart, they would stay outside, because flying into the kitchen meant certain death at the hand of Aunt Pearl and Gemma's trusty flyswatter. Something fairly large fluttered by us toward the light, and for a moment I thought a bat had ventured onto the back porch, ready to zoom around the light and feast on a few of the bugs.

"What kind of critter is that?" Grandpa asked.

When the *critter* decided to settle onto the screen door with his much smaller moth cousins, I realized what it was. "That's a luna moth, Grandpa. Isn't it beautiful?" Its huge pale green wings outspread on the screen gave the moth an exotic look, and it seemed so out of place. I never stopped being amazed that the luna moth lived in Georgia, because it looked more like something from the pages in the section about South America in my geography book.

Grandpa looked back at me, and in the yellow light I could see a proud look on his face. "You know the names of a lot of critters, don't you, Sissie?"

"Yes, sir, I do. I read all the time. You know how much I love animals."

"Well, in that case," Grandpa said, "let me tell you about my favorite animal." And then he started telling me about Old Pearly Fangs.

"There he goes again, telling that same story about a stupid snake drinking moonshine. That's just an excuse to glorify the use of alcohol," Aunt Pearl complained in her preachy voice. She was the only person I knew who could sound preachy even when she was reading off a grocery list.

I couldn't see Gemma or Aunt Pearl's faces, just their backs. Even though I could only hear what they were saying, I could imagine how they looked. Gemma in her white apron, continuing to straighten up the kitchen, not saying a word, politely ignoring her sister's sharp words. Aunt Pearl wearing that self-righteous look on her face, as if she would rapture away to heaven any minute.

Grandpa laughed softly and rolled his eyes. He pulled out the can of Prince Albert tobacco that was always in his overalls pocket, as well as a single thin sheet of cigarette paper.

While he was talking about the old timber rattler, he began to form a line of tobacco neatly on the paper. Then holding the paper with its tobacco between the thumb and index finger of both hands, he slowly slid the edge of the paper lengthwise across his tongue and then folded the paper onto itself, forming a perfect cigarette.

But before he could strike a match, Aunt Pearl's voice distracted him. He was holding the match in midair.

"Now you take my husband. Toolie is a godly man. Why, not a single drop of alcohol has ever touched that man's lips," Aunt Pearl bragged in a loud voice.

Grandpa looked at me, winked, and in a low voice said, "That's because he always used to drink it with a straw." I giggled, and the sound of my laughter made Gemma and Aunt Pearl suddenly realize that it had become really dark outside and we were still sitting on the back porch.

Gemma came to the screen door and looked out at us. "You two come inside before the mosquitoes eat you alive."

"Dang, I didn't get to smoke my cigarette."

"Just save it for tomorrow, Grandpa." I winked at him, and in a much louder voice I added, "You can smoke it while you tell me that snake story again."

We left our swing and stepped into the kitchen, now an

orderly place, with all the dishes put away.

Aunt Pearl looked at me in disgust and said, "Sissie, you should've been in here helping your grandmother and me with the dishes. It's not too soon for you to learn your place as a woman."

Gemma spoke up, "I asked her to sit and keep her grandpa company. He likes to hear about the poems she's writing."

"Huh!" Aunt Pearl looked at Grandpa and me as if we were crazy, and then she turned her attention back to Gemma. I guess that meant we were dismissed. "What are you cooking for the family reunion?"

Grandpa spoke up before Gemma could answer. "Uh, we're goin' to the livin' room and watch television. Come on, Sissie." Grandpa headed for the comfort of the living room, his old black and white television, and his rocking chair.

"Sissie, would you turn off the big light? There's a glare on the TV screen." Grandpa had already settled into his rocker, and once he sat down, he had a hard time getting back up. "And would you mind askin' your grandma to fix me a cup of coffee?"

"Okay, Grandpa." I turned off the light and headed back into the kitchen. For some reason I just knew to be quiet.

Mama had always told Biddie and me when we got too noisy, "If you'll be real quiet, sometimes adults forget about you and tell something you're not supposed to hear." Well, right outside the kitchen door, I heard Aunt Pearl telling something I wasn't supposed to hear. She was talking about someone I barely knew, her daughter Sharon.

"Sharon can't even show us the courtesy of coming to the reunion. I know I agreed to help her, and, don't get me wrong. I have no regrets about bringing up Rose. I love Rose like she's my own daughter, but Sharon acts just like nothing ever happened."

Gemma interrupted, "I'm sure that's not true, Pearl..."

"Yes, it *is* true. As far as Sharon's concerned, she has her two sons and her rich husband, and that's it. She's in Atlanta and never comes home to see her Daddy and me or her daughter. And then Rose went and made the same mistake. Spud, poor Spud, is growing up without a father. Rose is living a lie. I feel like *I'm* living a lie, too."

If I had been looking in a mirror at that moment, the reflection of my mouth would have looked like a capital O. I had never been that shocked before in all my life, except maybe that one time when I was five. My jeans had been outside drying on the clothesline, and when I put them on, a bumblebee had gotten into them first and it stung me on my behind. Well, that bumblebee would have to get in line, because this piece of news was even more shocking.

"Pearl, surely you believe Rose's story. If anyone is living a lie, it's Sharon. You did the best you knew to do. You've been a good mother to Rose, and Rose has been a good mother to Spud." Gemma didn't mention Pearl being a good grandmother to Spud.

I knew I wasn't supposed to be standing outside the door listening, and I almost shouted out loud from the shock. I had to bite my bottom lip and clamp both hands tightly over my mouth. I couldn't let Aunt Pearl and Gemma know that I had been listening in on their conversation.

I decided to back up slowly, very slowly, so as not to let the floor squeak under my feet. I could not make a sound. When I finally tiptoed into the living room, Grandpa looked at me with a puzzled look.

"What's wrong with you, Sissie? You look like you just swallowed a doughnut. And where's my cup of coffee?"

"Uh, Aunt Pearl and Gemma were talking, and I didn't want to interrupt."

"They're *always* talkin'. Surely to goodness they can stop long enough to fix an old man a cup o' coffee."

"Grandpa, you and I need to talk."

CHAPTER 21

Grandpa Spills the Beans

"We can't help who we're kin to, but we don't have to act like 'em."
– Grandpa

Grandpa and I needed some time together alone so we could talk without being overheard, and what better place was there for a private conversation than on the creek bank at the home place. Mama and Daddy were at work, and Gemma and I were drying the last of the lunch dishes. Grandpa cleared his throat and spoke up, almost like he was making some kind of big announcement.

"Honey, I think I'm gonna head up to the mountain for awhile. Is it okay if Sissie goes with me?"

"Are you going turtle hunting?" Gemma asked. "It's awfully hot outside." It felt about as hot inside, too. The rotating kitchen fan was just moving the heat around from one spot to another.

"Naw, I thought we might look for some dewberries. I sure would like one of your cobblers for supper."

I chimed in, "Me, too, Gemma. Can I go with Grandpa?"

"Well, I don't see why not," she answered, "but y'all be careful and watch for snakes."

Grandpa reached for his straw hat and his cedar cane and headed for the back door, with me right behind him. Gemma spoke up. "Uh, aren't you two forgetting something?"

Grandpa looked puzzled. "What?"

"Something to put the dewberries in maybe?" She reached into the cabinet and pulled out an old long-handled pot. "Bring me lots of berries, and I'll make a big cobbler."

As we started off the porch, I grabbed a weathered worn-out folding lawn chair and we put it in the car trunk. Grandpa and I headed toward the crossroads with the usual grinding of the gears in his old Mercury. How much longer could those gears possibly hold out? In what seemed like no time at all, we turned down the rutted dirt road and pulled up into what used to be the yard of the old home place.

"Where do you want to talk, Sissie?"

"I think I know just the place, Grandpa." I remembered one of my favorite spots by the creek, a tree that had somehow grown bent over and crooked. I could sit on that, and Grandpa could sit in the folding chair. Once we were settled into our seats, I was ready to ask questions, and I hoped Grandpa would be willing to answer them. A soft breeze whispered through the hardwoods, and I hoped that our secret conversation wouldn't somehow get carried along on the wind and be heard by others, sort of like in the Greek and Roman myths we had read in Mrs. Martin's class.

"I know I'm not a grown-up, Grandpa, but I have to talk to you about something." I could imagine that Grandpa must have started worrying about what he had gotten himself into.

"About what, Sissie?"

"You remember when you told me that someday you would explain to me all about Aunt Pearl and her hard life?"

"Yes, I do."

"Well, I don't think you can wait as long as you'd hoped, because Raleigh got ahead of you." I told Grandpa all about what Raleigh had told Spud and me on Christmas Day.

He looked at me with a raised eyebrow and said, "Oh, I see."

"And there's something else, Grandpa. I promised Spud I wouldn't tell, and I haven't told anyone but you, not even Gemma." I was on a roll. "And there's more, Grandpa."

"More?"

"Remember Sunday evening when I was supposed to go get

you some coffee, but I didn't bring you any coffee because I said that Gemma and Aunt Pearl were talking in the kitchen and you said they were always talking and…?"

"I remember, Sissie," he interrupted.

"Well, I eavesdropped on their conversation. It was an accident. I didn't really mean to."

"And what did you hear?" he asked, a look of concern on his face.

"I heard Aunt Pearl talking about Sharon and Rose. About how she loved Rose like her own daughter and how Rose had made the same mistake as Sharon. And how poor Spud is growing up without a father. She said she felt like she was living a lie."

"Well, sounds like you heard a good bit."

"I couldn't say anything to Gemma, Grandpa, because Aunt Pearl is her sister, and Biddie is my sister, and I would never say anything bad to somebody about Biddie."

"I can understand that, Sissie. But your grandma probably needs to know that you overheard their conversation. She and Pearl need to be more careful in the future. I'll tell her if you want me to."

"Okay, Grandpa, but what I really want right now is the truth. It's important to me. In fact, it's one of my New Year's resolutions."

"Is that right?"

"Yes, sir. Grandpa, family members shouldn't keep secrets from each other," I blurted out. "It's not fair that Spud has never been told the truth, especially since so many people know all about his grandmother and his mother, and he doesn't know a thing. He's been made into a big joke. He's been kept completely in the dark, and Raleigh was insulting him and Spud didn't even know enough to defend himself. That's not right. In fact, that's downright mean and cruel."

"You're right, Sissie, but it's a long, complicated story. Your grandma will have a fit if I tell you."

"Grandpa, trust me. I know a lot already and I haven't told a soul except you. I won't tell Gemma."

"All right. But this is between the two of us." I nodded and crossed my heart, and this time, I didn't have my fingers crossed behind my back.

* * * *

"Toolie wasn't Pearl's first choice for a husband. In high school she was crazy in love with Walter Smith, who is now your Uncle Toolie and Aunt Pearl's brother-in-law and Raleigh's great-grandfather. When Walter asked Pearl to marry him, Pearl's father refused to give his permission for them to get married because he said Pearl was too young."

"He probably really just wanted Pearl to stay home and take care of him and your grandma, because their mother was always sick and always wanted everybody to know about it. Their father was a self-righteous know-it-all, just like Pearl. It's no wonder their mother was always pretendin' to be sick."

"Anyway, Pearl was heart-broken. Later, Walter joined the army, and he met his first wife, Irene, and they had a son named Winston. Irene ran off with another man and Walter divorced her, but Winston stayed with Walter. Then Walter remarried, and his new wife just happened to be Toolie's sister Eleanor. And Winston became Eleanor's step-son."

"Meanwhile, Toolie courted Pearl for a while, and her father finally allowed her to get married, which meant Pearl's new sister-in-law was married to the man Pearl had wanted to marry to begin with. Pearl and Toolie had their two children – first Sharon and then Mitchell. When Toolie and Eleanor's mother, Aunt Sadie, died, Sharon sat with Winston at the family gatherin' after the funeral. They already kinda knew each other, of course, but I reckon that was the first time they had ever really talked to one another. They were teenagers and they weren't any kin, and so at first they started writin' to each other like friends."

I was trying to keep everything Grandpa said straight in my mind, and I nodded my head at him several times, just like I understood perfectly well. Actually, I was already starting to get a little confused and swimmy-headed.

"Then Winston started comin' around to call on Sharon, and they fell in love. They wanted to get married, but Pearl didn't approve of the marriage. She said Winston wasn't suitable since he came from a broken home. I figure mostly she was still mad because if she couldn't ever have Walter, then she wasn't goin' to let his son marry her daughter."

"Sort of like revenge?" I interrupted.

"Yep. Well, Sharon and Winston were pretty serious about gettin' married, because, unbeknownst to Pearl and Toolie, Sharon was expectin' Winston's baby. Lord, don't tell anybody I told you all this."

"I won't, Grandpa. Keep going." I listened even more carefully so I wouldn't miss a single detail.

"Anyway, when Toolie and Pearl found out, instead of makin' her marry Winston, they sent her straight off to live with a cousin in Florida until she had her baby, Rose. They brought Rose back to live with them and brought her up as their third child, like she'd been adopted. Sharon stayed in Florida and hardly ever came home again after that. Winston went his way, married a strange woman named Ruby Gail, and they had Raedean, who had Raleigh. Meanwhile, Sharon married a rich insurance man, had two sons, and moved to Atlanta. Are you with me so far, Sissie?"

"I think so, Grandpa." Were my eyes crossed? They sure felt like it.

"Rose grew up as Pearl and Toolie's daughter, and most everybody in the church and in the Valley, too, thinks that she really is their daughter. In the meanwhile Mitchell had a few scrapes with the law when he was still in high school. He got into a heap o' trouble."

"What'd he do?" I asked, so Grandpa could have time to take a breath.

"Well, he and some friends broke into a store and stole some things."

Grandpa shifted in his chair and brushed a bug off his sleeve. He paused and looked off for a moment like he was thinking hard about something, and then he went back to telling his story. "This is where what I'm tellin' you gets even sadder. Toolie and Pearl had their hands full of problems. The judge put Mitchell on probation and he didn't have to go to jail, but Pearl kept houndin' him about changin' his life. Mitchell got tired of all the bickerin' and Pearl constantly tellin' him what to do, so he joined the army so that Uncle Sam could tell him what to do all the time. Eventually he got sent to Normandy, and he got killed during the D-Day invasion. Pearl never forgave herself, even though he probably mighta got drafted anyway."

How did Grandpa keep all this stuff straight?

"The way I figure it, at least Mitchell died servin' his country and not servin' time."

I nodded my head in agreement. "But what about Rose?"

"Rose kinda made the same mistake as her mother. She fell in love with a boy who went to high school with her, Edward McKenna, Frank's boy."

"You mean the same McKennas who own the department store?" I asked.

"Yep. Rose and Edward planned to get married and, accordin' to Rose, they did secretly elope to a justice of the peace, because even though Pearl wanted her to finish high school and then go off to business school somewhere, Rose had other ideas. Her husband, Edward, was killed in a car accident a few weeks after their high school graduation and just a few months before Spud was born."

"Pearl refused to believe that Rose and Edward were really married. Claimed she never saw their marriage license and there wasn't a proper religious service. She said people in the community were talking about her. So Rose moved to Florida to stay with the same cousin Sharon had stayed with, and when it was time for Spud to be born, Pearl and your grandma went down to be with her to help out."

"A few months later Rose moved to Atlanta to be near Sharon, but Sharon wasn't much help, because Rose was part of her checkered past and Sharon's husband thought he was high society. Still does, from what I hear. Rose couldn't make enough money alone to support herself and Spud in Atlanta, so she moved back to live with Pearl and Toolie, even though it was the last thing in the world she wanted to do."

Good Lord, I was glad I was sitting down, because my head was spinning for sure. Thank goodness I had both my arms wrapped around the trunk of the bent tree I was sitting on. Sometimes Gemma and Aunt Pearl watched *Search for Tomorrow* and *The Edge of Night*, and I don't think either one of her stories could have ever been as complicated or as strange as the story of my family.

No wonder Grandpa didn't want to tell me about Pearl's hard life until I was older. It didn't really have anything to do with being an adult and understanding heartache. I needed a driver's license and a road map to follow his story.

"And that's about it, Sissie," he said, suddenly winding down his family history lesson and shifting his body once again in the uncomfortable folding chair.

I thought for a moment. "So this is the big family secret, Grandpa? Aunt Pearl was trying to run everybody's life and she made a mess of everything. What's so secret about that? She's still doing it."

"I reckon, Sissie, the saddest part of the story is that Pearl ever got that way to begin with. If her mama and daddy had been more concerned with their children and less concerned with themselves, Pearl's life might've been different. I don't know how in the world your grandma turned out the way she did. There ain't a day goes by that I don't thank God for your Gemma, because she and Pearl are as different as night and day. All I can say is your Uncle Toolie is a saint."

"I've always felt that way, Grandpa, even before you told me the family secrets. I've never understood how he and Aunt Pearl could be so different from each other. They never have seemed too happy together, not like you and Gemma. And I never could figure out why Rose would leave Atlanta and move down here to live with them."

"Well, now you know, and I can't believe I just told you all of this. Your grandma will be mad as a wet hen if she ever finds out I told you. In fact, she might even make me sleep with the chickens."

"I won't let Gemma find out, Grandpa. I won't break my

promise to you. But somebody needs to sit down and explain a few things to Spud. He should at least know that Aunt Pearl is his great-grandmother and not his grandmother. That ought to make him feel a whole lot better." It would sure make *me* feel better.

"Sissie, you can't tell any of this to Spud. Even though you may not agree with everything, it's not your place to tell him about his family. It's Rose's place, and nobody else's."

"I know, Grandpa. But at least maybe now I can know how to defend him better against Raleigh."

Grandpa looked up. Troubling gray clouds were moving across the deep blue sky, and some of them were beginning to look even darker gray, almost black. The breeze was picking up as well, and way off in the distance a soft rumble started up.

"Looks like it's comin' up a cloud, Sissie, and we've got work to do. We're supposed to be bringin' back a pot full of dewberries, so we'd better get busy pickin' before that rain sets in."

"I reckon so, too, Grandpa."

"Besides, it'll look awful suspicious to your grandma if we don't do what we set out to do. It's one thing for me to spill the beans, but it's another thing to go dewberry pickin' and come back home with an empty pot. She might make us explain."

"Well, Grandpa, I guess you could tell her we picked a whole pot of dewberries, but we stopped at Mount Olive Creek and they escaped." Grandpa laughed out loud, and I felt happy to see him looking better. This was a good day.

Grandpa slowly drove his car back down the bumpy dirt road from the home place to where it met the main road, never getting past second gear. Then I set to work, scampering over rocks and up the steep road banks, while keeping a sharp lookout for copperheads and rattlesnakes. I picked handfuls of the shiny black berries, leaving the unripe red ones for another time. I thought about what Mrs. Martin had said to us one day in English class about the dewberry's cousin: "Blackberries are green when they are red."

Sometimes the dewberry brambles snagged my arms and hands, leaving tiny dotted lines of blood, but one of Gemma's cobblers would be well worth all of my scratches. By the time we had picked over half a potful of dewberries, the thunderstorm was close enough that Grandpa didn't want us to risk getting struck by lightning. A few sprinkles of rain were falling, and as the rain began falling in earnest, we pulled away in his old gray Mercury, which for some reason had refused to crank only three times.

That evening our dewberries made another appearance, this time cooked and juicy, enclosed in a heavenly cloud of butter, vanilla, and sugar sweet dumplings. And, of course, Grandpa and I argued over who got the first dishful.

CHAPTER 22

Chinaberry Summer

"Children should be seen and not heard."
— Aunt Pearl

"Old busy-body religious fanatics should not be seen or heard."
— Grandpa

Sunday afternoons in the summer brought delicious dinners in Gemma's kitchen. They brought icy cedar, hand-cranked churns filled with different flavors of homemade ice cream - vanilla, strawberry, and banana. They brought long naps to escape the heat and humidity outdoors, even though it was almost just as hot indoors. Sometimes they brought annoying relatives who dropped in for unannounced visits.

"Raleigh, why don't you and the other children go outside and play?" There she went again. Aunt Pearl must have never been a child. I swear, when she was born, her mama looked inside the baby blanket and saw a little old lady with a wrinkled face and a bun in her white hair. And since when did Spud and I become "the other children?"

Why did adults do things like that to children? Why did they assume that, just because we were children, we should all like each other and want to play together? Did the adults all like each other?

I don't think so, especially after I always accidentally overheard the way Gemma and Aunt Pearl talked about some of the visiting relatives after they left.

And why did the adults always make the children sit at a separate table to eat? What was *that* all about? Did our manners offend them? Mama tried to explain, "We just want to have an adult conversation." Did they figure we couldn't hear them four feet away in the corner where they always made us sit like outcasts?

I looked at Gemma and gave her a look to let her know I was not happy. To my surprise, she gave me the same look right back. "Go on, Sissie, and do the best you can. Remember Philippians 4:13."

I thought for a moment: "I can do all things through Christ who strengthens me." Well, I wasn't sure if even Jesus would have wanted to play with Raleigh if they had met as children. At least now I knew Raleigh wasn't really kin to me. He was just a visiting annoyance.

Spud, Raleigh, and I went outside and stood on the front porch. Raleigh didn't want to play with us – *he hated us*. I couldn't think of a single thing that the three of us could do together. We couldn't play hide and seek, because who would go looking for Raleigh? We couldn't see-saw, because last year when we had built a see-saw with a long board stretched over one of Grandpa's saw horses, Raleigh suddenly got tired of see-sawing and jumped off while Spud was still in the air.

Finally, we did what any two normal eleven year olds would do when they are stuck with a snotty, whiny little bully: We ran into the woods and hid until Raleigh gave up calling to us and went inside to the living room to watch television.

I looked at Spud and whispered behind a hackberry bush, "Maybe he'll leave us alone if we don't say anything else to him." We sneaked out from behind the leafy bush and headed to my house through the woods, not by the usual path.

The weather was warm and the blue sky was full of gigantic, cotton puffy clouds. Normally on a day like today, Spud and I would have been sitting on an old quilt in the backyard making up stories about the cloud shapes, but Spud had another idea.

"Let's take turns riding your bike."

We pulled my bike down off the front porch, and I took a few turns around the driveway. I rode faster on each loop as soon as the bike's front wheel left the soft sand in the middle of the loop and rolled onto the harder ground.

Next it was Spud's turn. After he peddled his first loop around the driveway, I looked out to see Daddy and Mama headed home on the path. I waved, and turned my attention back to Spud, who was about to start the fastest part of his second loop.

Suddenly, from out of nowhere, Raleigh came running toward us. He must have sneaked around the back of our house, because we hadn't seen him coming.

He had a wicked gleam in his eye. He pulled his hand from behind his back and threw at least a dozen or more chinaberries at Spud full force. He must have pulled those off the gnarly old chinaberry tree in the backyard. Most of the hard green berries hit Spud squarely in his face, making him lose his balance for only a moment, just long enough to make his bicycle wobble madly.

At that same instant the bicycle's front tire hit a large patch of sand in the driveway as Spud headed out of the curve. The bike crashed to the ground, throwing Spud onto the ground in a heap. He cried out in pain, trying to get up, but holding his right arm, which now had a funny angle to it.

Daddy had looked up just in time to see Raleigh fling the chinaberries in the ambush, and he came running to help us.

Raleigh was screaming at Spud, "You can't have my grandpa. He's *my* grandpa! And you don't have a daddy. You're illiterate!" Before Daddy could get to Spud, Raleigh saw Daddy coming and started high-tailing it back, across our lawn and through the field, to my grandparents' house, never once looking back.

When Daddy reached Spud, he helped him sit up. We turned and watched Raleigh, who by now was running so hard he was almost kicking his own behind. "That little monster had better run home to Raedean. She's gonna hear an earful from me."

Meanwhile Mama was hurrying toward us. She looked over and yelled at Raleigh, "You'd better run, you terrible little brat! And stay off our property!" She was giving him her best evil eye, but he was so wicked it bounced right off him.

My attention shot back to the problem at hand. "Daddy, we have to get Spud to the doctor." I was crying now. I was afraid for Spud.

"I know, Sissie, but it's Sunday. We'll have to take him to the hospital. Run out to your grandma's house and get Rose."

Now I know that I ask a lot of questions, but Raedean asked the stupidest question I have ever heard when Daddy told her what Raleigh had done. She turned to her son with a surprised look on her face and said, "*Raleigh*, did you *do* that?"

How was it that anyone with any sense whatsoever knew that Raleigh was a horrible, snot-nosed bully, but Raedean thought that he was a perfect little angel? If Patsy Stephens had seen what Raleigh did to Spud, she would have spelled out plenty of words to describe him, most of them too bad for me to repeat.

Walter and Raedean suddenly were in a hurry to get back home. In fact, their car was about to pull out of Gemma and Grandpa's driveway as Rose and Daddy sped down the road in our car taking Spud to the hospital.

Mama was furious with Raedean and Raleigh. "I can't believe that woman. When it comes to her precious little Raleigh, she's like a mule wearing blinders. She just looks straight ahead, and never sees a thing he does. And that boy is mean as a snake." Frankly, I didn't see any reason whatsoever for Mama to insult snakes.

The next day Spud was sitting on Aunt Pearl's couch behind a TV tray, looking miserable and eating chicken noodle soup with a spoon in his left hand, or at least trying to, because he was right-handed. *The Edge of Night* was blaring out from the television. Even Spud's broken arm couldn't keep Aunt Pearl from her stories. Wasn't the Stevenson family drama enough for her?

I sat down on the couch next to Spud. "Does it hurt much?" I asked. I wanted to touch the cast, but I was afraid I would hurt him more.

"It's not so bad right now. I hurt in too many other places to notice." Spud was wearing a T-shirt and shorts, and his legs and knees were covered in bruises and scrapes from his fall on the rocks and dirt in our driveway. It was a wonder that he hadn't broken something else.

I spoke up with anger in my voice. "Spud, if Raleigh Brown was here right now, I would…"

"*No*, Sissie, you wouldn't, because that would make you as mean as him, and you're not like that. You're not cruel. But Mama and Grandma said that he had better *never* set foot on this property. And Grandma said that goes for Raedean, too."

"I hope he never comes back here at all, not even to Gemma's house either," I fussed.

Spud looked down at his cast. A look of aggravation passed over his face like a dark thunder cloud. "I have to wear this stupid cast for at least six weeks. That means almost the whole summer I can't go swimming or ride a bicycle or anything. All because of those stupid chinaberries."

"No, all because of that stupid Raleigh Brown."

"I haven't even had this dang blasted thing on for more than a day, and my arm already itches where I can't scratch," he fairly growled.

In all the years I had known Spud, I don't think I had ever seen him so ill-tempered. He was mad at Raleigh. He was mad at Raedean. He was mad at chinaberries. He was mad at his cast. I decided I'd better leave and go on home before he got mad at me.

CHAPTER 23

A Come to Jesus Meeting

"A praying knee and a dancing foot don't grow on the same leg."
— *The Preacher*

The fourth Sunday in July was always the date for our family reunion. I don't know who in the world had made that decision years before. Whoever it was managed to pick a date that would ensure that the weather would be blazing hot and that the yellow jackets and mosquitoes would be fighting each other to see which ones could be the most worrisome.

But before our reunion dinner could get underway each year, our church held a special Sunday morning worship service that officially began our annual revival, which always lasted for one solid week. Uncle Toolie was the head deacon at Mount Olive, and he and Aunt Pearl liked to make the two events coincide because that meant more people would be in attendance on Reunion Sunday. Since most of the people there were kin to us in some way or another, maybe some of them might come back for the revival. They never did.

Grandpa once warned me, "Sissie, be careful about who you criticize in our church, because likely as not, you're kin to 'em somehow." Well, I didn't worry too much about criticizing the people at church. I just learned to be careful to do it behind their backs so they didn't hear me. I learned that the best from Mama.

Speaking of which, Mama walked down the hallway, peered into my bedroom, and gave me a stern look. It was too soon for a guilty look and not necessary for her to give me the evil eye yet.

"Sissie, hurry up, or we'll be late. Now put on all the clothes that I laid out for you to wear." Mama just never could accept the fact that I was a tomboy. That instamatic camera snapshot of me that she had pictured in her mind was not the same as the real me. Once again, I despised the torturous feminine outfit she had devised for me to wear: A new scratchy, lacy slip with elastic smocked across the back of the bodice. A crinoline starched so heavily that it could stand up alone, each ruffle a different pastel color, like a stiff rainbow with an elastic waist. A yellow flowery dress that buttoned impossibly in the back, along with a sash that I could never reach, much less tie correctly into a proper bow.

If I did manage to tie a bow, the knot always hit in the middle of my spine, so that if I leaned back against the pew, I felt a huge, uncomfortable lump in the middle of my backbone. There was a pair of black patent leather shoes, the kind with the strap that could be worn across my foot or folded down on the back of the shoe, along with thin white socks with lace around the tops. And last, a yellow and white hat that looked like a flattened bouquet of white daisies with yellow fuzzy centers. *This was worse than Easter.*

I couldn't believe that silly hat. "Maybe those daisies will tame that wild cowlick you have," Mama commented. "At least, maybe they'll cover it up." If she thought my hair needed taming, then why did she insist on giving me home permanents?

Biddie hummed happily as she put on her new outfit. She was taller and thinner than I was, and her new soft blue nylon and satin dress flattered her teenaged figure. My dress, along with my starchy crinoline, made me look like a silly goose fluffing its feathers to shake off rain water. And what's more, everything I had on either scratched, itched, or was too tight. Little did I know that much more misery was yet to come.

"Hurry, everybody, get into the car." Mama was finishing her covered dishes for the dinner on the ground, gathering bowls of food covered with aluminum foil and putting them into the refrigerator. The kitchen felt almost as hot as the oven, but an even hotter blast of heat hit us as we opened the door and headed outside to the car. It had rained during the night, not enough to help, though, just enough to make the day really steamy.

Biddie and I scooted into the back seat of Daddy's new white Plymouth. Biddie was all prim and proper as she sat down and straightened her skirt. She had even slipped on a pair of white gloves. I cringed as my back touched the hot vinyl of the car seat. The heat went straight through the fabric in the back of my dress and the elastic in my slip. I could even feel it through the sash knot that was boring into my spine. This was going to be a very hot July day.

* * * *

Our old white, clapboard church seemed to have put on its best appearance for the day. Even the steeple seemed to rise taller and prouder than usual. The bright morning sun made the window panes shine like diamonds, and the grass around the church had been freshly cut. The deacons had worked for hours to spruce up the yard, and they had even mowed all the grass in the cemetery.

The sign out front had been freshly painted with the name of our church, Mount Olive Baptist Church. Of course, not one single olive tree grew on the church property and the sanctuary wasn't on a mountain. I had always wondered how that name was chosen. I guess that someone back in 1858 must have just liked the name Mount Olive.

As I started to get out of the car in the church yard, I bumped my head on the car door and the daisy bouquet resting on top of my head went flying into the air and landed in the edge of a shallow mud puddle. I grabbed the hat as fast as I could, and Mama immediately pulled out some tissues from her purse and started wiping off the mud.

"Oh, Sissie, you are *impossible*! Can't you try just once to act like a lady? What will people think about you?" She continued wiping off the flowers, and when she felt that she had cleaned off the specks of mud well enough, she handed the hat back to me. "Here, put this back on. No one will notice the mud. It blends in with the daisy centers."

Why should I care what people thought about me? The main thing that mattered was what God thought about me. I figured that God didn't care if I wore that stupid daisy hat to church or not. If God had wanted daisies on my head, they would be growing there.

Inside the church the ceiling fans turned their paddles slowly, but like the smaller one in Gemma's house, they mostly just stirred the heat around. I wasn't too excited about going to the reunion service, not only because of my fancy uncomfortable clothes, but because we had a guest preacher. I hadn't heard too much about him, but I just hoped he wasn't another one of those who yelled. I could hear perfectly well, thank you, and I did not need anyone to scream at me. I hoped he would just try to do a better job than our regular preacher, Brother Eddie Edwards. Of course, we never called him Brother Ed or Brother Eddie. We just called him The Preacher.

The Preacher was all right when he was just walking around talking to people like a normal person or conducting the Easter sunrise service. But when he stepped into that pulpit, something came over him that made him think that everyone in our little church sanctuary had suddenly gone deaf. I guess he figured if he screamed at us, maybe we would pay closer attention, or his words would stick in our minds better. Of course, I had mastered the fine art of *The Preacher Face*. When he started yelling, I could look like I was really listening hard, but I had tuned him out, just like I had learned to do in Mrs. Melba Colley's classroom.

Now the best seat in the house was held by Mrs. Grace Johnson, our church pianist. We always called her Miss Gracie. She was wearing a yellow cotton dress with a matching belt covered with the same fabric as her dress, and she had on large yellow clip-on earbobs with gold-colored jewels in them plus a necklace with three strands of crystal beads. She always curled her hair with bobby pins, so the back of her head was a sea of tight little brown curls.

A mirror ran across the full width of the upright piano. Even though Miss Gracie sat with her back to the congregation, she could play music from her hymn book while keeping an eye on who was coming in late. She always had chewing gum in her mouth, but no one ever really noticed it unless we sang a hymn that was kind of fast. Then she chewed her gum harder to match the beat.

Gemma wasn't so subtle. She sat on the end of the pew at an angle near the front of the church. This position afforded her the ability to watch The Preacher give his sermon, see who was coming in late, and make sure that Grandpa hadn't fallen asleep on Reunion Sunday.

"Your grandma has the sharpest elbow I have ever felt," Grandpa complained after last year's Reunion Sunday. "She can crack a rib with that thing. It'll take me until next year for my rib bone to heal."

Wedged into the third pew were Gemma, Grandpa, then me, Spud, Daddy, Mama, and Biddie, who wasn't happy sitting with us. "Mama, why can't I sit in the back with the other teenagers? I don't want to sit here," she had whined on the way down the aisle.

"Because we need to sit together as a family. And a lot of times the teenagers talk and misbehave in church. I don't want you acting like that. What will people think?" Mama argued. Yeah, and Mama couldn't turn around and give Biddie the evil eye all the way in the back of the church either. What would people think?

Uncle Toolie, Aunt Pearl, and Rose sat in the pew behind us so that Aunt Pearl could poke Spud if he misbehaved. We liked to sit near Gemma, because she always had a pack of Juicy Fruit in her pocketbook, and she passed that down to Spud and me if we got restless. It was good to have Grandpa in church so I could sit with him. He was wearing dark navy blue pants, a brown plaid shirt, and a blue tie, the only one he owned, I guess, because I never saw him wearing a tie except on Reunion Sunday.

"A tie is just a silly waste of cloth, Sissie. Somethin' to catch gravy stains," Grandpa always said. He was right, because I could see a few of those stains that Gemma had tried in vain to wipe off with a damp washcloth.

In the little rack behind each pew, along with the usual hymn books, brand new funeral home fans had been placed for us to fan away the heat. I wondered why the funeral home always chose that same picture of snow-covered peaks, probably somewhere in the Rocky Mountains. I guess while we were sitting there melting in the blazing Georgia heat, we could look at the beautiful wintry scene and imagine how it would feel to be cold.

On the back of the fan, the funeral home had printed *Nelson and Bigham Funeral Home. Its our pleasure to serve your needs. We will always be their for you and your loved ones.* Be *their* what? And what happened to the apostrophe in *its*? Good grief, I was only eleven and my English grammar was better than that. If Miss Maude Jones had been in our church and had seen those mistakes on her fan, she would have whipped out a red pencil from her pocketbook and drawn big circles around the grammar errors. And shown them to the people in the funeral home.

The Preacher stood up from his oak and red velvet chair and carried his hymnal to the pulpit. "We will now sing 'Shall We Gather at the River.' Everybody please stand and sing this great old hymn of faith."

Why did we always have to sing that song? I always thought that song was pretty peculiar for us to sing at Mount Olive, since there wasn't a river around us for thirty miles. We should have sung "Shall We Gather at the Creek," since that's where we all gathered to be baptized. Miss Gracie played a verse to get the congregation into the proper tempo, and she started chewing her gum a little faster, four fourths time.

The congregation was standing to sing. I shared a hymn book with Spud, and we were lucky. We got one of the hymn books that one of the teenagers had written in. At least I hoped it was a teenager and not an adult. The offender had turned the hymnal into sort of a scavenger hunt. While everyone else was singing about gathering at the beautiful river, Spud and I followed the clues scribbled in our hymn book. "Turn to page 107." When we reached that page another note scrawled in pencil read, "Now turn to page 347."

Every page we reached told us to find another page. At last we reached the end of the line. We found the hymn "Leaning on the

Everlasting Arms," and the unknown scavenger had added words in the title and changed it to read, "Oh, Baby, You're Leaning on My Everlasting Arms."

I'm not sure that the new song title was all that funny, but it sure seemed funny, because we were in church and we couldn't misbehave. Spud and I began to giggle, but we didn't dare laugh out loud. So we just stood there, our heads bowed and our shoulders shaking, trying to keep from laughing. Spud was even holding his nose so that no bubbles could come out. Aunt Rose poked Spud in the back, and Aunt Pearl thumped his right ear. Mama snapped her fingers at me and gave me the evil eye. "Behave!" she fussed in a loud whisper that I could hear over the music.

With the hymn finally finished, The Preacher closed his hymn book and asked the question: "Shall we pray?"

I really dreaded The Preacher's prayers, because they seemed to go on for at least half an hour, except when he was blessing a meal – then they were quick. Daddy had explained that to me once during Sunday dinner.

"Daddy, why does The Preacher pray for so long on Sundays?"

He thought a moment and answered, "Well, I think The Preacher must not pray all week long, so he has a lot of catchin' up to do on Sunday mornin'."

Grandpa added his explanation. "Naw, that ain't it. I reckon his wife talks all week long and doesn't let him get a word in edgewise, so on Sundays The Preacher just enjoys hearin' the sound of his own voice."

I have to confess that during The Preacher's prayer I bowed my head, but I kept my eyes open. All the time that he was praying his lengthy catch-up prayer, I was looking at that beautiful snow-covered mountain on my fan. I wondered if it was anywhere near the continental divide. I wondered if it was in Colorado. I wondered why the people at the funeral home printed an advertisement on the back of dozens of church fans if they didn't know proper English grammar.

"All these things we ask in your name, Lord, amen and amen," The Preacher concluded his prayer. At long last he let the Lord's ears rest. It was time for the offering. Two deacons went forward with the offering plates, and The Preacher called on Daddy to bless the offering we were about to give. As long as he had talked, why couldn't The Preacher have asked God to bless the offering himself? Finally, Miss Gracie broke out into her usual three verses of "Bringing in the Sheaves."

I once looked up the word *sheaves* in a school dictionary. It was one day in Mrs. Colley's class when she was talking endlessly about termites. I didn't learn a thing about termites, but I found out that sheaves were bundles of grain tied together. So while Miss Gracie was playing that hymn, I was sitting there wondering if anyone had ever actually put sheaves in the offering plate, and I'm not sure exactly how it happened, but when the offering plate got to me, I handed it over to Spud, and maybe he just wasn't prepared, or he still had his hand in his pocket looking for his other nickel, or he was still trying to scratch the itch under his cast. But somehow he dropped the offering plate. That metal plate must have bounced at least five times on the hardwood floor, scattering dollar bills and coins everywhere before rolling a few feet, wobbling noisily, and finally coming to rest under the front pew.

Everyone started scrambling to pick up change and coins and get the plate moving again before Miss Gracie finished the third verse. We got everything put back into the plate, plus a few extra items we found under the pews, passed the plate along, and got settled in. I looked over at Mama, and she was giving me the evil eye again.

When I was younger, I used to wonder when I was reading stories about strange gypsy women who could give someone the evil eye: *What the heck is the evil eye?* Then I thought about Mama when Biddie or I misbehaved. I don't know if her version was the same as the one in the storybooks, but that look was plenty scary to Biddie and me.

"And now the choir has a special song they would like to sing," The Preacher announced to us. It was a beautiful song about how Jesus died and rose again. Well, it *could* have been a beautiful song.

I looked at the members of the choir. Most of them looked either dead tired or uninspired. They were singing a song about the resurrection of Jesus, and they didn't look joyful at all. In fact, they never looked up from their music at all. I wanted to stand up and shout to them, sort of like The Preacher, "For Pete's sake, you're saying that Jesus rose from the dead. Can't you people show a little joy?" But I figured Aunt Pearl would poke me instead of Spud.

Speaking of Spud, he had turned his funeral home fan so that he could push the handle down into his cast and scratch his itchy arm, which sort of made him wave his fan around. When Aunt Pearl poked him hard in his back, I wondered if she had ever had to wear a cast in the summertime.

Finally it was time for the sermon, and The Preacher stood up. "We are privileged to have Reverend Homer Snow with us today and for our revival all this week. Brother Snow, will you come now and speak to us?"

An older, white-haired man rose from the other red velvet chair and came forward.

Homer? Spud perked up immediately. Here was a fellow sufferer. The way he walked up to the pulpit made me feel that Brother Snow knew what he was talking about and that he believed what he was talking about, too.

"Good morning, everyone," Brother Snow began. "Today I'd like to take you fishing with Jesus and his disciples at the Sea of Galilee. Then this week during our revival I'd like to take you for a walk with Paul on some of his journeys."

I braced myself and got ready for the yelling to commence, and I couldn't believe my ears. Brother Snow must have talked for over thirty minutes, and he didn't yell at us a single time. He just talked in a normal voice about Jesus and Paul. He had even been to all the places he described for us.

Brother Snow was a good preacher, but Spud did take exception to one thing. In the middle of Brother Snow's sermon, a big brown spider walked across the floor up near the pulpit. Miss Gracie cringed, and people as far back as the fourth pew started watching the spider instead of Brother Snow. Mrs. Lois Davis, who was seated in the pew in front of me, picked her feet up. I don't know why so many people are that afraid of a plain old woods spider.

Without stopping his sermon, Brother Snow walked over, stepped on the spider, and returned to the pulpit, leaving the spider in a heap on the floor. Spud elbowed me softly in my side and whispered, "What did I tell you about people killing spiders?" For that, he received another poke in the back from Aunt Pearl.

As Brother Snow was continuing to tell us about Paul's travels, all eyes suddenly went back to the heap on the floor. The crumpled spider had somehow managed to stand up and continue its doomed journey toward the altar. Again Brother Snow, still preaching, walked over, stepped on the spider even harder, and returned to the pulpit.

He looked back at the now lifeless heap. "I guess that spider must've been a Baptist."

Meanwhile the heat was getting worse inside our little church. Even though the windows were wide open and the overhead fans were spinning their wooden blades, a trickle of sweat started to roll down my back. The creepy elastic smocking in my slip was digging into my back, and the sweat aggravated my skin, making it itch even more. The stiff lace on my new slip was scratching under my arm pits, and my patent leather shoes were beginning to get tighter against my heels. Every time I tried to adjust the way I was sitting, I managed to sit on that starched crinoline, which was pressing a mesh pattern like a screen door into the backs of my legs. If I leaned back against the pew, the knot in the bow on the back of my dress pushed hard into my spine like a small rock.

I guess that The Preacher wasn't satisfied that Brother Snow hadn't yelled at us and warned us about Judgment Day and about all the people who were going to hell, so after Brother Snow sat down, The Preacher had to stand up and have his say. I reckon he figured that he had only one chance a year to yell at some of my relatives, because they never darkened the door of the church on any other Sunday of the year, and that included Grandpa.

I thought, "Lord, don't let him start talking about the evils of dancing, or we'll be here all afternoon for sure."

When The Preacher finally finished his sermonette, he led us in our altar call hymn. I sure hoped he didn't ask us to raise our hands if we were ready to go to heaven. The lace on my slip was already carving an everlasting scratch in both of my arm pits, and if I raised my hand, the smocked elastic in the back of my slip would crawl up my sweaty shoulder blades and irritate the prickly heat rash that was already forming there. And, besides, I wasn't ready to go to heaven – I hadn't even made it to Florida yet.

Now there are only so many times that a congregation should repeatedly sing all the verses of "Amazing Grace" in one service. The Preacher never seemed to get tired of singing verse after verse over and over again. The more verses Miss Gracie played, the slower the overheated congregation sang. Pretty soon we would all be asleep in our pews. I began to hope that someone would come forward to the altar and confess his sins just so The Preacher would turn us loose and I could go home and change my clothes.

At last, it truly did feel like the Spirit was moving among the members of our little congregation, when suddenly a giant buzzing cicada flew wildly in through the open front doors and hit the fan right above us. The loud scratchy noise of the giant winged insect as he was flying in and then the commotion as his body was being blasted to smithereens on the people below merged with the sound of spinning fan blades, and, well, that brought on the last verse of "Amazing Grace."

In the book of Ecclesiastes, The Preacher says that there is a time for every purpose under heaven. Hallelujah! It was time for the church service to be over.

It was time for me to change clothes. It was time for our family to gather. It was time to eat dinner on the ground.

CHAPTER 24

Shall We Gather

"If the Devil doesn't get you, Mama will, and that's worse."
— Biddie

A few weeks before the family reunion, I had accidentally overheard a discussion between Mama and Daddy. I was outside carefully observing the behavior of honeybees buzzing in the althea bush located directly under the open kitchen window. Their little brown and yellow bodies were so powdery and loaded down with pollen that, I declare, I didn't see how they were able to lift off, much less fly. I'd had a few encounters with them in my life, and they really knew how to sting.

Just as I was thinking about what Mrs. Martin had taught us in science class about the queen bee, Mama's voice drifted out the window. "Jeb, I just don't want to go to the reunion. I'll cook plenty of food for you to take out to your mama and daddy's house. And I'll go to church. But I don't want to go to the reunion. *And that's final.*"

"Honey, please reconsider," Daddy was pleading with her.

Now if the truth be told, Mama didn't like most of Daddy's family. "Jeb, you're asking an awful lot of me. I don't force you to go to a reunion for *my* family every year."

"Yeah, but *mine* is different."

"How is yours any different? *I am curious to know.*" She had a nasty tone in her voice.

"My family is next door. It'll be a little hard for them not to notice that you aren't there. What can I tell everybody? How can I explain why you're not at the reunion, especially if you go to church?"

"Tell them I'm sick. Tell them I got a headache during church. Lord knows, The Preacher could give anybody a headache," Mama sniped.

"You know they'll just all come pilin' in on you here to check on you," Daddy headed her off.

I couldn't see her face, but I could imagine the look in her eyes. I could have sworn I heard the cabinet door open and the aspirin bottle rattle. "Jeb, do you know how I feel about most of the people who show up at your family reunions?"

"How?"

"I wouldn't have a thing to do with them if they weren't kin to you. And you feel the same way, too, you just won't admit it."

Daddy sounded hurt. "I do not."

"Yes, you do," she insisted.

"Now, baby, come on. If you'll go to the reunion, I promise I'll do something extra special for you. I'm probably gonna get some bonus money later this summer. How would you like to go to Florida one week-end?" Of course, that offer included Biddie and me, I hoped. I got so excited I almost put my hand on a huge bumblebee that was backing out of an althea blossom.

"Oh, all right, but it had better be a special trip to make up for me having to spend all Sunday afternoon feeling like I'm stuck in a box of animal crackers with some of your loony relatives."

"I'll make it up to you, honey, I will. I *promise.*"

And so Mama had cooked half the night and had even gotten up at six o'clock on Sunday morning to finish cooking the food she was taking to the reunion. Daddy had gone to bed early on Saturday night and slept like a log.

* * * *

With the Sunday service now over, the congregation streamed

out of the stuffy heat in the sanctuary and into the blazing heat in the front yard of the church. Many people were giving each other hugs while others were simply shaking hands politely. A few used their yearly visit to our church as a time to walk over to the cemetery to pay their respects to family members who were buried at Mount Olive.

"Come on, Aunt Ida, let us help you," Gemma offered. She and Aunt Pearl helped their elderly aunt make her way across a low brick wall to visit the grave of her husband William, my great-great uncle, who had died in 1925. It was sort of a miracle that he was buried in the church cemetery, even though he had always been a member of Mount Olive.

Gemma had told me all about him. "He joined Mount Olive when he was a boy. Years later, after he failed to attend three regular church conferences in a row, his name was removed from the church roll and he was asked to move his membership to another church. He never went back to church anywhere. When Uncle William died suddenly one hot summer afternoon, Aunt Ida took on the deacons and the preacher at Mount Olive."

The story was that Aunt Ida was wearing white lace gloves, and she shook her lacy fist at the preacher. "My husband spent his life in this church. If you don't let me bury him here, you'll never see me or a dime of my money again." Uncle William was buried in the church cemetery the next day and no one ever crossed Aunt Ida again. I wondered if any other people buried in our cemetery had been like Uncle William, or if they had all just died as quiet Baptists.

After everyone had had a chance to visit outside the church, cars full of relatives began to pull out of the gravelly church yard and head toward Gemma and Grandpa's house. We hurried to our house to collect all the food that Mama had made.

In the car on the way home Daddy said, "Now, Mama, make sure I know which dishes you cooked. I will not eat anything made by Ruby Gail, Raedean, or Aunt Ida. Ruby Gail and Raedean don't know how to cook, and God only knows what might be floatin' around in Aunt Ida's food. She's got 'bout forty 'leven cats." By the time we arrived at our house, cars were parked alongside the dirt road, down Gemma's driveway, in our driveway, and even into the edge of the woods.

I do not know what hell is like, unless it's anything like being stuck somewhere in a locked room forever with Raleigh Brown, Rusty Jackson, Miss Maude Jones, and a swarm of angry hornets thrown in for good measure.

However, I do think I know what heaven is like. I experienced heaven when I ran into my bedroom and shed all the misery of those hot, scratchy, itchy clothes and slipped into the joy of my sleeveless blouse and shorts. I put on my socks and tennis shoes, went outside, and ran around the house twice just to feel the breeze on my skin. Then I ran to Gemma's house before Mama had time to notice that I wasn't wearing a skirt.

Under the pine trees Grandpa and Uncle Toolie had already laid sheets of plywood over sawhorses the day before to create long tables, and Gemma and Aunt Pearl draped the plywood with ironed white cotton bed sheets. Trunk lids and car doors popped open, and like magic, casseroles began to appear almost out of the thin air. When all the coolers were opened and all the dishes of food were placed on the makeshift tables, I declare I think we could've probably fed a small town.

I have never smelled so many different kinds of perfume in all my life. Every aunt who hugged me to her bosom was wearing a floral fragrance, mostly too strong. One smelled like gardenias, another like honeysuckle. Aunt Georgia was surrounded by a heavy cloud of perfume that smelled like old fashioned roses. For some reason, Aunt Ida smelled like vinegary, fermenting June apples.

Grandpa's cousin Dovie hugged me. She smelled like lilacs. "I declare, Biddie, you get prettier every time I see you." Well, I wasn't pretty and I wasn't Biddie, but at least she was trying.

The mouthwatering aroma of Southern fried chicken mingled with the other aromas of every possible kind of casserole that was set out on the tables alongside heaping bowls of potato salad and slaw. Platters were heaped with pimento cheese sandwiches cut into little triangles. Cakes of every color and flavor added their own wonderful smells to the delicious, fragrant cloud hanging over the tables. A large dish of Aunt Pearl's banana pudding was nestled among apple pies and peach cobblers. Some of the cousins used church fans to keep flies away.

Hungry relatives piled food on thick paper plates that always made my flesh crawl if I scratched them with my fork. People were laughing, talking, and eating at the same time, holding on to their plates and somehow balancing their waxy paper cups of sweet iced tea and lemon slices.

I saw Biddie once. She and three other giggling girls who were our teenage cousins had hurried through the line and headed for the back porch. The idea was to escape Spud and me, because we were too young to be cool. I hated it when Biddie acted like a teenager instead of my sister.

Rose was busy helping Gemma and Aunt Pearl, so she was constantly running back and forth to the kitchen. "Sissie, could you please help Spud? He needs help fixing his plate and carrying his tea."

"Sure, Aunt Rose." I found Spud in line, trying to make a decision about what to eat. He wasn't really having any problems putting food on his plate, though, because two aunts who kept referring to him as a "poor little baby" were spooning out potato salad and squash casserole onto his plate, right next to a fried chicken leg.

"I'll come back and help you get your tea, Spud." I hated the feel of those paper plates, but I didn't have any choice if I wanted to eat, so I started through the line, too.

Someone touched me softly on the shoulder. It was Aunt Rose again. "Here, Sissie." She quietly handed me one of Gemma's kitchen plates. "Use this. Your grandma said just bring it into the kitchen when you get finished."

"Why, thank you, Aunt Rose," I said, running my fingers over the plate and enjoying the touch of the smooth glass.

I started down the line putting a sample of everything that looked good to me on my aqua blue china plate. Gemma came by with a pitcher of tea.

"You remembered, Gemma." She knew I couldn't abide the scraping feel of those rough plates. I just couldn't eat off one them to save my life, even though I always tried.

"Of course, I remembered," she whispered.

Uncle Toolie and Aunt Pearl had invited The Preacher and Miss Thelma, and from the looks of his plate he must have truly believed all his sermons about Judgment Day, because he was eating like there was no tomorrow. "Don't forget your dessert, Thelma honey, there might not be any when we come back through the line," The Preacher cautioned his wife.

Under our feet the crunchy pine straw felt like a thick, inviting brown rug, and relatives were sitting wherever they could find a place – on the porch steps, in the swings, in folding chairs borrowed from the church. Uncle Toolie had set some homemade benches around as well, and a few people were sitting on quilts spread out on the pine straw.

I looked around at the assortment of people gathered, and I realized that I had not seen Raleigh even once. Where was he? I had to agree with Mama – I wouldn't have had anything to do with Raleigh except for the fact that he was in our family. Spud was trying to carry his plate in his left hand and use his cast to hold his iced tea against his chest.

"Spud," I called out. "Wait!" I went to help him, but I was having trouble balancing everything myself. "Where do you wanna sit?"

He looked around at all the people sitting everywhere. "How 'bout in your dining room?" he asked, and he wasn't teasing.

"Very funny. I wish we could." We headed slowly toward the porch just in case there might be an empty seat up there somewhere. Surely someone would feel sorry for a boy with a broken arm.

"Here, you children sit down right here on the steps. There's room for you." Several cousins were seated on the cement steps. "Y'all scoot over and give them some room." A friendly, red-headed woman invited us to sit down: Ruby Gail. The porch step cousins obliged and scooted closer to give us enough space to sit on the top step.

Ruby Gail got up from her chair and helped Spud. "Here you go, sugar. I'll hold your plate while you sit down." Then she returned to her seat in the glider and began eating a large fried chicken breast. Maybe she was strange, like Grandpa had said, but she was also kind.

"Good Lord, these eggs are delicious – Ruby Gail, where's little Raleigh?" Aunt Georgia asked, between bites of deviled eggs. "I haven't seen him today." I knew I was smelling old fashioned roses for some reason.

"Oh, honey, let me tell you. Raedean sent him to a Catholic boarding school up near Atlanta," Ruby Gail said, in a half whisper.

"But it's the summer time. School's suppose to be out," Aunt Georgia continued, as if Ruby Gail didn't have sense enough to know that it was summer.

"Not at Mother Mary's School for Troubled Children. School's never out," she said firmly.

I wondered if Mother Mary was ready for Raleigh. I didn't know much about Catholic schools except what I had read in books or seen on television, but it was my understanding that some of the nuns would sometimes hit students with a ruler for misbehaving. I wasn't sure that only twelve inches of thin wood would do Raleigh much good. I figured after the first week the nuns had probably stopped using rulers and had started whacking him over the head with a yardstick, or maybe even a two-by-four board.

Aunt Ida piped up from her seat in the swing. "Why in the world did she send him to a *Catholic* school? She's a Baptist."

"Well, he got into a little spot of trouble," Ruby Gail continued. I wondered if she was silently nodding her head toward Spud, since we were both eating quietly on the step with our backs turned to them. Or maybe she had just forgotten we were sitting there, like Mama always said.

"What kind of trouble?" Aunt Ida persisted. Not only was she bossy, she was apparently very nosey, too.

"Don't tell Raedean I told you, but he threw rocks and broke a bunch of car windows in their neighborhood. The judge gave Raedean two choices. Raleigh would be arrested and get locked away for six months in a reform school or he could go to Mother Mary's School," Ruby Gail explained. So that was Raleigh's *little spot of trouble.* What did she call breaking Spud's arm?

"Oh, my goodness," Aunt Ida gasped. "Where in the world was Raedean when all this rock-throwin' happened?"

Ruby Gail continued, her whisper much louder now. "She was at the beauty parlor. Carl was supposed to be watchin' him, but, well, you know Carl. Raedean's really upset. Raleigh's so young, and he's usually such a sweet little boy. He just got in with the wrong little friends." Suddenly Spud got choked on a mouthful of potato salad, and I had to slap his back a time or two before I was sure he was breathing okay.

Aunt Pearl walked up on the porch steps holding an empty tea pitcher in each hand. She had to wade through all the aunts, uncles, and cousins seated every which way in folding metal chairs. As I watched her make her way to the kitchen, I couldn't help but think that she looked a lot like a righteous Moses trying to part the Red Sea.

Aunt Ida spoke up, "Is this your famous banana pudding, Pearl?"

"Why, yes, it is." Pearl paused to enjoy the moment, almost forgetting the empty tea pitchers in her hands. "I made it using Mama's old recipe."

"Well, it's absolutely delicious. " Aunt Ida cooed, her voice velvety sweet.

Ruby Gail chimed in. "It sure is, honey. I declare, if that dish had a divin' board on it, I'd just jump right into it." Aunt Pearl beamed with pride.

One of the cousins got up from her folding chair to open the screen door, but Rose met Pearl at the screen door. "Here, Mama, I'll take those. You need to go get something to eat. Go on now. I'll bring some more tea out in a minute."

Pearl turned around and crossed back over to the other side of the Red Sea and headed out to get something to eat, a saintly look on her face. But I knew she had said plenty of unkind things about Ruby Gail and Aunt Ida in the past, because I had overheard her talking to Gemma in the kitchen. She may have considered herself righteous, but as she left the porch, she never once stopped to ask Spud if he needed anything.

As she walked across the yard, a cousin stopped her. "Pearl, your banana pudding is heavenly, as usual."

We could hear Aunt Pearl all the way up on the porch. "My daddy always said that no matter how bitter your life is, you can always sweeten it up with a good dessert."

Aunt Ida said in a low voice, "Lord, there she goes again with one of her pearls of wisdom."

"Humph," Aunt Georgia added, "her pearls of wisdom dropped out of a cheap dime store bracelet."

Aunt Ida spoke up again, this time in her normal voice, sounding like she really cared. "Where's Sharon? I thought maybe she might come this year."

Ruby Gail spoke up. "Ida, you know she doesn't come to these family reunions. My God, she doesn't even come home to see her mama and daddy."

"Well, who could blame her?" one of the other aunts spoke up, the one who smelled like honeysuckle. "If I was Sharon, I wouldn't come home either. If Pearl was your mama, would *you* want to come home?"

Spud was chewing very slowly and quietly, but he reminded me a lot of a praying mantis sitting perfectly still on a flower watching an unsuspecting spider. He barely moved a muscle, but his antennae were up, his eyes were moving, and he was listening to everything that was being said.

Three cousins decided they had had enough to eat, or maybe they had had enough of Ruby Gail, Aunt Ida, and Aunt Georgia. They took their empty plates and headed down toward the serving tables. Grandpa, Toolie, and Walter were sitting in folding chairs near the serving tables, and I could tell from Uncle Toolie's outstretched hands that he was in the middle of a fishing tale. Eleanor and Gemma were sitting together near them, and Pearl settled down in an empty chair beside them, her plate of food balanced on her lap.

The three empty chairs on the porch spelled trouble, because Raedean, her mousey husband Carl, and Winston had just arrived at the reunion late, and they were headed toward us carrying plates piled with food. Raedean was dressed in a pink suit and white high heels, and she was wearing a pearl choker and large matching pearl earrings. A flat white hat with roses on it was perched on top of her curly blond hair. Her husband Carl, dressed in shorts, a plaid shirt half hanging out and half tucked in, and tennis shoes without socks, walked behind her, never saying a word to anybody.

When they reached the porch steps, Raedean looked down at Spud and me and suddenly noticed my plate. "Well, how did you rate a china plate? I guess your mama didn't think paper plates were good enough for you."

"My mother didn't give me this plate," I answered back. "My Aunt Rose did." I probably didn't sound too respectful when I said it, but I didn't have much respect for her anyway.

"Ooh, your *Aunt* Rose. I see. Well, little Homer, how is your arm?" What a cold, unconcerned tone she had in her voice, like she was asking but she didn't really want to know.

Spud looked as if she had just poured hot grease on his head. "It's all right," he mumbled. He stared down at the remaining food on his plate, like he had just lost his appetite.

I spoke up, mostly to Spud, but for Raedean's benefit. "It's *not* all right, Spud, you've had to wear a cast all summer."

"Well, I'm sure it was just an accident. These things sometimes happen when children ride bicycles," she added, like his broken arm was somehow all Spud's fault, like he was being careless. If my friend Patsy Stephens had been on the porch listening to Raedean, she would have taken one look at Raedean and spelled out i-d-i-o-t. Or something much worse.

Winston spoke up all of a sudden. "Dang, I knew I was forgetting something. I forgot my drink. Raedean, would you mind going back to get me some tea?"

"Daddy, I told you not to forget to get something to drink," she whined.

"I can go get your tea. I'll be right back," I volunteered, mostly to get away from Raedean. I started to get up from the step.

"No, he asked *me*. I'll go get it." Raedean put her plate down in her chair and stormed off the porch. She acted worse than any child I knew, including her son.

"Why are y'all just now gettin' here?" Ruby Gail asked Winston. "I thought you'd be here in time for church."

"You know Raedean. When I got to her house, she had to do half a dozen things before we left. She's in a foul mood. She didn't want to come. You shouldn't have insisted." Raedean's husband Carl, seated right next to Winston, never opened his mouth, except to stuff food into it.

Ruby Gail apparently ignored his comment, because she suddenly stood up and said, "I'm going back for some more dessert. Are you finished, Ida?"

"Well, I wouldn't mind having another small slice of cake, if you don't mind." Another small slice? The first piece I had seen on her plate wasn't a slice – it was a wedge.

His wife and daughter out of earshot for a few minutes, Winston carried his plate over to the steps. Two more cousins had left, leaving a little space beside us, so Winston sat down next to Spud. He put his arm around Spud's shoulder, gave him a quick hug, and asked, "Spud, how are you doing?"

"Uh, I'm okay, I guess," Spud answered in an uneasy voice.

"Is that arm giving you much trouble?" he asked, sounding concerned.

"No, sir, it mostly just itches a lot," Spud explained, his voice a little unsure. He must have been wondering why Winston was interested in him and his arm.

"I'm sorry that happened to you, son. I wish it hadn't. That was a very thoughtless thing that Raleigh did." Spud's mouth dropped open in surprise.

Before Spud could think of something to say, Mama came up the walkway. "So this is where you two finally ended up sitting. I'm just going in the kitchen and help Rose. I don't think she's eaten a thing yet."

I couldn't help noticing the look on her face as she took in the scene with Winston sitting next to Spud, talking to him. She walked up the steps onto the porch and stopped to speak to some of the ladies before going inside and closing the screen door behind her.

Raedean was headed up the walkway behind her with

Winston's cup of iced tea. She didn't miss the scene with Winston and Spud either, and a dark cloud of anger swept across her face. "Here's your tea, Daddy. I see you two are talking like a couple of lost buddies. Raleigh would probably be jealous. That's one thing I can say for Raleigh. He loves his granddaddy. He refuses to share him with anybody."

"Raedean, *hush*," Winston said in a low voice, his face turning red.

"Well, it's the truth. He should be here today with me, instead of away in that awful school." Her voice got louder. "Nobody seems to believe in that boy but *me*."

"Raedean, this is not the time or the place," Winston said firmly.

"Well, *what is* the time or the place, Daddy?" she shot back, her voice getting even louder. "I go get your tea, and while I'm gone, you sit with this fatherless boy and forget all about your own grandson who's suffering away from his family."

"This boy *is* my own grandson," he blurted out, "and he's suffered plenty, too." Gasps could be heard from the remaining relatives on the porch, and I wondered if Aunt Ida or Aunt Georgia would have a heart attack. Spud and I were motionless, afraid to move. We'd secretly listened in on plenty of adult conversations before, but we had never actually been in the middle of grown people arguing like Winston and Raedean were doing.

"Well, maybe you'd better be more concerned with your legitimate family!" She was so mad she was spitting when she talked, and she threw his cup on the sidewalk, splattering tea everywhere and sending little pieces of ice in all directions.

"*Raedean!*" A voice called out from behind us on the porch. It was Mama. And she had the same tone I had heard only once before – when she was on the phone with Miss Maude Jones. I looked around so fast my neck joint popped, and the look on her face was not look number one, two, or three. In fact, I had never seen that expression on Mama's face before. It was way beyond the evil eye.

"Don't you dare say something like that in front of that child. *What is the matter with you?*" She and Rose were coming out the front door at about the same time Raedean had started her loud speech about Spud.

"Well, I didn't figure it was any big secret. How old is he? Ten? Eleven? Somebody should've told him what he is by now."

"Raedean, *hush this minute!*" Ruby Gail hissed behind her, holding saucers of cake in both hands. "You're embarrassing us and making a fool of yourself."

"Spud, Sissie, go inside the house. *Now!*" Mama snapped out the order so fast that neither of us dared to argue. Of course, that didn't mean that we couldn't stand inside the living room doorway and listen through the screen door.

"Look how you're acting. No wonder Raleigh acts the way he does," Mama fussed at Raedean.

"Everybody picks on Raleigh," Raedean fussed back. "Raleigh didn't mean any harm. He just thought Homer already knew the truth about his real grandfather and his daddy. And Spud and Sissie wouldn't play with him." Her voice had become whiny.

Mama didn't back down. "He called Spud names. He told him his mother and father weren't married. He made Spud have a bicycle wreck and break his arm. He told Spud he couldn't have his grandfather. Raleigh is a bully. He has problems, Raedean. *Are you so blind that that you can't see what everybody else sees?*"

"Well! I have never been so insulted in all my…" she started saying, but the next voice we heard interrupting Raedean was Aunt Rose.

Quiet, sweet, saintly Rose. "Raedean, you've been spreading that lie about Edward and me for years, and I'm sick of it. You need to drop it and quit living in the past. Everybody knows you wanted Edward McKenna for yourself, and you were jealous when he picked me instead of you. And for your information, and for everyone else's information here, Edward and I were married by a justice of the peace." This was better than watching one of Aunt Pearl's afternoon stories, because we were actually in one of them.

Rose was on a roll, like she had been holding back for years and was letting everything go. "Yes, it's true, we weren't married in a Baptist church in front of fifty people, with flowers and a white frosted cake, but we were legally married when our son was born.

Your reputation hasn't exactly been lily white either, Raedean. You might think about that. For God's sake, just because I'm your sister and there's not a thing you can do about it, don't take that out on my son." More gasps from the relatives on the porch.

Even after my long talk with Grandpa at the creek, my mouth must have made another capital O. I had never actually thought about the fact that if Winston was Rose's father and he was Raedean's father, too, then they were half sisters. So that made Raleigh Spud's first cousin, or half first cousin, or half a cousin. How disgusting was that? In fact, he was closer kin to Spud than I was. And since Raedean was Rose's sister, then she was a sorry excuse for an aunt.

CHAPTER 25

Troubled Waters

"You've got all the answers, and nobody has asked you the questions."
– Daddy

Well, that certainly was a family reunion to remember. Throughout the whole scene on the front porch, Carl had never said a word. Raedean stormed off with her mousey husband in her daddy's car, but Winston and Ruby Gail actually stayed on for a while longer. I would have thought that he and Ruby Gail would be so embarrassed that they would high-tail it on home, too, but they weren't. In fact, they acted at ease, like they were finally free of something very heavy that had been weighing them down for a very long time and they had finally laid it down.

And other strange but wonderful things happened as well. While we were gathering all of Mama's empty dishes and putting them into a cardboard box to take them home, Rose hugged Mama good-bye even though we were just going next door. It wasn't a quick hug either. It was a grateful hug that let us all know that Mama was no longer just Rose's cousin by marriage – she was Rose's friend.

Meanwhile gossip about the argument on the porch had moved through the crowd of relatives at the reunion like a wildfire in a dry September cornfield. Most people were whispering about it, except Aunt Ida, of course. She just talked right out loud about everything she had heard. Aunt Pearl wasn't too happy about the fracas, but when she found out about how Mama had stood up for Rose and Spud, I saw her quietly wiping her eyes with her apron.

Gradually the reunion began to break up, and all the assorted relatives with their empty casserole dishes and cake plates, coolers, and quilts, loaded into their cars and headed off in all directions to parts unknown, at least until the next Fourth Sunday in July. I was already dreading July 1961.

The woods and the yard at Gemma and Grandpa's house gradually returned to normal after Uncle Toolie and Grandpa took down all the makeshift tables. Nothing was left of the reunion except the memories of fading voices on the breeze.

"Winston and Ruby Gail can't help how Raedean acts," Daddy said to us later that afternoon. "She's a grown woman, I guess, at least *age-wise* she's grown."

He and Mama were sitting at the dining room table, having a cup of coffee. I declare, they could drink coffee in one hundred degree weather.

"Well, I think she's worse than Raleigh," Biddie added.

Mama sighed, "I have to agree with Biddie. Raleigh can always change as he grows up, but Raedean, well, I expect she'll always be Raedean."

I spoke up, trying to add something meaningful to the conversation.

"It's just like Grandpa says, 'A copperhead will always be a copperhead. He won't ever be a king snake no matter how hard he tries.'"

Daddy turned and looked me straight in the eye. "You know, Sissie, you've got all the answers, and nobody has asked you the questions." I took exception to that remark. In fact, I thought Daddy got that comment backwards. I had questions, lots of questions, and nobody had ever given me all the answers, although Grandpa sure tried.

Daddy looked over at Mama. "Now, I believe I owe you a

vacation in Florida." Did I hear Daddy correctly? I almost reached up and hit both sides of my head with the palms of my hands to make sure my ears were clear.

"When, Jeb?" she asked, for the first time in forever looking excited about something. Her eyes suddenly had a warm brightness as she looked at Daddy.

"How 'bout in two weeks? Mid-August. A customer told me about some place his friend owns. He called them *villas*. We can reserve one for the week-end, and we can all go."

I wasn't sure I could read the look on Mama's face. It was a mixture of both excitement and dread. *We can all go.* Did Daddy think those words really went together well with *vacation*?

Later I headed out next door to sit on the porch with Grandpa. As I cut through Gemma's kitchen, everything was in order, just like the reunion had never happened. She was lying down in the bedroom resting, and Grandpa was sitting in the back porch swing rolling up one of his cigarettes.

I quietly opened the screen door and went out to join him. We sat there not saying a word for a long time, and I thought about the events of the day as the sun slowly started dropping in the west. I figured Grandpa was thinking about a lot of things, too. Finally I spoke up, "You're sure quiet tonight, Grandpa."

"I'm awful tired," he sighed. "I'm gettin' too old for all this reunion nonsense. This one really took a lot out of me. Out of your grandma, too." He struck a match and lit up the end of his cigarette.

"You mean, Raedean and the way she acted?" I asked.

"Well, that's part of it, but just movin' everything and gettin' tables set up. Then takin' it all down again. It's too much work," he said, rubbing his right arm and drawing in a puff of smoke. "And it's a lot of the same people comin' every year. Most of 'em don't care a lick about us or about each other, for that matter. We won't even see most of 'em again 'til next July. It's just a chance for some of 'em to get together, eat too much, and gossip."

"Well, Grandpa, at least Winston settled the issue about him being Spud's grandfather. And we know about Rose and her husband being married when Spud was born. But nobody's explained to Spud that Aunt Pearl isn't his grandmother, that she's really his great-grandmother. He needs to know that. Like I told you before, I expect he'll be mighty glad to know that."

I sat there just shaking my head. Adults always seem to think that children don't know how to behave, but there sure had been a lot of misbehaving by the adults in the Stevenson family down through the years, including Raedean's embarrassing scene at the reunion.

Grandpa looked me in the eye, not with a mean look, but with a kind look. "You're just gonna have to be patient, Sissie. I think Rose realizes that now. Even Pearl is startin' to show some weak spots in that wall she's put up around Rose and Spud. Pearl's not really a mean woman, Sissie. In her own way she just thinks she's been protectin' her family."

"And some of those people, like Winston and Ruby Gail, might've done more for Spud all these years, but Pearl has made them keep their distance," Grandpa went on. "Even the McKennas. They've got to know that they haven't done right by their grandson. Pearl is just one old woman. If they'd really wanted to see their grandson, they could've done it by now. They don't seem to have much backbone, if you ask me."

I didn't add anything to that. I just looked off in the distance, watching the sun slowly sink even lower in the west, until I became aware that Grandpa was watching me. "What is it, Sissie? You have that look on your face."

"What kind of look?" I asked.

"A troubled look. You know, the kind you get when you have some questions that need answerin'. Like you're really studyin' somethin' in your mind."

Grandpa could read my face as well as Biddie could read Charles Dickens.

"Well, I was thinking about this morning in church." I looked down at my hands lying on my lap. "I know it's a hymn and all, but don't you think it's silly to sing about gathering at the river? There aren't any rivers close around here."

"Yes, but we do have creeks. People forget all about creeks. And a creek is really a river of sorts. When it rains real hard for a long time, a creek can almost become a river. And, besides, all the creeks run into other creeks and eventually they all run into a river somewhere anyway. And then the rivers run into the ocean," Grandpa explained. "So I guess they're all relatives."

"You mean, like at our family reunion? We all gather together, big and small, old and young, and then we all become the Stevenson family. Is that what you mean?"

"Well, I reckon so. Except for Raedean. Now she's an exception," Grandpa laughed.

"What is she then, Grandpa?" I asked. "She's not really a Stevenson, I know that much."

"Yeah, but she considers herself part of the family, so I figure she's not a creek or a stream. She's just a big mud puddle. She's got a lot of possibility, but she's mighty shallow. She likes to be in everybody's way and make a big muddy mess. Then she dries up and goes away 'til the next storm blows in." Grandpa thought for a moment. "I think Raedean is just lookin' for a place to belong."

I had to agree with his explanation, but I was still thinking. "So the creek where you go turtle hunting finally flows into a river. I reckon then the creek water must end up in the ocean." I had taken in all that Grandpa had said, and I was mulling it over in my mind.

"Pro'bly so," he agreed, drawing in another puff of his cigarette and coughing a time or two before stamping it out in an old green glass ashtray sitting between us in the swing.

"So that means that all the branches and streams and creeks kind of know which way to go," I added.

"That's right," he said. "But the river we sang about in church today is a religious river, not just a river around here someplace. So I reckon, just like the creeks and rivers, we're all tryin' to figure out which way to go before we finally come together one day."

"You mean in heaven?"

"Yep."

As I sat there thinking, the sun was going on down, and little twinkles of light began flashing around in different places at different times in the back yard. The lightning bugs were out. To me they had to be the most fascinating insects in the whole world, at least in my part of it. How many insects carried their own light with them in the darkness? Even humans couldn't do that. We needed flashlights and batteries.

Suddenly I realized that night had fallen and we were sitting in the dark with no lights except the lightning bugs. "Do you want me to switch on the porch light, Grandpa?"

"Naw, that'll just draw a bunch of pesky bugs. Candleflies will be all over the screen door. Let's just sit here and enjoy the lightnin' bugs." In no time at all dozens of sparkles dotted the back yard. Then the cicadas started singing – the July flies.

In the summertime sometimes their singing was so loud that I wanted to close my bedroom window, but I couldn't, because I needed the night air to keep me cool. Tonight was no exception. The July flies would sing like this all night long.

And so the cicadas provided the musical accompaniment while the lightning bugs gave us a light show. Then the crickets, not wanting to be left out, started chirping their evening song. And last, but not least, in my opinion, the tree frogs started singing in their higher pitch. Grandpa and I sat in the swing together and enjoyed our own private musical concert, free tickets compliments of Mother Nature.

From inside the house the telephone rang a long and a short. "That's probably Mama calling to tell me to come home," I said, and I was right.

Gemma stepped out onto the porch. "Sissie, your mama said you need to get on home. It's late. You'd better watch for snakes on the path. Here, take one of our flashlights with you, okay?"

"Yes, ma'am." I reluctantly gave Grandpa a hug and left him sitting in the swing. "Night, Grandpa. Thanks for always answering my questions."

"You're welcome, Sissie, anytime," he said, and I knew he meant what he said. "'Night. See you tomorrow."

Gemma hugged me. "Sissie, thank you for looking out for Spud today. I hope you know how much he loves you."

"Just as much as I love him, Gemma. Just as much as I love him. 'Night." I headed out toward the field and followed the path home, shining the beam of my flashlight on the ground ahead of me. I loved snakes, but I sure didn't want to step on a rattlesnake or a copperhead, because the offended snake wouldn't love me back.

As I looked at the lights of my house shining in the darkness ahead, I thought about what Grandpa had said about all the creeks and rivers and streams. I thought about the continental divide and how Mrs. Martin had explained it to us in her geography class. No matter where they were, in the east or in the west, the creeks and the rivers and the streams managed to follow their true direction before finally joining together to make their way home.

Sunday night a thunderstorm started up around midnight. Maybe that was what all the singing and chirping night critters were trying to tell us, because they just seem to know when a storm is coming.

Lightning flashed its bright lights through my bedroom window, lighting up my room briefly, and then returning it to darkness. The wind picked up as well, and Biddie got into bed with me just as a heavy rain started pounding on the roof of our house. After about half an hour, the winds died down and the rumble of thunder moved off into the distance. By daybreak on Monday morning, the sun was shining, and the storm was only a memory.

* * * *

Biddie and I were sitting in the dining room crunching on our bowls of cereal, and Mama and Daddy had already left for work. Suddenly we heard the sound of grinding gears and looked out the dining room window just in time to see Grandpa pass by in his old gray Mercury.

"There goes Grandpa again. Turtle hunting, no doubt," I commented. "He probably figures the heavy rain might've troubled the waters in the creek and caused the turtles to get out and look for a sunny spot on the creek bank." In my mind I could see a turtle just sitting out on a big rock, basking in the early morning sun before the day got too hot.

I got dressed and headed out to Gemma's house. Biddie had another exciting summer day planned. She was going to stay home, read *Jane Eyre*, talk to Elizabeth if Aunt Pearl wasn't on the phone, watch *Search for Tomorrow*, and get supper started. As for me, Spud was coming over to Gemma's house, and we were going to help her work in the garden.

I accidentally slammed the screen door behind me as I walked into the kitchen. Spud looked up from the table, where he was enjoying a leftover biscuit with butter and a big spoonful of pear preserves. "I need my strength to work in the garden. It's gonna be a hot day today," he explained guiltily. Pear preserves were shining in both corners of his mouth.

"Gemma, did Grandpa go turtle hunting?" I asked.

"Yes, he did, Sissie. That man is impossible. He still didn't feel too good this morning. That reunion almost did us both in. I told him not to go, but he wouldn't listen. Said the home place would make him feel better."

"There's a lot of truth to that," I agreed. "He loves to go there."

"Yes, he does. All right then, if we're gonna get any work done in the garden today, we'd better head on out before it gets too hot," she said, stirring us into action.

Not very long after that, it did get too hot, so we came in and had some ice water to cool down. Grandpa still hadn't come back home. We didn't worry much at first, but when he didn't come back by lunchtime, Gemma began to have a concerned look on her face.

Daddy came home at lunchtime, and Gemma was waiting for him at our house. "Jeb, your daddy went turtle hunting hours ago and he hasn't come back yet. I'm worried sick. Maybe he's had car trouble. That old car could play out at any time, and it's so hot outside. Or he could've gotten snake bit. Could you ride up in the mountain and look for him?" I glanced over at Spud and Biddie, who both had fearful looks on their faces.

"Of course, Mama. Come on. Biddie, you stay here by the phone in case someone calls. And make sure Pearl is not on the phone. This is an emergency. Sissie, you and Spud come with us." We hurried to get into the car and we sped out onto the dirt road. Daddy barely stopped at the stop sign at the cross roads and headed straight up the mountain road.

We turned down the rutted road through the woods and

headed toward the home place. Our drive wasn't pleasant and carefree, and no one was reaching out rolled-down windows and touching the overhanging leafy limbs or stopping to wade in the cool, pebbly stream that crossed the road. This drive wasn't like the one I had taken with Grandpa when we went turtle hunting or on the afternoon when we all went looking for Christmas trees. Today we were on a mission, looking for Grandpa, and I could sense dread by the look on Daddy's face. Gemma was biting her bottom lip, trying to keep from crying. The two of us were silent in the back seat. This wasn't the time for questions or polite conversation.

Daddy pulled up into what was once the yard at the old home site. Grandpa's dusty old Mercury sat there empty with no sign of him anywhere. We hurried out of the car and started down the path into the woods.

"Everybody fan out and call to him," Daddy directed.

"Daddy, he's probably not on the branch. Spud and I'll look at the creek. That's where he finds the big turtles." Daddy didn't even stop to wonder how I knew that.

"Be alert, you two," Daddy warned us, "and for God's sake, watch where you're steppin'. You can step on a snake in a minute in all these old leaves and branches. Holler if you find him."

Daddy and Gemma took off in the direction of the branch and the Devil's Land. Spud and I headed toward the creek. And there we found him.

Grandpa was on the ground, his eyes closed, half way sitting up, but mostly leaning against an oak tree near the edge of the creek, his cedar walking stick lying on the ground beside him. A few feet away a huge turtle was sitting on a rock in the edge of the water, not paying the least bit of attention to the turtle hunter who was lying only steps away from him. But the turtle hunter was no threat to him.

At first no sound would come out of my mouth, but suddenly Spud started yelling, "Over here by the creek. He's here." Then I was able to find my voice, and we started yelling. Spud pulled his whistle out of his pocket and its shrill sound filled the woods. We could hear Daddy's footsteps on the leaves, running through the woods, with Gemma right behind him as fast as she could go.

I knelt down on the ground and took Grandpa's hand. "Grandpa, Grandpa, it's me. It's Sissie. Please don't be dead. Please, Grandpa. Don't be dead," I was pleading, tears welling up in my eyes.

Spud took his other hand. "I'm here, too, Grandpa. It's Spud. Please don't die." Tears began rolling down his cheeks.

Grandpa's eye lids fluttered slowly, and he opened his eyes. He tried to focus on our voices, but his eyes were moving from side to side. The right side of his mouth drooped strangely lower than the rest of his mouth, and a stream of saliva was running down his chin. I wiped his chin with my shirt tail. "It's okay, Grandpa. We've found you."

"Oh, Lord," Daddy yelled. "He's here, Mama." Daddy knelt down on the ground and tried talking to Grandpa. "Daddy, can you hear me? Can you speak?" Grandpa said nothing.

Gemma knelt down beside me and took Grandpa's hand from me. "Honey, can you hear me?" His lips moved softly, but no words came. His eyes started to focus.

"I think he's had a stroke, Mama, a bad one. Much worse than the others. We've got to get him to a hospital," Daddy said urgently. "Right now."

Grandpa's eyes focused for just a moment, and seeming to use all the strength he could find, he shook his head. Daddy didn't agree. "We've got to, Daddy. You can't stay here."

Gemma, who had been simply holding Grandpa's hand, now patted it softly. "Do you want to go to the hospital, honey?" Grandpa shook his head slowly. "Do you want to go home?" He nodded.

"Take us home, Jeb," she instructed Daddy, just like he was a little boy.

"But, Mama," Daddy protested. "He needs to see a doctor now."

"And he will, Jeb. Take us home," she repeated calmly.

"Grandpa, we're gonna take care of you. You'll be all right," I said, trying to make him feel better the only way I knew. He looked straight into my face, and then he moved his eyes toward the creek several times. "Did you leave your turtle hook over there?" He slowly shook his head, and then he moved his eyes toward the creek again. "The creek, Grandpa?" He nodded.

Grandpa was completely paralyzed on his right side, and there was no way he could walk out of the woods. Daddy moved our car down the path into the woods as close as he could, and it took the four of us to carry Grandpa and get him into the car. We headed back home, but this time, Daddy didn't waste a minute. I'd never seen Daddy drive so fast. Gemma sat in the back seat, holding on to Grandpa and talking softly to him, words we couldn't hear in the front seat.

As soon as the car stopped in the driveway at Gemma and Grandpa's house, Daddy barked out instructions, "Sissie, call Dr. Frazier. Now! And if anyone is on the line, tell them to *get off*. This is one time you don't have to be polite. Spud, run get Toolie and Pearl. We need 'em."

Uncle Toolie and Daddy got Grandpa into bed, and Dr. Frazier arrived within half an hour and went in to examine Grandpa. Mama came home from work as soon as Daddy called her, and the kitchen became a crowded place with everyone trying to think, to whisper prayers, and to pace.

Cups of untouched coffee sat on the table, and even Gemma's glittery Florida napkin holder couldn't put any sparkle in the room. Rose nervously washed dishes. Biddie sat in a chair and shook her foot on the floor. Spud and I set up the Parcheesi game on the table, but we never made a single move.

Dr. Frazier and Gemma came into the kitchen, and she fairly collapsed into one of the kitchen chairs. Aunt Pearl pulled her chair next to her, put her arms around her sister, and held her close. Then Dr. Frazier gave us his opinion.

"Well, it was a stroke. A terrible one. You can take him to the hospital if you want to, but, I'm sorry, there's really nothing anybody can do at this point. Even if he had had the stroke in the hospital, we probably couldn't have saved him. I doubt if he will live through the night. I've known Woodrow for many years, and I don't think he would want to stay alive in his present condition. I also think he would prefer to die at home in his own bed." He looked down at Gemma to see what her response was. All of us were looking at her.

Her eyes filled with tears, and as they began to run down her face, she took a napkin from the sparkly napkin holder and wiped them away. Daddy knelt beside her chair. "Mama, what do you want to do? This is *your* decision."

"I want him to stay here, surrounded by the people who love him," she said, wiping her nose with the napkin. "I always knew this day would come, and I have to do the right thing for him, Jeb. He has always made me promise that I would let him die at home with dignity. That's all I can do for him now." More tears flowed down her cheeks, and our tears began to fall as well. Somehow our tears were little streams that flowed together in one direction, as we silently waited for Grandpa to make his final journey.

Gemma had made her decision, and throughout the night while everyone else was in the kitchen keeping a vigil, she stayed by Grandpa's side, holding his hand. Biddie and I went in around midnight to see Grandpa, and we both kissed him on the forehead. "We love you, Grandpa. We always will." We both prayed that, even though Dr. Frazier had said that he had gone into a coma, somehow he understood what we were saying to him.

Spud stepped in softly behind us, and patted Grandpa's left hand. "I love you, too, Grandpa." That was the second time that day that Spud had called him Grandpa, and that was fine with us, because that was the way Spud loved him.

The next day at about ten o'clock in the morning Grandpa slipped away, so Biddie, Spud, and I went in to say good-bye to him. He was lying in bed with the sheet pulled over his body, and Daddy raised the sheet for us to see Grandpa's face. He looked like he was asleep, just having a peaceful rest.

Dr. Frazier left, and Daddy called the funeral home. Half an hour later a big black hearse from Nelson and Bigham came to take Grandpa away. In the early afternoon Gemma and Daddy went to the funeral home to make final arrangements for Grandpa. He would be gone for a little while, but he was coming back home the next day.

CHAPTER 26

Gone to Glory

*"So I reckon, just like the creeks and rivers, we're all tryin' to figure
out which way to go before we finally come together one day."*
— *Grandpa*

Early Wednesday morning Grandpa came home one more
time. The same hearse from the day before pulled up to Gemma's
porch. Four men climbed out, and one of them came up on the
porch and shook hands with Daddy, before turning and shaking
hands with Biddie and me. He was dressed in a black suit, a
starched white shirt, and a black tie.

"Hello, I'm Mr. Nelson, from Nelson and Bigham Funeral
Home. I'm sorry to hear about your loss, young ladies."

"Thank you, sir," we both chimed in together. I had to bite
my tongue to keep from asking him why he hadn't seen the two
big grammar mistakes on their church fans.

"Where shall we place the deceased, Mr. Stevenson?" he
asked Daddy.

The *deceased*? Grandpa had a name.

"In front of the fireplace, if that's okay," Daddy answered
politely.

Mr. Nelson peeked into the living room like he was looking
into a cave. "Yes, that will do nicely. That way I don't think we'll

have to move the furniture, and you'll still have plenty of room for visitors to move about in the room."

Daddy helped Mr. Nelson and his three assistants wheel the gray metal casket into the living room on a special black velvet-covered rolling stand and place it in front of the empty fireplace that had been swept clean.

Flower arrangements on wire stands or in baskets had begun to arrive in delivery trucks from the florist shop in town, and Mr. Nelson put the flowers around the casket and on tables in the room. Then he spread an American flag over the casket and folded it neatly back to the right.

Gemma stood between Daddy and Aunt Pearl, who both had an arm around her, while the rest of us stood behind them silently as Mr. Nelson slowly raised the left half of the lid of the casket. And there was Grandpa, dressed in a nice new gray suit and starched white shirt, his hands resting neatly on each other across his stomach. I didn't recognize the tie he was wearing, because it wasn't the one he always wore on Reunion Sunday.

Suddenly I was filled with a bitter anger that seemed to boil up my throat and into my mouth, and my mind began spinning with questions. Why was Grandpa in a suit? I had never in all my life seen Grandpa in a suit, even on Reunion Sunday. Did he have to get all dressed up to get into heaven? Was heaven a fancy place? Wouldn't God have been just as happy to see Grandpa in his overalls and a long-sleeve shirt?

"They did a good job at the funeral home. He looks natural," Aunt Pearl spoke up. *Natural?* Natural would be Grandpa in his overalls, his walking stick in one hand and his turtle hook in the other, stepping slowly along the creek bank looking for turtles. Or sitting with me in the porch swing listening to the night creatures' concert. Or talking about Old Pearly Fangs. I left the room.

I needed to be in a familiar place, away from this casket and from Grandpa, who was all dressed up like someone I had never known. I needed to be outside to breathe in the fresh air. Not the scent of death and funeral flowers, but the fresh alive smell of the flowers and trees in Gemma's yard.

As I walked through the kitchen, Grandpa's cedar walking

stick stood all alone in the corner of the kitchen by the back door. He wouldn't be needing that any more. Quietly I opened the screen door and closed it behind me.

As I sat down in the swing, I suddenly felt guilty, and Mama wasn't even there giving me one of her special looks. I made myself feel guilty all on my own. How could I be angry at Grandpa? He didn't want to die, and I knew for a fact that he would never have chosen to dress up in a fancy gray suit, a starched white shirt, and a new tie.

I thought about his walking stick in the kitchen, and then suddenly I felt a tiny sparkle of happiness, almost like a lightning bug had somehow turned on its light in my mind. For a moment I was happy for Grandpa. I figured, in heaven, everybody walks just fine, and nobody has to worry about strokes or any other kinds of sickness. Grandpa was free from his pain.

The screen door opened slowly, and it was Gemma. Without saying a word, she sat down beside me and wrapped her arms around me. We cried together, Gemma for the loss of her husband, and me for the loss of my grandfather. And together we both cried for the loss of innocence. We had been touched by death in what we thought was the safest place in the world, a little white house on a dirt road in Georgia.

After lunch Rose and Daddy took her car to the home place to bring Grandpa's car home. Spud and I went with them, and I rode back with Daddy. It was the strangest thing. The old Mercury cranked the first time, and not one single time did the gears make a grinding sound. I reached out my hand and stroked the dash of the car, almost as if I was reaching out to touch Grandpa.

Daddy parked the car under a shady oak tree in Grandpa's usual parking spot. He opened the lid of the trunk, and we both peered inside. Grandpa's turtle hook was still in the trunk.

"I'll be dadgum," Daddy said, looking at me and scratching his chin. We both understood. Grandpa hadn't gone turtle hunting at all – he was paying his final visit to the woods and to the creek.

The creek? *The creek?* I left Daddy standing beside the car and ran as fast as I could.

"Sissie, what's the matter? *Sissie*?" Daddy called after me, but I didn't stop to answer him. I just kept running.

Not to my room. Not to the front porch. But to my favorite perch in the mimosa tree, because I had to think.

Hummingbirds were flitting around the pink powder puff flowers, but for once I wasn't interested in trying to catch one. My thoughts were all about Grandpa when we found him and about our final conversation together on the porch.

Why had Grandpa moved his eyes toward the creek? I had checked to see if he had left anything there, and he hadn't. Was he calling my attention to the big turtle on the rock? No, I understood exactly what he was doing. Grandpa knew how sick he was, and he was trying to tell me that he was like the creek. It was time for him to join the other creeks and find his way home.

Then another worrisome question suddenly edged its way into my grieving mind. Grandpa had died at ten o'clock. Had the old clock been a bad sign? Since I was the one who brought it down from the loft, was I somehow responsible for Grandpa's death?

* * * *

Cars started arriving at Gemma's house. Neighbors carrying platters and bowls of food dropped by to pay their respects and to sign the book that Mr. Nelson had left in the living room. The book rested on a wooden stand and was lighted by a long brass attached light that cast a soft glow on the open pages. Throughout the day, the list of names signed in the book grew longer and longer. Grandpa had thought none of the people at the reunion would see us again for a whole year, but he was wrong.

Finally by late Wednesday afternoon, Gemma was exhausted, and she went into her room to rest. I sat down on the edge of her bed. "Gemma, I was thinking. Do we have to ask The Preacher to speak at Grandpa's funeral? He'll probably just yell and talk about hell. Can't somebody else speak at his funeral? Can't we ask Brother Snow? I want him to talk about how Grandpa is in heaven."

Gemma smiled as she reached out and took my hand. "Sissie, I'm one step ahead of you, dear. The Preacher is going to read some scriptures, but Brother Snow is going to conduct the funeral service. I don't think my husband's funeral is the place for The Preacher to yell at anybody either," she agreed. I had more respect for my grandma at that moment than I had ever felt before.

Someone knocked on the bedroom door. "Mama, can I speak to you for a moment?" Daddy's voice called out. "Everyone has finally left, and Toolie needs to see you in the living room. Sissie, you stay here."

"No," Gemma said, "she stays with me." And Daddy didn't bother to argue.

In the kitchen everyone in my family was gathered for a late afternoon supper. Casserole dishes and paper plates were everywhere, and we could hear low conversations around the table as we headed into the living room. Uncle Toolie was waiting quietly in the room beside Grandpa's casket, and Gemma walked over to join him.

"Did you get it, Toolie?" she asked softly, almost in a whisper.

"Yeah, I did. It took a little doin', but I got in touch with a few people I once knew." He slipped her a paper sack. "Not a word of this to Pearl. She can't know."

"I understand, Toolie." She looked over at Grandpa and back at Uncle Toolie, sort of like she was speaking for Grandpa. "Much obliged, Toolie. Much obliged."

When Uncle Toolie left the room, Gemma put her hand into the paper sack and pulled out a new can of Prince Albert tobacco. Then she pulled out something else, something I had never actually seen, but I knew exactly what it was the moment I saw it: a pint jar of moonshine. She made sure the lid was nice and tight, and then she put the two items back into the sack and slipped them down into the foot of Grandpa's casket where no one could see them. She spoke to me in a very low voice, "You mustn't tell another living soul, Sissie. Especially your Aunt Pearl." I nodded.

Gemma put a pint of moonshine and a can of Prince Albert in the foot of Grandpa's casket? I wanted to put something in there, too. "Gemma, I have to go. I'll be right back, all right?" Before she could answer, I ran out the front door and headed straight home to look for the right thing. What did I have that was worthy to stay with Grandpa forever, a sort of keepsake? I had nothing of value that I could lay at his feet in his casket.

In my bedroom my eyes quickly scanned my dresser and my walls. A map of Florida? Of course not. The milk glass vase on my dresser? No. I ran out of my bedroom feeling even sadder than before, if that was possible. I went into the kitchen to drink a glass of water, to clear my mind for one moment.

As I leaned against the cabinet, tears began to well up in my eyes. *What was I thinking?* Grandpa wouldn't want anything that cost a lot of money. That was not the kind of man he was. I looked around the kitchen, trying hard to think of something, something of mine that I could give to him before Aunt Pearl or some other relative could intervene and somehow stop me.

A slight breeze floated through the kitchen window, and suddenly my eyes came to rest on a fluttering piece of paper on the refrigerator door. My poem. Grandpa loved my poem about the rat snake. In fact, he was the only person who didn't think I was crazy for loving snakes. I quickly pulled the poem from its taped place of honor on the refrigerator and ran out the kitchen door, across the yard, and through the field to Gemma's.

Almost breathless, I handed her the poem without saying a word, and without saying a word herself, she folded my poem tenderly and put it into Grandpa's casket. But she didn't put it at Grandpa's feet with the paper sack. Instead, she gently lifted Grandpa's hands and slipped the folded piece of paper underneath it.

"I defy anybody to say a word about this piece of paper, Sissie. And I don't want to hear a single comment from your Aunt Pearl."

Throughout that day I had barely spoken to Spud. Was he avoiding me for some reason? While Gemma and I were standing together looking down at Grandpa and my poem, we heard soft footsteps behind us. We turned and saw Spud standing quietly in the doorway.

"Is it all right for me to come in?" he asked nervously in almost a whisper. His eyes were full of sadness.

"Of course, it's all right for you to come in, Spud," Gemma answered at once. "Why wouldn't it be all right?" she asked him softly, reaching out her hand to him.

"Grandma said this was a private time for you and your grandchildren, s-s-so I d-didn't want…" he stammered, and I could see a tear running down his cheek.

Before he could finish his sentence, Gemma pulled him close to her, wrapped her arms around him, and kissed him on top of his head. "Spud, I love you like you're my grandson, and Grandpa loved you the same way. Sissie's not like Raedean and Raleigh. She's happy to share her grandpa with you, aren't you, Sissie?"

"Yes, ma'am. Grandpa's love was big enough for all of us," I said. "We'd never leave you out, Spud. *Never.*" Gemma put an arm around me, and we all three stood there together.

Suddenly Spud noticed the piece of paper under Grandpa's hand. "Hey, what's that?"

"That's my poem about the rat snake. I wanted Grandpa to keep it."

"That's nice, Sissie. That's real nice."

Biddie's voice sounded behind us. "Can I hug you, too, Gemma?" Without saying a word to Biddie, she just reached out and pulled her in so that we all formed a little knot, with her arms around us all. I could understand why Biddie loved baby chicks so much, because Gemma reminded me of a mother hen, raising her wings to shelter her baby chicks from harm.

As she hugged us, she praised us, "I couldn't have any better grandchildren if I searched the whole world over."

* * * *

During the night, lamps stayed on in the living room and different relatives had agreed to come and sit with Grandpa. "It's a sign of respect," Daddy explained to us. "And it also gives us a chance to go home and get some rest," which we all did. We knew that Thursday was going to be a very busy day.

Before daylight Biddie came into my room and sat down on the edge of my bed. "Sissie, wake up. I've got a question for you." I woke up fast, because Biddie never had a question for *me*. I always seemed to have a question for *her*.

What is it, Biddie?" I asked, as I sat up in bed, still half asleep.

"I saw your poem in Grandpa's casket, and Gemma asked me if I wanted to put something in, too. I would, but I don't know what I have that Grandpa would have liked to keep close to him always. I want to put something in before it's too late." The look on Biddie's face was the same expression that must have been on my face while I was searching frantically for the right gift to give Grandpa.

I thought for a moment, the fog of sleep slowly lifting. "Don't worry, Biddie. I know just the thing."

We both got dressed in a hurry and headed to Gemma's house. We didn't have to dress nicely yet, because the funeral wasn't until three o'clock, and I wasn't about to put on anything scratchy before I absolutely had to.

The lights were still on in the living room, and when Biddie and I tapped on the front screen door, Aunt Georgia and Aunt Ida cautiously peeked out to see who was at the door.

Aunt Ida lifted the latch on the door and let us in. "My goodness, you girls are here mighty early. Your grandma is still asleep."

"We didn't come to see her. We came to see Grandpa," I explained.

"Oh, I see. Well, come on, Georgia, I sure could use a cup of coffee. And since these girls are in here, we're not really leaving Woodrow alone."

As soon as they went out of the room, Biddie and I stepped over and looked down on Grandpa one more time. "Where should I put it?" Biddie whispered.

"I think you should put it under his hands on top of my poem."

"I'm not sure I can do it, Sissie," she whispered again, looking almost fearful.

"It's okay, Biddie, we can do it together," and I knew we could. Slowly I reached out and touched Grandpa's sun-spotted hands. They were cold. Not the kind of cold that his hands were in the wintertime, but a lifeless waxy cold. My heart was breaking, but I had to do this. "Here, Biddie, give it to me." I reached out my hand, and Biddie dropped her treasure onto my open palm:

Her favorite white rock from the home place – the arrowhead.

Gently I lifted Grandpa's hands and slid the arrowhead underneath them so that it rested on top of my poem. Just as I finished slipping the stone into place, something shiny in the casket caught my eye. I looked closer. Right beside Grandpa, deep in a fold of the casket's creamy satin lining, something had been pushed in so that only a bit of it showed. What was it? I had to look – *I couldn't help myself.* I reached my fingers in to lift it out, but when I touched the object and realized what it was, I immediately pushed it back down again. It was a brass compass.

Thursday morning passed quickly, and lunch at Gemma's was a blur. Then it was time to get dressed for the funeral. At least Mama showed me a little mercy and didn't make me wear that stupid crinoline. When I walked into my bedroom after I returned home from lunch, Mama had laid out what she wanted me to wear: the tight black shoes, lacy socks, and another scratchy dress. This time it was a light blue one with a white lace collar that had a little white stiff fabric flower in its center, placed exactly where it would scratch my neck every time I looked down. I took that as a sign that I would have to look up and try not to be so sad.

The summer heat in my bedroom was almost unbearable, and as I dressed I tried to keep my mind occupied. I couldn't help thinking: *I wonder if Raleigh will be at Grandpa's funeral.* I hope not. Maybe he's still at Mother Mary's, being smacked by the nuns. I didn't want Raedean to be there either.

Every single thing that happened that afternoon was new to me, and I made a point of trying to remember every single thing I could. So I carried my journal everywhere and wrote down what I heard and saw.

Mr. Nelson returned to Gemma's house and closed Grandpa's casket. This time the deacons of Mount Olive carefully moved his casket to the hearse that was waiting near the front porch steps.

The hearse moved into position in the driveway, and our cars began lining up behind it. Then as the many aunts, uncles, and cousins who had assembled at Gemma's house moved their cars into position one by one, they switched on the headlights of their cars. Among them were Winston and a teary-eyed Ruby Gail, but, thankfully, no Raedean or Raleigh.

The funeral procession pulled out of the driveway onto the dirt road before inching slowly toward Mount Olive. On the way to the church two cars that were coming from the opposite direction pulled over and stopped out of respect.

Before the Stevenson family entered the church for the funeral service, all of the other people in the church had already taken their seats. Then Mr. Nelson directed family members into the sanctuary. More than half of the left side of the church was reserved with big white ribbon bows, and as we began walking down the aisle, everyone stood up. Miss Gracie was playing well-known hymns from one of our usual hymnbooks. I hoped she wasn't using the same hymnal Spud and I had used Reunion Sunday.

Gemma walked with Daddy and Aunt Pearl. Biddie and I walked down the aisle together behind Mama. I noticed Mrs. Martin on the right side of the sanctuary, standing among all the people who had crowded into Mount Olive Church. In fact, so many people had come to Grandpa's funeral that many of them had to sit in folding chairs around the back wall of the sanctuary or out on the front porch because there wasn't enough room for them to sit in the pews.

The ceiling fans were turning full force, trying to cool down the stifling heat, but even with the front doors and windows wide open, the air around us was still humid and heavy with the scent of funeral flowers and women's perfume. *No uninvited cicadas today, Lord, please,* I prayed.

As we filed into our seats, I heard a gasp ahead of me. Aunt Pearl had almost stopped in her tracks as she turned from the aisle to move down to the end of the front pew. I turned my head without thinking, and I saw what had surprised her. Sitting on the first pew immediately behind the reserved section was a beautiful woman, nicely dressed in a pale blue suit, a woman I had only seen once or twice in my life: Sharon.

When the family began to be seated, Spud slipped over and sat beside me.

The Preacher, all dressed up in the same brown suit he had worn Sunday but wearing a different tie, read scriptures to us.

"In my father's house are many mansions…" Somehow I couldn't imagine Grandpa living in a mansion forever. He was probably very pleased if God had just offered him a cabin near a slow-moving creek.

When The Preacher finished reading from the Bible, Miss Gracie played a hymn, but this time she added extra notes and made the song more flowery than usual. How odd – it was "Shall We Gather at the River?" And Miss Gracie's chewing gum beat four beats to the measure.

Brother Snow stood up and walked to the pulpit. I was praying, *"Please, Lord, no spiders today either."* In front of the altar was Grandpa's casket, now closed and completely draped with the American flag.

"Many of you may not know this, but Brother Stevenson's mother, Mrs. Hannah Stevenson, was a midwife. And sixty-five years ago, she helped my mother bring me into the world. And so today, I have the honor of helping Miss Hannah's son as he leaves this world for a much better place. I tell you this with all the faith I have known throughout my life: Brother Woodrow Stevenson has gone to glory."

By the time Brother Snow had finished the service, he had made everybody in the church feel that Grandpa was the lucky one, not us. He even told some funny stories he knew about Grandpa when they were boys attending classes together in that one room school Grandpa had often talked about. But Grandpa had never told me Brother Snow's stories. I didn't think it was possible that there was a single story Grandpa had ever forgotten to tell me.

Brother Snow ended his service with these words, and I wrote them down the best I could: "Woodrow Stevenson was a good man who lived a simple life. He didn't have much money, but he was rich in friends. He knew he wasn't perfect, so he didn't spend his time criticizing and judging others. He loved folks the way they were, and they loved him the same way in return. He was a storyteller, a keeper of the family history, and a man with a good sense of humor. He loved his family. He loved his grandchildren, and he spent time with them, passing on to them the wonders of life. A simple measure of his kindness to others is the number of people who are gathered here today to bid him farewell."

Across the road in the church cemetery we stood around Grandpa's grave as soldiers fired their rifles into the air, and another soldier played "Taps" with a bugle. Gemma reached out and received the American flag, folded neatly into a triangle and handed to her by one of the soldiers. Grandpa had always been proud to be a veteran of World War I.

I looked over at the grave of Aunt Ida's husband. Maybe Grandpa *didn't* have a lot of money, but at least Gemma didn't have to shake her fist and create a ruckus to get him buried at Mount Olive. Grandpa died like a quiet Baptist.

After the funeral, we stood in the church yard greeting people who had come to the funeral. I wasn't sure if Biddie and I could survive so much hugging and strong perfume in one week.

Mrs. Martin came over to speak to me. "I mainly came here because of you. I know how much you loved your grandpa." She hugged me, not the hard, perfumed hugs of my relatives at the reunion, who were glad to see me once a year and didn't give me a thought the rest of the time, but the soft, gentle hug of someone who wanted to offer me comfort.

"I think that sometimes grownups believe they're the only ones who are sad and lost and hurting, and the children get forgotten in the confusion of all the sadness," she said to me. She was right. My heart felt like a deep, empty well, and I didn't think I would ever be able to fill it with happiness again. "Take care of your grandmother."

As she started walking to her car, I called out, "I'll see you at school in September, Miz Martin."

She came back over to me and put her arm around me once again. "I guess you haven't heard. I won't be back in September. I'm a grandmother now. My son and his wife had a baby in May, that day I was absent, and they want me to move closer to them. So I've taken a job at a school in North Georgia. I'm moving next month."

Could I deal with two terrible losses in the same week? My heart was already broken after losing Grandpa, but now Mrs.

Martin, too?

She must have seen the look on my face. "I'm so sorry you had to find that out today, but I'm not going away forever. You can always write to me. And I'll come back to the school sometime to visit. I promise."

The empty well in my heart grew even deeper. "I'll never forget you, Miz Martin. Never."

"And I'll never forget you either. Keep writing your poems and stories. I'm sure that's what your grandfather would want you to do."

"I will, I promise." And I meant exactly what I said.

As Mrs. Martin walked away, she looked back and waved at me once more. "I'm proud of you, and I'm certain that someday you'll find your true direction in life." As I watched her drive away down the dusty road, I realized that not a single person in my life had ever told me that before.

* * * *

When we arrived back home, Biddie and I hurried to put on the most comfortable shorts we could find. A blue cotton shirt freed me from the scratchy flower than had left red marks under my chin. I went into the kitchen to fix a glass of ice water. Mama and Daddy had changed clothes, too, and they both walked into the kitchen. Daddy looked sad and exhausted, and Mama had the look of someone who had spent way too much time with Daddy's relatives. She opened the cabinet and reached for the aspirin bottle.

"We're gonna stay here and rest for a few minutes," Daddy said. "Then we're all gonna have supper together at Gemma's."

"We're going on out to her house now. Spud's meeting us," I explained.

"Okay, don't y'all play out there in this heat too long now," Mama warned us, "and watch for snakes." Biddie and I both hurried back to Gemma's house where Spud was already waiting for us on the ill-fated front porch steps. The three of us sat there for the longest, not saying a word.

A few of the visiting aunts, uncles, and cousins lingered for a while, but when the sun started getting lower in the west, they got into their cars and began to head back to parts unknown. Because Uncle Toolie was the chairman of the deacons, he had stayed at Mount Olive to help put away chairs and to oversee the placement of the flowers in the cemetery.

I had overheard him talking to Aunt Pearl in the cemetery as everyone was leaving. "I've gotta stay busy, Pearl, I can't go home and sit down right now. I've gotta keep movin'." Uncle Toolie was going to be lost without Grandpa.

Spud, Biddie, and I weren't really interested in sitting around on the porch or in the living room talking with the relatives, because we had already seen enough of them on Reunion Sunday, and, besides, children weren't really welcome in the adults' conversations anyway. So the three of us went out into the back yard and sat in Grandpa's Mercury.

Even with the windows rolled down, after a while we got too hot. As we climbed out of the car, Rose's voice called out to us through the screen of the open kitchen window. "Children, come on inside and wash up. It's about time to eat supper."

We slowly left Grandpa's old car behind us and stepped up on the back porch. Biddie reached out her hand to open the screen door, and that was the exact moment when the big family argument started up in the kitchen.

CHAPTER 27

The Rose of Sharon

"An apple doesn't fall far from the tree, but when I hit the ground I rolled as far away as I could."
— Sharon

Aunt Pearl stopped us in our tracks. "You children go back outside and play," she snapped. And for the first time in my life, I realized that she reminded me of a giant snapping turtle.

Spud tried to protest. "But, Grandma, it's hot and the sun's going…"

"Then go next door and watch television," Aunt Pearl interrupted him.

Without saying a word, Biddie primly turned around, and trying to maintain her teenage dignity, walked down the porch steps and headed toward our house. Meanwhile Spud and I did what any two normal eleven year olds would do in our situation. We pretended to leave, circled around through the woods, ran back to Gemma's house, and squatted down outside the kitchen window so we could hear everything that was going on inside.

We looked up and saw Biddie, who had turned around and seen exactly what we had just done. To our surprise, instead of acting like a high and mighty teenager and tattling on us, she quickly circled around, too. Then she hurried over to where we were and squatted down under the window with us to listen.

We weren't going to miss a single word. What was going on in the kitchen was far better and much more interesting than all of the afternoon stories that both Aunt Pearl and Gemma watched on television all rolled up together. We could hear Sharon's voice loud and clear through the screen of the open kitchen window. We didn't even need to turn up the volume.

"Well, I'm sorry I wasn't born a perfect saint like you, Mama."

"I have never claimed to be a saint," Aunt Pearl protested.

"Mother, please," Rose begged Sharon. "Let's not do this now, not here, not right after Uncle Woodrow's funeral."

"No, Rose, we're going to get this all out into the open once and for all."

"I cannot believe, Mama, that you have allowed this festering lie to go on for eleven years. You've allowed people to think that my daughter wasn't married to Edward McKenna and that Spud was illegitimate. How *could* you? He's your own flesh and blood."

"I have never encouraged people to think that way about Spud."

"Yeah? Well, you never did anything to stop it either, so that means you allowed it," Sharon argued back. "You're not a bit better than Raedean Brown."

"Don't you dare compare me to that awful woman, Sharon. What could I say? How could I stop it? Besides, I don't recall ever seeing a marriage license…"

"*Mama!* I've always told you that our license was in the glove box of Edward's car when he…" Rose protested, with a hurt sound in her cracking voice. "Besides I got a copy…"

Even though Rose was trying to explain, Sharon cut her off and started in on Aunt Pearl again. "And I'm sure that some of your saintly sisters at church were counting the months on their fingers."

"Well, you have to admit, it looked suspicious that right after Rose graduated from high school, she announced to us that she was pregnant and then conveniently added that she had been secretly married to Edward McKenna. Anybody might question that." Whose side was Aunt Pearl on anyway?

"She couldn't tell anybody sooner that she was pregnant because she would have been made to drop out of high school. She wouldn't have gotten her diploma. She's your granddaughter, Mama. You should love her no matter what. And if seeing their marriage license had meant so much to you, you could have bought your own copy at the courthouse."

Aunt Pearl answered shakily, "Well, that wasn't really necessary…"

"Mama, you know perfectly well why you wouldn't accept Edward McKenna as Rose's husband. We all know."

"Sharon, please, don't…" Aunt Pearl interrupted, "I'm begging you."

"Mitchell didn't just break into some unknown store. He robbed McKenna's Department Store. And you knew you couldn't stand spending the rest of your life seeing your granddaughter married to a McKenna. It would be too embarrassing for you to have to rub elbows with the McKenna family. It was easier for you to let Rose be the scapegoat. Your pride has kept those poor people from knowing their only grandchild."

Rose spoke up, actually raising her voice to Aunt Pearl. "You *never* told me that, Mama. You've just always said that Mitchell got into some trouble with the law."

Aunt Pearl fired back, seeming to ignore Rose's comments. "I haven't tried to keep Rose and Spud away from them. I've tried to *protect* them."

"Protect them from *what*, Mama? There's a difference between protecting your children and cutting them off from the rest of the world. The McKenna's are good people. They wouldn't have harmed Rose and Spud. If it hadn't been for Frank and Helen McKenna dropping the charges, Mitchell would've gone to prison."

The three of us looked at each other. Aunt Pearl was always good at dishing out a good tongue-lashing, but I had never heard anyone dare to give *her* one, not even Uncle Toolie. And Sharon didn't show any signs of letting up.

"You've put your pride ahead of everything else in your life. You've never known my two sons. You've never really appreciated the great-grandson that Rose gave you. And you've pushed me away ever since I got pregnant with Rose."

We looked at each other in disbelief. Spud's mouth was a perfect capital O.

"I didn't agree with what you did, Sharon. It was sinful. And what Mitchell did was sinful, too," Aunt Pearl answered back.

"Was that any reason for you to punish *everybody*? You never see the good things people do, Mama, only the bad things. You act like you're perfect, but you're not. You're self-righteous. And that's as big a sin as any."

We started hearing a strange sound – crying. Not just crying, but sobbing.

Who was it? It couldn't have been Sharon, because her voice was clear and strong.

"Mama, Mitchell was a grown man. You weren't responsible for his decisions. *He was responsible*. He decided to get into trouble. He decided to bring shame on himself and this family. He decided to leave home. He decided to join the army. My God, Mama, don't you realize? Mitchell finally grew up. He died in service to his country. He died a hero. Think about that. Why are you still dwelling on the mistakes he made? That I made? *Let 'em go!*"

For the first time Gemma spoke up. "She's right, Pearl. It's time for everybody in this family to stop living a lie. Life's too short to waste it on regrets. Let go of the past."

"Mama, Spud has grandparents who have never known him," Sharon continued to peck away at Aunt Pearl like a persistent hen. "He's never known that I'm his grandmother. He's eleven years old, and he's a stranger to me. Don't punish him because you want to punish *me*."

Right about then Spud got a cramp in the calf of his right leg. "Ouch!"

"Shh!" Biddie shushed him, and I put my hand over his mouth. All this squatting was taking its toll on us, but we couldn't leave. Spud halfway stood up, bent over, and quietly walked the cramp out of his leg.

"You could've come home any time you wanted to, Sharon, and spent time with Rose and Spud. I never tried to stop you."

Aunt Pearl wouldn't give up, but her voice sounded different, not preachy anymore, just sort of scratchy.

I thought about what the cousin had said on Gemma's front porch at the reunion, "If Pearl was your mama, would *you* want to come home?"

"How *could* I, Mama? How can you blame me for never coming home? Every time I have talked to you on the phone, you have never once asked me about Jamie and our sons, who incidentally are your grandchildren, too. You spend the whole time criticizing me for something I did when I was eighteen years old. Look at me, Mama, I'm forty-seven! You've missed almost the past thirty years of my life!"

In the middle of all the arguing and squabbling, I couldn't help but think about the story Grandpa had told me about the Devil's land. Aunt Pearl was fussing and telling her side of the story. Sharon was fuming and telling her side of the story. Neither one would give in, and the rest of the family was stuck in the middle, fenced in by pride on both sides with no place to go.

"You should never have gotten mixed up with Winston Smith. He was no good."

Aunt Pearl still refused to give up.

"No, Mama, Winston Smith *was* and *is* good. He's stayed in touch with me all these years. While Rose was growing up, he sent money for her every month, money I sent on to you, the same money that you always refused from him."

"I didn't want his money," Aunt Pearl almost hissed like a snake.

"Unfortunately, Winston's biggest fault was that he was Walter's son. And, by God, if you couldn't have Walter, then you weren't going to let me have Winston. Your father did a cruel thing to you, and you turned right around and did the same cruel thing to me," Sharon hissed back. "Your own child."

"That's not true, Sharon," Aunt Pearl protested.

"Yes, it is, Mama."

"Yes, it is, Pearl," Gemma added.

We were listening so intently outside the window that we didn't even notice Mama and Daddy walking toward us. The sun was going on down, but there was still enough light to see clearly. When I realized that they were both standing a few feet away from us, I elbowed Biddie and Spud and braced myself for the look that we were about to receive full force from Mama. I thought about Perseus and Medusa and closed my eyes in a hurry. Which one would it be: The stern look? The guilty look? Or the evil eye? When I opened my eyes, Mama just looked puzzled.

"What are you children doing?" she asked.

While Biddie and I withered in guilt, Spud put his finger on his lips. "Shh!"

"What's goin' on?" Daddy asked in a low voice.

"Aunt Pearl and Sharon are having a big argument in the kitchen," Biddie explained.

"Yeah," Spud added, "and I'm finally gettin' some answers."

Sharon's voice was so loud that it almost echoed. "Don't you think Winston has suffered enough? Hasn't he had enough punishment being married to Ruby Gail and having that awful Raedean for his daughter? Don't you think Walter has suffered? Don't you think *I've* suffered enough?"

Mama looked at Daddy and spoke in a low voice. "Jeb, we can't just walk in right now. We'll be in the middle of a free-for-all."

"Yeah, and this argument should've happened years ago, and if we go bustin' in, they'll stop. We shouldn't interrupt," Daddy said almost in a whisper.

Mama looked confused. "Should we go back home then?"

"Naw, just be quiet. I'm tryin' to listen."

"Jeb!" she whispered, a little too loudly. Then Daddy got the evil eye.

"Shh!" Spud and Daddy both put their index finger on their lips.

Aunt Pearl's teary voice was continuing, "I'm sorry, Sharon, about Winston. I know you hate me." Now Aunt Pearl was feeling sorry for herself, trying to get Sharon's sympathy.

"Mama, I don't hate you because you wouldn't let me marry Winston. I forgave you for that years ago. I'm happy with my marriage. I love Jamie. He's been a wonderful husband. If I'd married Winston, Rose might've turned out like Raedean. Who knows?" God forbid. "Instead, she has become a wonderful woman and a good mother. I'm very proud of her."

Gemma spoke up again in a sorrowful voice. "Pearl, Sharon, this has been a terrible day for me. Please, for Woodrow's sake, let something good come out of it. Make your peace. He would've liked that."

Yeah, and I was sorry that Grandpa wasn't here to witness this argument, even though Gemma would've been elbowing him the whole time.

Sharon's voice now sounded scratchy. "I love you, Mama. You and I both have made mistakes, but somehow good things have come out of them. Let's stop bickering. For Rose's sake and for Spud's sake."

"Come on," Daddy whispered, and we all followed him around to the front porch. "Remember. We don't know a thing."

Just as we reached the front porch steps, Uncle Toolie was about to go in the front door. We hadn't even heard him drive up. He opened the front screen door, and we hurried in behind him as if nothing had happened and we were all together. He looked surprised. "Jeb, I didn't even see y'all behind me."

Mama and Daddy were good at pretending, but Biddie and I had guilt written all over our faces. Spud couldn't even look anyone in the eye when we walked into the kitchen.

Daddy asked a little too brightly, "Are we too early?" Mama poked him in the back.

Sharon gave us all a suspicious look and then a sweet smile. "Nope, I believe y'all are just in time."

Meanwhile, Uncle Toolie was looking around the room at all the teary, red eyes and wet cheeks and Sharon and Pearl standing with their arms around each other. He asked a good question. "Did I just miss something?"

"Yes, Daddy, you missed this," Sharon said, as she walked over, put her arms around Uncle Toolie, and hugged him like she hadn't hugged him for thirty years.

After supper Spud and I left the stuffy kitchen, went out on the front porch, and sat down in the glider to enjoy the cooler night air. The althea bushes by the side of Gemma's house were in full bloom with lavender flowers that during the day were buzzing alive with bees. Now the blossoms were closed up and silent for the night. Gemma had once told me that there were pink ones and white ones, too, so I had looked for altheas in her flower catalog. I had discovered that the althea's real name is The Rose of Sharon.

Sharon and Rose stepped quietly out onto the front porch. They sat down in the swing and looked over at Spud and me. In the glow of the porch light, I could see that they were not smiling, but grinning, as they made the swing move slowly to and fro.

"So, how much of the argument did you two hear?" Sharon asked.

"Most of it," Spud confessed.

"Yep, pretty much," I chimed in.

Sharon turned her attention to me. "I had to come home for Uncle Woodrow's funeral. Your grandpa never judged me, Sissie. He was a very good man."

She looked at Spud, who was slowly gliding and watching her. "Spud, your grandfather Winston called me and told me about what happened at the reunion. He felt awful about it. He and Ruby Gail really are good people, even though she's a little bit strange sometimes."

We sat there silently for a long time, just listening to the songs of the night creatures, and then Spud spoke up, his voice a little shaky and uncertain. "Mama, I want you to tell me the truth. What happened to my daddy? Is he really dead or is that just a lie?"

"Yes, Spud, your daddy really is dead," Rose answered softly, wrapping the fingers of her right hand around the chain in the arm of the swing, like she was holding on tight. "At least we didn't lie to you about that. Lord knows, we've lied about everything else in this family, that is, when we've been willing to talk about things at all and not pretend they never happened."

"How did he die?"

Rose had already told Spud that story a hundred times.

"He died in a car accident when I was expecting you. We had just graduated from high school. He worked late at the store, and on the way home that night it was very foggy. He must've been tired and sleepy, and he missed a curve in the road. His car hit a tree, and he was killed instantly."

"Did Daddy suffer a lot, Mama?"

"I don't think so, honey, it was over so fast. In fact, I don't think he had time to know what had happened."

Spud looked thoughtful, trying to take in everything Rose was saying, like it was the first time he had ever really listened to her.

"When he died nobody knew yet that we were married and that I was expecting a baby," Rose explained. "We couldn't let anybody know earlier, or I wouldn't have been allowed to finish high school. Your daddy and I had planned to sit down and tell your Grandma Pearl and Grandpa Toolie that we had been secretly married and that I was expecting you. They had always dreamed that someday I would have a big church wedding with all the trimmings, but I didn't want all that."

"I had to tell them about you all by myself. Your grandma didn't take the news so well. She was very angry with me and ashamed, but I loved your father, Spud, and he had been so excited about becoming a daddy. He just never got the chance to know you. Mr. and Mrs. McKenna were so heartbroken, they never mentioned Edward to me again."

"I wish I could've known him."

"I do, too, honey. I'm sorry, Spud, you deserved to hear the complete truth from *me*, not from Raleigh or Raedean with their messed up jealous version of the story. I had wanted to tell you all of this when you were older. I should've told you the whole story a long time ago. I'm just like your Grandma Pearl in that respect. I thought I was protecting you, but I was wrong."

"So you and Daddy were really married?" Spud asked uncertainly.

"Yes, we were really married," Rose said, nodding.

"Raleigh told me I was illiterate, and Sissie told him I know how to read."

"Good for Sissie," Sharon answered, with an almost wicked sparkle in her eyes.

Spud looked at Sharon, and I could tell he didn't quite know what to call her yet. "So why did you leave my mama with Grandma and Grandpa?"

"When I was expecting your mama, I decided I had to let her go. I wasn't married, and I figured that unmarried mothers didn't have much of a future, nor did their children. It was a very hard thing to do, but I had to do what I thought was best for Rose."

She looked over at Rose and patted her knee. "I've made a lot of mistakes, and I hope someday you'll be able to forgive me, Rose."

Rose took her mother's hand and held it tightly. "Mama, not only do I forgive you, I understand completely. Life isn't so simple for women, is it? We have to make some hard choices sometimes."

Two miracles happened that night. Before we all left Gemma's house and went our different ways, everybody hugged each other. Somehow, after all the hurt we had felt when Grandpa died and after the sadness of his funeral, the love we felt in Gemma's house was a soft cloud of healing that seemed to wrap itself around each of us. We breathed it in, and it seemed to move deep inside us and mend our broken hearts.

The other miracle was that, instead of driving back home that night, Sharon stayed with her family. The next day after we had all eaten lunch at Gemma's house, Sharon headed back to Atlanta, but not before she had hugged Spud at least ten times.

"I'm sorry, honey, but I've got a lot of catching up to do." She hugged Rose. "Remember your promise. You and Spud are coming up next week-end to visit."

"I will, Mother. I promise." And Aunt Rose's fingers weren't crossed behind her back.

Sharon reached into her pocketbook, took out some money, and handed it to Rose. "Please use this to buy Spud some new school clothes. Why don't you take him to McKenna's Department Store?" Rose nodded, as if she knew perfectly well what Sharon really meant.

Spud and I went out and sat in the front seat of Grandpa's

Mercury for a while after Sharon left. I looked over at Spud, and once again, he was thinking hard, his tongue touching the left corner of his mouth.

"What is it, Spud? What's the matter?"

"Remember when I made a wish on that pully bone at Thanksgiving?"

"Of course, I do. You wished Gemma was your grandmother."

"That must've been a mighty powerful pully bone. First, I got Gemma, like I wished for. Now suddenly I've got more grandparents than I can shake a stick at."

"Well, there is a *really* extra, extra bright spot in all this mess, Spud, and I don't think you've realized it yet."

"*What?*"

"At least Aunt Pearl isn't your grandmother – she's your great-grandmother."

"How's that a bright spot?" he asked with a puzzled look on his face.

"I figure that means she's a little less kin to you. Maybe some of her meanness got watered down before it got to you."

He pondered that idea for a while, his chin moving sort of like a cow chewing on her cud. Then a worried look started moving across his face like a cloud covering the sun.

"Now what's the matter, Spud?"

"I'm slippin' on down, Sissie."

"What do you mean?"

"Well, now Mama is your daddy's *second* cousin, so that means I'm your third or fourth cousin. I can't keep up. I just know we're gettin' less and less kin to each other."

"Spud, I don't give a dang about what order cousin you are to me. I've got aunts, uncles, and cousins that are a lot closer kin than you on the Stevenson family tree, but as far as I'm concerned, we could just lop their branches right off our tree. They don't care about us, 'cept on Reunion Sunday. The ones that love you, those are the ones that are *really* kin to you. And that includes friends."

* * * *

That night after I went to bed, I listened to the July flies singing outside my bedroom window. Their noise was so loud I couldn't hear the crickets or the frogs for all the ruckus they were making. A lightning bug outside lit on the window screen, and for a few moments its little light blinked and shone brightly in the darkness of my room.

I thought about all that Grandpa had told me the day we saw the dead rat snake on Uncle Toolie's fence and about that day at the home place when Grandpa told me all the family secrets. I thought about what Brother Snow had said about Grandpa, how he didn't judge people.

I tried to think about Aunt Pearl the way Grandpa described her to me. "Pearl's just had a hard life." The sad thing to me was, maybe Aunt Pearl caused some of her hard life. I figure some women are good at having babies, but they're just not too good at being mothers.

Then I thought about Gemma. For the first time in her life, she was in her house spending the night alone. Daddy had asked her at least twice, "Mama, don't you wanna come stay with us for a few days?"

"No, Jeb, this is my home. I need time to be alone. I'll be fine. I'll call if I need anything."

What in the world was she ever going to do without Grandpa?

Then I thought about myself. What in the world was I ever going to do without Grandpa?

* * * *

On the second day of August, Spud finally got his cast off. Rose brought it back home with them from the doctor's office and asked Spud, "Honey, do you want to save this cast as a souvenir?"

"Mama, pitch that thing in the trashcan. I don't ever want to see it again." He walked around all day rubbing his arm and scratching it.

"Does it still hurt, Spud?" I asked him.

"Nope, it just feels good to be able to scratch where it itches."

The first two weeks on the August page of our kitchen calendar dropped off very slowly, and on a Thursday night it was finally time to start packing for our vacation in Florida. Daddy had already asked Gemma to go with us. He was standing in the kitchen, drinking the last of his second cup of coffee, talking to Mama. "I think it would do her a world of good to get away for a few days, don't you, honey?"

"I'm sure it will, Jeb." Was that a new expression I saw on her face?

Daddy set his empty cup in the sink and started to walk away. Suddenly he turned around and looked at Mama.

"Oh, I almost forgot. Throw in a few extra rolls of toilet paper, Mama. Spud's goin' with us."

CHAPTER 28

White Sugar Sands

*"There is no need to pay for air. Just roll down the
windows and you've got free air."*
– Daddy

I couldn't sleep, I just couldn't, and it was nearly midnight.
We had to get up in three and a half hours to start loading the car.
Mama and Daddy had a carefully organized plan.

"It'll take us about four hours to get to Florida, and we don't
want to travel in the heat of the day. So we need to be on the road
by five o'clock," Daddy had explained to us the night before.

Mama had added, "We'll pack food for breakfast and stop
somewhere to eat. Then we'll head into Florida by about nine
or ten."

Well, so much for carefully organized plans. Gemma had
a suitcase. Spud had a suitcase. And the four of us each had a
suitcase. Mama took one look at the biggest suitcase and said,
"Biddie, we're only going to be gone two nights. You can't take
everything in your closet. Repack with Sissie."

"Mama, no, please," she protested. "I'll take a smaller bag."

Then there was the cooler, a quilt, beach towels, and three
large cardboard boxes of groceries. Gemma was putting in her
extra stuff, which included a flashlight and a large paper sack with

the top neatly folded down. "I remember how much fun it was to walk on the beach at night."

Daddy looked disgusted as he took stock of all the suitcases, boxes, and bags assembled by the car. Mama was carrying out another small box, and Daddy looked at her in dismay. "It's already after five o'clock, Mama. This isn't gonna work. Is all this stuff necessary?"

"*Yes*, and I still have a few more things in the kitchen, too," she added, turning on her heel and going back into the house.

"Oh, Lord, where are we gonna put everything? Some of this stuff'll have to go inside the car," Daddy complained as he shuffled the suitcases and boxes around, trying to fill every available inch in the trunk.

Shortly after six Daddy announced, "Everybody get into the car."

Mama and Biddie sat down in the front seat, while Gemma, Spud, and I climbed into the back seat. Then Daddy passed the quilt and towels to me, and he put one of the cardboard boxes in the floorboard at my feet.

"Daddy, where am I s'posed to put my feet for four hours?"

"I don't know, Sissie, but I'm sure you'll figure somethin' out."

Daddy got in, rolled down his window, and cranked the car. Then turning to Mama, he asked, "Is everything turned off, locked, fed, watered, and flushed?"

"I think so, Jeb," Mama answered, looking concerned. "I just hope I didn't forget anything." I couldn't see Daddy's face at that moment, because he was putting the car into gear, but I was willing to bet that he was rolling his eyes.

Our car pulled out of the driveway, completely packed. I felt like a hot bottle of Coca-Cola in a six pack carton. Why did I have to hold a quilt and a stack of towels in an un-air-conditioned car in August? And why were we taking a *quilt* any way?

"Air conditionin' costs extra," Daddy had explained when he bought the new car, "and there is no need to pay for air. Just roll down the windows and you've got free air."

Well, the free air was hot, and when the car windows were rolled down, Mama complained about the wind messing up her hair. Besides, none of the air ever seemed to make its way to the back seat anyway. And how long could I be expected to sit with my legs and feet around a cardboard box, not to mention the thick folded quilt and towels in my lap.

The fully loaded car hummed down to the crossroads, and Daddy took a right, heading south. We had been on the road for only about fifteen minutes when it happened.

Even with practically no sleep, I realized something new about myself. No doubt about it – I was a morning person. I had just discovered all of the answers to all of life's mysteries at six o'clock in the morning, and I had to share them with my family. I couldn't help myself.

Then Biddie got snippy with me, and Mama got snippy with Biddie for being snippy with me. The quilt in my lap was hot, and I got a cramp in my right foot because I couldn't get it to fit around the cardboard box and my ankle was stuck between the box and the car door.

Spud tried to move over closer to Gemma, because the heat of my body under that dang quilt was making him even hotter. "It's hot back here, and I can't feel any air," Spud whined to anyone who might be listening.

Daddy spoke up, in a voice somewhere between a growl and a snort, "I'm tryin' to drive, and y'all are messin' up my concentration. Do y'all want to go to Florida or *what*?"

Being sandwiched together in a hot, airless car brought out the worst in all of us in a hurry. Finally in desperation, Mama spoke up in a falsely bright voice, "Let's all play *Break the Sugar Dish*. The first person to speak breaks the sugar dish. One. Two. Three. Go!" Of course, Biddie kept clearing her throat, and Spud sneezed twice. I read comic books until my stomach started feeling really queasy.

Two hours later we broke the silence and stopped at a roadside picnic table to eat breakfast. Mama had packed snack-sized boxes of cereal, plus bananas and milk. We poured the milk right into the little boxes. Somehow she had forgotten to bring a knife, so we had to break the bananas into pieces to put them on our cereal. Then we started to load back up and get on the road again.

"Mama, I think it's only fair for Biddie and me to take turns. She should sit in the back the rest of the way…"

"You know very well I can't sit in the back seat, Sissie," she interrupted me in mid-sentence. "I'll get car sick and throw up."

"Then can't we at least put the quilt and towels in the back window?" I begged. "It's too hot."

"No, then Daddy can't see behind him when he's driving," Biddie snapped back.

Mama reached into the back seat. "Here, Biddie, since you can't sit in the back seat, you can hold the quilt." Biddie didn't need to play *Break the Sugar Dish* anymore, because she didn't say another word the rest of the way to Florida, even when we stopped at a roadside stand to buy a watermelon that Spud had to hold on his lap.

As we drove farther south, the land became flat and I could see for miles. As we entered the state of Florida, a bright yellow and green oval sign proclaimed "Welcome to Florida." Painted oranges and orange blossoms decorated the edges of the sign. I couldn't help but think about Gemma's napkin holder in her kitchen. I guess the only thing missing was a good dusting of glitter on the oranges.

How different the land looked when I compared it to our valley. The pine trees were tall and pencil thin. The dirt wasn't red like it was at home. Instead, it was sandy, and spiky plants grew alongside the road. The ditches looked marshy, and every now and then I spotted a beautiful white wading bird, unlike any I had ever seen in the lakes at home. And I wondered about the snakes. Where were they hiding?

At last, when I looked out my window, I saw a huge body of water and cried out, "*This is it, Spud. It's the ocean!*"

"Didn't you just break the sugar dish?" Biddie asked me in a way that only a snotty teenager knows how to ask.

I snapped back at her. "Game's over. We're at the ocean now."

"That's not the ocean, Sissie. That's just the bay," Gemma said in a low voice. "Look off in the distance." And there it was, the wonderful blue ocean. It was so blue that I almost couldn't tell where the sky ended and the water began.

Before we reached the villa where we were staying, I noticed a long white brick building, with pictures of turtles and snakes painted over the white bricks. The tall sign in front printed in huge letters announced *Snake World*, and below the name the sign read, "Come inside and see live amphibians and reptiles of Florida. We have air conditioning."

Hmm, right away I started thinking about how I could talk Mama and Daddy into taking Spud and me there.

Spud elbowed me softly in my side. "Did you see that sign?" he whispered.

"Yes, I did. Do you want to go see the snakes?" I whispered back.

"Uh, huh."

Mama spoke up. "You two quit making plans back there. We did not come to Florida to look at snakes. We have snakes in Georgia, and I don't like to look at them there either." Gemma put her finger on her lips and winked. Spud and I quit talking about snakes immediately.

After the second time we passed Snake World, Mama made Daddy stop at a service station to ask for directions. At last we pulled into the parking lot of The Pink Flamingo Villas. I had already looked up the word *villa* in my dictionary at home, and the villas didn't look anything like Mr. Webster's description. In fact, each villa was actually a cement block house painted with the strangest pink color I had ever seen.

There were no flower gardens, just beds of small white rocks surrounding spiky plants that were similar to the ones I had seen beside the road, just larger versions. Tall plastic pink flamingoes were standing on metal stakes in the rock beds, and an occasional flower pot sat by the front door of a villa. And there were palm trees, which may have looked tropical, but they didn't give a lick of shade from the Florida sun.

We thought we were hot in the car until we climbed out and stood on the pavement outside the check-in office. A wave of heat washed over me, and the top of my head was already starting to burn. At the same time, heat was also coming straight up from the pavement into our faces. At last Daddy emerged with the key, and we located our own personal two bedroom, one bath villa.

Once Daddy turned the key and opened the bright pink front door of Flamingo #6, we all stepped inside and looked around.

"How are we gonna sleep?" Biddie asked with a concerned look on her face.

"We'll share a room with Gemma," I volunteered. "There are two big beds in that room." I pointed to a room with two big windows whose Venetian blinds were open, revealing the bright reflection of the ocean several hundred feet away across the road.

Daddy spoke up, "Spud, do you mind sleeping on the couch?"

"No, sir." Even if he minded, what choice did he have?

"All right, then here's your suitcase." Daddy started passing down our suitcases like water buckets at a fire.

Mama was already in the kitchen, checking out the stove and refrigerator and putting away the groceries. "The kitchen looks good, but I'm not too sure just how clean it is. I'll have to do a little cleaning in here. We'll have to buy perishables later."

I had waited way too long to walk on a real, honest-to-God beach, and I didn't really care whether the kitchen was spotless or not. "Let's put on our swimsuits and go to the beach. I wanna see the ocean," I interrupted. "*Please.*"

Mama looked at Daddy, "You go on, Jeb. I'll be down there directly." In ten minutes, we had all gathered in the living room, dressed in our swimsuits and flip flops and heavily coated with suntan lotion. Daddy was wearing a pair of blue shorts featuring every color of little fish that could be imagined, and he was wearing black socks and black lace-up shoes. He smelled like coconuts.

Biddie looked him up and down. "Oh, Daddy, tell me you're not…"

"I'm gonna take off the shoes when I get to the beach," he quickly assured her.

She looked at me and whispered, "I'm walking in the back of the line, *way* in the back."

* * * *

Spud ran up and down the beach, letting the waves hit him

full force a few times. Getting salt water in his eyes was a new experience. Biddie didn't dare get wet, because the water might mess up her hair, but I sat down directly on the wet sand. The ocean water couldn't possibly do any damage to my wild hair.

It was the most wonderful feeling to sit in warm, white sand and let my bare feet enjoy its softness while the rest of me thought about all that had been happening in my life. I looked out across the big, wide ocean, and foam washed up around me and washed back out again, like it was trying to take my sorrows with it.

I started thinking about Grandpa. He never got to see the ocean. He would really have loved to see the waves and the beach. But I reckoned he had been happy walking along the banks of the little branch that flowed through the old home place, with the ferns springing up around the gnarled roots of trees that leaned over the water. And he had been at peace, slowly walking along the sandy banks of the creek, looking for signs of turtles.

I moved over onto my beach towel, and I brushed the sand off my legs. As I shielded my eyes with my hands, I could see Spud running in the edge of the surf, foamy water covering his feet and splashing on his legs. I didn't remember ever seeing Spud so happy. I looked up at the clouds. The ones nearer the shore were fluffy and white, almost like cotton balls. But in the distance, hanging close to the horizon, the clouds were getting black and stormy.

"Well, Grandpa, looks like it's comin' up a cloud." I looked up at the puffy clouds above me, and I added, "Grandpa, I sure wish you could lean down, call out to me, and tell me exactly what heaven is like." I bet he already knew his way around, and if there was a creek up there, he would have already found it.

That night we had a fine supper of fresh fish and French fries cooked by Mama. Gemma made a big bowl of slaw and sliced up the juicy watermelon that we had bought at the roadside stand. Later Daddy found a comfortable chair in the living room and watched television.

"You know, it's kind of interesting to watch TV in another state," he remarked. I didn't see why, because he was watching the same programs he always watched at home on Friday night, just on a different station and channel.

Spud, Biddie, and I washed the dishes, and while we worked, we made secret plans for Saturday. Spud and I had our sights set on Snake World, and Biddie wanted to look at souvenir shops along the beach. Gemma overheard our whispering, and she started planning with us.

Along about midnight we had a terrible thunderstorm. At first there was a low rumble, then a weak distant flash of light. As the storm came nearer, a loud boom and a bright flash of light immediately after the boom let us know the storm was right overhead. I sat up in bed. I couldn't believe it – even the thunderstorms sounded different in Florida.

Biddie sat straight up in bed beside me. "What in the world? I've never heard such a storm."

The bedroom door opened softly. Spud was quietly slipping in. By the time the third loud boom sounded and shook the house, Gemma was awake, and three grandchildren were huddled in the bed with her.

Early Saturday morning the sun was just beginning to rise, and a few rays managed to sneak through the slits in the closed Venetian blinds in our bedroom. Even though I was awake, I thought everyone else was asleep. Someone suddenly shook me. It was Gemma.

"Get up, Sissie, Biddie, Spud. The storm's over. We've got things to do."

"Oh, Gemma, it's too early," Biddie and Spud protested.

"That's just the point. We have to get there first."

We scrambled out of the bed. Was somebody sick? What was so important? Mama and Daddy were still asleep, and we all tiptoed into the living room, where Gemma opened the large paper sack she had packed in the trunk of the car. She pulled out three colorful little sand buckets and gave one to each of us. We silently slipped out the front door.

The rays of the rising sun were so bright on the ocean that the water looked like shiny liquid silver. It hurt our eyes just to look at it.

We hurried down to the water, where only a few people were

already awake and walking on the beach. Gemma explained, "We're looking for shells and driftwood. See if you can find an interesting piece of wood that washed up during the night. After that horrible storm, I'll bet we'll find all kinds of stuff."

Spud went with Gemma in one direction, while Biddie and I went along the beach the other way. Tiny white crabs scurried across the sand before disappearing into smooth little holes, and the crabs blended in so well we almost didn't see them.

Ten minutes later, we met back to compare what we had found. My bucket had dozens of little shells that looked like pairs of closed angel wings. Some of the other shells were very thin and had little holes in them. Biddie had found part of a sand dollar and a piece of mother of pearl, plus lots of tiny round or open wing-shaped shells.

Spud and Gemma had found the same kinds of shells, too, but Spud had found one that was much larger than the others. "I had to dive down and get it before the ocean carried it back out again," Spud explained to Biddie and me, "and Gemma kept yelling and telling me not to drown."

Gemma was holding two interesting pieces of wood. They were twisted and looked heavy, but when she handed one of the pieces to me, it felt light.

"It's been drifting in the ocean, no telling how long, before it finally washed up on shore. I'm gonna put it on my dresser at home."

We carried our treasures back to the villa. Mama was in the kitchen cooking bacon and eggs, and Daddy was in the bathroom shaving. Mama and Daddy didn't quite seem to understand the word *vacation*.

After breakfast I sat down on the living room sofa and unfolded Daddy's road map. We weren't actually on the Atlantic Ocean. We were on the Gulf of Mexico which was connected to the Atlantic. I located where we lived in Georgia and traced my finger down to where we were in Florida. Maybe our creek in the mountain flowed into the Chattahoochee River before eventually flowing into the Gulf of Mexico and on into the Atlantic. Maybe just a bit of Grandpa's memory was out there right now in the gulf.

"What do you kids want to do this afternoon?" Daddy asked. "We can go back to the beach, or we can all just get in the car and ride around, you know, see the sights." Piling into that car like a bunch of steaming sardines and riding all over creation was not what we all had on our minds.

Biddie spoke up first. "Uh, I could go look in some souvenir shops. But I'd like to just stay here in the air conditioning and read a book." Lord, sometimes Biddie was a little old lady dressed up like a teenager.

Daddy looked at her and shook his head. "You can read a book at home, Biddie. You need to do somethin' different sometime."

Then Spud and I spoke up at the same time. "*We want to go to Snake World.*"

Suddenly Mama had a strange look on her face, almost as if she had just felt a really bad pain somewhere. I wondered if there were any aspirins in the villa's kitchen cabinet. She said firmly, "I *refuse* to go to Snake World. Jeb, why did you ask them? Why didn't you just tell them what to do?"

"Because this is a vacation. They're supposed to have fun. Tell you what, you and Biddie go look in the shops, and the rest of us will pay a visit to Snake World."

This time, it was Gemma's turn to have a strange look on her face. "I –I don't know, Jeb. This isn't what I had planned. I figured Biddie and I could look in the souvenir shops together, while the rest of you go to Snake World. I'm not crazy about snakes."

"I'm not either, but I think I'll be all right if I don't have to get too close to the things," Daddy said.

"Come on, Gemma, *please!*" Spud and I begged together. We practically carried her out to the car. It was roasting hot outside, and the inside of the car was even hotter. But even though I was already a little bit sunburned and the blistering vinyl car seat bothered my back, I was prepared to suffer if Daddy would just take us to Snake World.

CHAPTER 29

Turtles and Gators and Snakes

"The words 'beautiful' and 'snake' don't belong
together in the same sentence."
– Gemma

I wanted to learn as much as I possibly could about snakes. Daddy dropped off Mama and Biddie at the end of the street with all the souvenir shops and arcades near the villas.

"We'll meet you back here in about an hour and a half at that shop on the other end. What is it? *The Sand Dollar*," he answered himself, squinting at the storefront sign.

Mama didn't look too happy about the time limit, but she had a spring in her step as she and Biddie walked away. I imagined that spring had something to do with the fact that she didn't have to go and look at snakes.

Once again, Daddy drove around completely lost. We wasted thirty minutes looking for Snake World, and we even passed it twice before we could get him to slow down and pull in. I declare, it was a good thing God didn't ask Daddy to lead the Israelites through the desert – we never would have received the Ten Commandments.

When Daddy held out my entrance ticket and I reached for it, my hands were trembling.

"Are you all right, Sissie? Are you sure you really want to do this?" Was Daddy sure *he and Gemma* really wanted to do this?

"Yes, sir, I'm fine. I'm just so excited. I can't wait."

Spud took his ticket from Daddy and the four of us passed through the entrance gate. Two of us were filled with excitement, and two of us were not. We meandered around looking at the different exhibits, and we noticed a crowd starting to gather near a large enclosed cement pit that was about a third full of murky water.

When we joined the crowd, Spud peered over the rail. "Wow! Look, Sissie."

An alligator, so dark green that he was almost black, was swimming around in the water, and a keeper started explaining all about alligators to the audience. He touched the alligator gently with a long metal pole, and the alligator obliged him by making a strange noise that the keeper said was the gator's "warning."

And then after a few minutes, the keeper turned his attention toward a huge rock near the pool, and using a large pole with a hook on the end, lifted up what was the biggest timber rattlesnake I had ever seen in my life, even in my books. That snake had to be ancient. The keeper started telling us all sorts of interesting facts about rattlers.

"Rattlesnakes are very nervous creatures." What was new about that? I'd be nervous, too, if somebody was always trying to hit me in the head with a hoe or run over me with a car. "They know they can't eat something as big as a human, but they do have to defend themselves." Spud needed to learn a few defense lessons from rattlesnakes.

I looked behind me for a moment. Daddy was next to Spud, taking in everything, not missing a single word. Gemma, however, was looking around, looking up, looking back, looking anywhere but at the snakes.

When the keeper finished his speech about rattlesnake facts – most of which I had already learned from Grandpa – he used his long hook to lift up a cottonmouth moccasin. I'd seen a few of them, too, down at the creek on the home place, swimming around. They looked plenty scary when they opened their mouth to give *their* warning – a large cotton white lining inside accompanied by two very sharp fangs loaded with venom.

When the snake and alligator program had ended, we wandered around to look a little more. All I had to do was study the expression on Gemma's face to know that she had already gotten her money's worth for her entrance ticket.

In one of the glass cages, something colorful caught my attention, and I walked over to see what it was. It was a coral snake. I had seen plenty of them in pictures, but I had always wanted to see a real one. "Over here, Spud, quick. It's a coral snake!"

Spud hurried over. "Wow. It's even more beautiful than the ones in your snake book. You'd never guess it's so dangerous."

Gemma looked at Daddy. With a note of disgust in her voice she told him, "The words *beautiful* and *snake* don't belong together in the same sentence."

"It's okay, Gemma. Coral snakes won't bite you if you don't bother them. They don't go looking for trouble. And a coral snake looks like another snake that's completely safe, a kind of king snake. You only have to look at the colors of his bands to tell the difference. Just remember: *Red on yellow, dangerous fellow. Red on black, okay, Jack.*"

"Humph," she said, "what I want to know is what Jack is doing so close to the snake to begin with."

"Have you children seen enough?" Daddy asked. "I want to go back and sit on the beach."

Spud looked at me, and I looked at him. I knew perfectly well that we both could have stayed there all afternoon, but I reluctantly answered, "Well, all right, Daddy, I guess we're ready."

Just as we were about to find the exit, a sign caught my attention. *Turtles of Florida.* "Spud, look!" I cried out, as I pointed to the sign.

"Oh, Daddy, *please*, just a few more minutes," I begged.

Daddy looked over and saw the sign. "All right, Sissie. Are you okay, Mama? Do you mind staying a few more minutes?"

"No, Jeb, I'll be all right. I'm fine with turtles, but snakes are a whole different story."

We entered a separate area filled with cement pits and water tanks. I had never seen so many different kinds of turtles in all my life – big ones, little ones, snappers, soft shell, adults, and babies. All I could think about was Grandpa, but I couldn't let myself cry, because Gemma didn't need me to make her feel any sadder.

I turned my back away from her and peered down at the big snapping turtle that was swimming around in one end of the pool of water. Large rocks were in the shallow water and around the edges of the pool so that the turtles could come out and sit for a while.

I spoke softly to the snapper, "You're a mighty pretty turtle. And I'll bet you have lots of stories to tell." His eyes looked sad to me, and I wondered if maybe he longed to be swimming in the freedom of a sandy creek or a lake with the warm sunlight shining on him. I felt a tear slide down my cheek, and I wiped it away quickly before anyone could notice.

Just then I heard a man's voice behind me. "Young lady, if you ever need a job when you grow up, you come back and visit us, you hear? I can tell you really love turtles." It was the man who had told us all about alligators and snakes.

"Yes, sir, I do, and I love snakes, too."

"Well, that's mighty good to hear. I mean it now – you come back and visit us real soon."

"I'll plan to do just that." I wondered if it was too soon to make a resolution to come back to Florida the next summer.

On the way back to our villa, we met Mama and Biddie at *The Sand Dollar* souvenir shop, and we all went inside for a quick look. Shells of every imaginable kind were piled in different baskets around the walls of the shop. Daddy's eyes lit up when he caught sight of a statue of a hula dancer.

"Don't you even think about it, Jeb," Mama warned him.

I picked out a small mesh bag that contained a variety of shells of different colors, but Spud's sights were set on a shell twice as big as his hand.

One of the clerks in the store told Spud, "That's a conch shell, son. Put it up to your ear and you can hear the ocean." Spud listened for a few moments, and then he put the shell up to my ear. Sure enough, I could hear waves.

"Let's get one of these, Sissie, and then we can listen to the ocean when the weather gets cold again."

At the cash register, Daddy paid for all of our purchases, including the new napkin holder Gemma was clutching in her hands like a prized treasure. This one was aqua blue and covered with sparkly little fish. Biddie wanted to show Mama something else she had found, and as soon as Mama turned her attention away from Daddy for just a minute, he managed to purchase a large plaster of Paris statue of a pink flamingo. By the time Mama saw what he had done, the man at the cash register was giving Daddy his change and putting everything in bags.

When we got into the car to leave the shop, Biddie had a look on her face that I had never seen there before. I had to look up the best word in my thesaurus to describe it: *radiant*.

Driving back to the villa, I nudged her and whispered, "What's with you?" I couldn't believe that her new sand dollars had made her that happy.

"MYOB," she said through lips that barely moved.

"So, are you Patsy Stephens now?" I asked back.

"Not now," she said through her teeth. Had Biddie suddenly decided to become a ventriloquist? Was I the dummy?

Later that afternoon the sun was beginning to get lower in the sky. Spud and I sat down on our beach towels and watched the waves rolling in, their white foam swirling around our sandy feet. Spud was looking out across the ocean, deep in thought. I figured he must be thinking about Grandpa again.

He sighed deeply and asked, "Sissie, why did my mama name me Homer?"

Oh, Lord! "Spud, I've explained that to you at least a thousand million times. He was a famous Greek…"

"I know all that. But I hate my name. And you know something else, Sissie? I hate my nickname, too. It's *stupid*. It's about *potatoes*. I want people to take me serious, and they never will as long as I'm named after potatoes."

"Well, let's think about this, Spud. I mean, let's give it some serious thought." Now the soft, foamy waves of water were coming farther in and washing completely around us. "Your middle name is John. How about John? Or Johnny?"

"Naw, I don't think so. A boy named Johnny made fun of me all the time in first grade." Dang, I'd forgotten all about Johnny Mac Hudson. At least when we came back to school after Christmas holidays that year, Johnny Mac had moved out of the county. Patsy Stephens said his mama moved every time the rent was due.

"Then I guess I shouldn't suggest Mac either," I added.

"*No!* I can just feel the pain and hear Rusty Jackson now. 'Looka there, boys, I can smack a Mac.' It's just no use. I'm doomed."

A light came on in my mind. "I've got an idea. *Homer John McKenna*. You could call yourself H.J. McKenna. That sounds strong. H.J. That name sounds like you're a great writer or a rich businessman. Who knows, someday you might work in McKenna's Department Store. What d'ya think?"

"H.J. McKenna. I like it just fine," he said, and I swear he would have grown two inches taller if he had been standing up.

"That will be a good name at school, but I'm still gonna call you Spud."

We both stood up and gathered the wet, sandy beach towels. I looked toward the ocean just in time to see Biddie strolling along the beach, talking to a boy, one I was sure she would call "dreamy." Hmmm, was that why she had been acting so strangely?

* * * *

Once again Mama cooked up a wonderful supper. This time we had fried oysters and tossed salad. After all the dishes were washed and the kitchen was put back in order, we took Gemma's flashlight and walked on the beach. The wind blowing in off the ocean felt really cool after all the fiery heat of the day.

We shone the light and watched the tiny white crabs, like scurrying ghosts, running across the beach. Even though we had the beam of our flashlight, the moonlight shining down on the white sand was bright enough for us to see where we were walking.

That night, after all the excitement of the day – the snakes and turtles, the souvenirs, the ocean, the foamy waves, and the dreamy boy – we all headed for bed. Spud took the quilt and a pillow and made himself a bed on the floor at the foot of Gemma's bed. When I closed my eyes, I could still see snakes and turtles. That was a good thing for me.

* * * *

During the early morning something caused me to wake up. Biddie was fast asleep, and Spud was making short snoring sounds as he slept soundly on the quilt on the floor. I didn't know at first what had caused me to come out of my sound sleep. Then I realized that it was Gemma who had made me wake up, the sound of her crying so soft that I heard only little sobs and short breaths.

I sat up in bed. "Gemma, are you all right?" I asked in almost a whisper.

The sun was just beginning to come up over the ocean, and once again tiny rays of light were shining through the slits of the Venetian blinds. I slipped over to her bed and sat down beside her.

"What's the matter, Gemma?"

"I miss him so much. He was the love of my life, the only man I ever loved. You'll understand one day, Sissie." She took my hand and held on to it, and I squeezed her hand softly in return. I felt a sudden stab of guilt.

"Gemma, something's been bothering me a lot. Can we talk about it?"

"What, Sissie?"

I hesitated for a few moments. I felt a small shiver suddenly run through my body. I wanted desperately to ask Gemma my question, but I didn't want to make her even more unhappy. And what if she hadn't thought about it herself already? She might suddenly start hating me.

"Go ahead and ask, Sissie. It's all right."

I took a deep breath. "You remember the old clock I brought down from the loft?"

"Yes, I do. Why?"

"Did the old clock cause Grandpa to die? Did I cause Grandpa to die?"

"No! Absolutely not," she tried to assure me.

"But I was the one who brought it down from the loft. It chimed ten times, and Grandpa died at ten o'clock."

She sat up and put her arm around my shoulders. "It's true. You brought down the old clock, Sissie, but it was my idea to go up in the loft to begin with. If it was anybody's fault, it would be *mine*. But it's *nobody's* fault."

"But what about the rabbit's foot?" I asked, blinking back tears.

Gemma hugged me again. "No rabbit's foot could have saved him either, Sissie. Don't believe in Pearl's superstitions, not even for one minute. Your grandpa was very sick. We just didn't realize how sick he was."

"I miss him, too, Gemma."

"I know you do. But instead of thinking about how sad it was for him to leave us, I reckon we ought to be happy about all the time he was with us."

"I'll try to do that," I promised her.

"I will, too, but it's gonna be hard."

"We can help each other," I said, and I meant it.

* * * *

Early Sunday morning we had a quick breakfast before we had to pack up and pile back into the heat of our car and make the same trip all over again, just in a different direction.

Daddy said something that really surprised us. "You know, we don't have to check out until noon. Why don't you kids go to the beach one more time before we leave? No tellin' when we'll get back this way."

Spud ran for the bathroom, while Biddie and I ran for the bedroom to change out of our shorts and shirts and into our swimsuits. Mama called after me, "Sissie, you need to wear a tee shirt. You're already sunburned."

Five minutes later we snatched the beach towels off the clothes line behind the villa and headed to the beach. Biddie's face was full of hope. Maybe, just maybe, the mysterious teenage boy would be walking on the beach this morning, and she was prepared in case she saw him. I had seen her slip a pen and some paper into a little pink vinyl bag to take with her.

We spread out our towels side by side on the sand, and Biddie started walking along the beach, letting the foamy waves roll gently in and wash over her feet. Spud sat down on one of the towels, and I sat down on my towel next to him. Then he lay back, his elbows folded, resting the back of his head on his upturned hands. I could tell he was really thinking.

"The clouds here are so beautiful. You know what? I'll bet we could come up with lots of ideas about their shapes," he said as he looked up, studying the clouds.

"Pro'bly so."

"You know somethin', Sissie?"

"What?"

"I'm glad we got to see all those snakes yesterday. That was fun."

"I thought so, too. I'm glad you love snakes, Spud."

"I don't love snakes, Sissie. I *like* snakes. I *love* spiders."

"I like spiders, too, Spud. Maybe sometime we can find a place called *Spider World.*"

"I doubt there is one of those, Sissie, 'cause most people don't like spiders at all. But *I* do. I think they're interesting. They don't seem to worry about anything, and I don't suppose they ever feel sorry for themselves. I don't think a spider sits around wishing his mama had laid her eggs someplace better so he could've hatched out into a nicer life."

"That's true, Spud." I looked over at his face. I wasn't sure he was actually talking about spiders, and he was getting way too serious. "And I bet she never regrets the time she acted too fast and ate her husband by mistake."

"Or the four or five other husbands," he laughed. Then he was quiet for a minute before he said, "You remember that spider that died at Mount Olive during the sermon on Reunion Sunday?"

"Sure." How could I forget?

"That poor old spider, even though she got stepped on, she managed to pull herself up and keep on going. And even though she finally died a horrible death under Brother Snow's shoe, I had to respect her."

I had felt a few things for that poor spider myself, but respect wasn't one of them.

"Did you know that the orb weaver is nearly blind, Sissie? But every day she redoes her web all over again. She just does it and she doesn't complain about it."

"Yeah, and I've never seen a more beautiful pattern anywhere, not even in Biddie's algebra book. And orb weavers don't have to go to school to learn that."

"If they do go to spider school, I hope they have better teachers than some of the ones we've had, Sissie. I hope none of their teachers have huge moles or yell at their spider students or wear bright red lipstick."

"Hey, Spud, when a spider raises his hand to ask the teacher a question, which one does he raise? After all, he has eight." Spud laughed so hard, I was glad he wasn't drinking milk.

"You'd make a good spider, Sissie. With that many legs you could ask a teacher a lot of questions at one time." I wasn't sure if that comment was really funny.

Then he got serious once again. "So, I guess when we get back home, we've got to keep goin', even without Grandpa. And we've gotta go back to school and not worry about Rusty Jackson. And, Raleigh, well, I'm not sure yet what we're gonna do about Raleigh. I'm still thinking about that one."

"That's right, Spud, if we get stepped on, we'll just have to pull ourselves up and keep going. We'll just have to be on the lookout for a very big shoe."

* * * *

Daddy called to us, "Okay, y'all need to load up." I dreaded that trip back home so much. When I climbed into the back seat of the car, the heat of the vinyl seat almost blistered the back of my legs that were already almost blistered. My sunburn had reddened my back and shoulders as well as my thighs, and I could feel heat rising from the burned areas of my skin.

We stopped at a roadside table, and we had to practically unpack the car trunk to get to the cooler. While we had been playing on the beach that morning, Mama and Gemma had made pimiento cheese sandwiches and packed them in the cooler. We fought off the buzzing yellow jackets that wanted our food, finished our lunch, reloaded our car, and headed off again, surrounded by the smothering airless heat of our car.

I noticed that Biddie was much quieter than usual, and I hadn't even picked an argument with her to cause that. She hadn't once complained when Daddy made her sit in the back seat so that Gemma could sit up front for awhile. She kept holding on to the little pink vinyl bag, like it contained something very valuable.

I elbowed her softly and whispered, "What's going on with you?"

"None of your beeswax," she popped back.

"Well, something's going on," I insisted. Dad blame it, I hated the times when she stopped acting like my sister and became a rude teenager.

"If you must know, Miss Nosey, I got Jeff's address," she whispered.

"Jeff? Who's Jeff?"

"Shh! The boy on the beach, silly. He's from Dothan, Alabama, and his family was staying in one of the villas. I met him at one of the souvenir shops, and he met up with me on the beach yesterday. I saw him again this morning. He promised to write to me, and I promised to write to him."

Later on, as Daddy steered the car up the highway toward Georgia, I began to notice a very bad smell, weak at first, but then growing steadily stronger.

Mama looked in the rear view mirror. "What is that *horrible* odor? It seems to be coming from the backseat. I hope none of you children have lost your manners."

But the odor smelled more like something dead, like very old fish. The smell finally became so strong that Mama asked Gemma to roll her window all the way down. I guess she didn't care so much about messing up her teased hairdo after all.

As the heat in the car became worse, the odor became even stronger. My sunburn was really hurting, and I couldn't bear to sit too close to Biddie or to lean back on the car seat. I was beginning to feel really queasy.

Biddie reached down into the floorboard of the car and picked up my sand bucket. "Aha, this is the culprit." My beautiful angel wing shells turned out to be mussels, and the little animals had apparently still been at home when I picked up the shells on the beach. Now their dead bodies were beginning to decay in the heat.

"Oh, throw those things out, Sissie, for heaven's sake. We still have at least two hours or more before we get home," Mama complained.

"Please don't make me throw them away," I begged.

Daddy pulled the car over to the side of the road and put my bucket in the trunk, which turned out to be a blessing, because we got to open the car doors and let in some fresh air.

Once we were back home, it was strange to look out the living room window and not see the ocean. But in Florida, I couldn't go out on the porch and see the mountains either.

It was getting late in the day and the sun was going down, yet I headed outside to the mimosa to sit and think for a little while. As I climbed up and sat down on my favorite perch, I realized that even the mimosa tree seemed to know that it needed rest. When the sun went down and all the night sounds began, its fernlike leaves closed up for the night.

I thought about our family vacation. Florida was mostly everything I had expected it to be, but in some ways it was nothing like I had imagined. I got the worst case of sunburn I had ever had, but I did finally get to see the ocean and the palm trees. I walked on the sugar sands of the beach and picked up real shells, not Mama's macaroni, and I felt the foamy waves washing in around my feet.

Spud came home with a new name, and he had flooded a toilet in a pink villa. Biddie flirted with a dreamy boy on the beach and got his address, and Gemma found another glittery napkin holder for her kitchen table. Daddy bought a pink flamingo statue and got to watch his same favorite shows on Florida television stations. And Mama, well, Mama got to cook and clean in a different state.

CHAPTER 30

Home at Last

"The same rain that falls on the lilies falls on the poison ivy."
– Grandpa

The following Sunday morning, we went to church at Mount Olive. The August heat was holding on tight and showing no signs of cooling down any time soon. We were already steaming hot and perspiring after the ten minutes it took for Daddy to drive from our house to the church, and it was about as hot inside the church as it was outside, only stuffier. Most of the Sunday school students took chairs outside, and the teachers set up their classes in any shady spot they could find.

Gemma had already warned us on the way to church, "The heat's gonna be bad for the next few weeks, because we're in the dog days of summer, so try to keep as cool as you can."

During the week since we had returned from Florida, my sunburn had become a little less painful, but a new problem had set in: Now my skin was itching for real. I begged Mama, "Please don't make me wear anything hot and scratchy today. This sunburn is *not* just my imagination."

Mama had mercy on me, and I wore a plain white, sleeveless cotton blouse and a blue polka-dot skirt that had once belonged to Biddie. Even though I sat down next to Spud in the third pew, he was very careful not to sit too close so he scooted over closer to Gemma.

"I don't wanna hurt your sunburn." I appreciated that.

During the church service, The Preacher prayed for so many people for such a long time that I thought maybe while we had our eyes closed, he was reading names in the telephone directory. I just had to peek.

During his sermon he yelled at us, as usual, and I mostly tuned him out with my Preacher Face. I used the time to think a lot, mostly about Grandpa. I still had lots of questions to ask, and Grandpa would never again be able to give any answers.

During the school year, Mrs. Clara Sue Martin had helped us to see that the world was a very big place, much bigger than our valley, much bigger than our county, much bigger than the little part of the world where we lived. We had learned the names of the continents and the oceans. We had learned the names of the longest and widest rivers, as well as the tallest mountain ranges.

"Now you can't forget about the United States, for goodness sake," she had reminded us, and so we had learned all fifty states and their capitals, including the new ones, Alaska and Hawaii. But there was one place that I had never seen on any of the maps we studied in geography class: Heaven wasn't on any of Mrs. Martin's maps.

After the service was over and people were standing around in the church yard talking to one another, I walked over to the cemetery to visit Grandpa's grave. I knew he wasn't really there. Like Brother Snow had told us, I knew that Grandpa had gone to glory, but it was a good place to go and think about him and all he meant to me. It was also a very good place to think about questions that needed answers.

I laid some of my seashells on the soft, red dirt that covered his grave. I bent down to straighten up a vase of artificial roses that Gemma had put on his grave, when all of a sudden I noticed a silky, almost invisible web. From the plastic branches of the grave flowers, an orb weaver had spun a beautiful web that stretched over to a small shrub growing near Grandpa's grave. The sun was shining, and the orb weaver, who knew how to make a perfect web, was basking in the sunshine, waiting for a tasty, unsuspecting meal to fly into her web. I didn't disturb her Sunday dinner plans.

I started thinking about when Spud and I were on the beach talking about orb weavers. Then the strangest thing happened. For some reason, Raleigh's name popped into my mind. Why in the world would I be thinking about Raleigh Brown at this very moment?

Then I thought, maybe Raleigh's life was sort of like the way Spud described the orb weaver's eggs. If Raleigh had been born somewhere else, to another set of parents, he might have had a different life and been a nicer person. Raleigh couldn't help the fact that Raedean was his mother.

Then I thought about what Brother Snow had said about Grandpa at his funeral. *He didn't spend his time criticizing and judging others. He loved folks the way they were, and they loved him the same way in return.*

Spud wasn't sure what he was going to do about Raleigh, but I knew what I had to do. I was going to have to find a way to love Raleigh, just the way Grandpa would want me to do. If Raleigh didn't love me in return, well, that was his problem.

* * * *

I never let anybody know that Grandpa had already told me all the family secrets. I felt proud that he had trusted me, like he needed to pass all of the secrets on down before he left, like somehow I was the family history keeper. Or was he just talking it all out, trying to make sense of it all like everybody else?

Some things changed, and some things never did. I was ready to begin the sixth grade at the same school, but Slippery Branch Elementary School would never be the same again, not without Mrs. Clara Sue Martin there. Spud was going to change his name, but how? Would everybody understand, or would he be laughed at even more than ever?

I had a feeling that Aunt Pearl would always be the same, even though Sharon had tried to set her straight. I guess it was too late for her to change, so she was just one of those people we would have to love the way Grandpa had taught us to love.

Pip and Copper both turned out to be roosters. Over four months after Biddie and I rescued them from their feed store prison, they were getting bigger and already starting to strut and crow in Gemma's chicken yard. I was sorry that Biddie hadn't named them Rusty and Raleigh.

The day we came home from Florida, Mama looked through the mail and handed me a letter Patsy Stephens had written to me. Patsy was the sweetest person in the whole world and my very best friend, except Spud, of course, but she had one annoying problem with her writing. Her letter was five paragraphs long, and it contained only five sentences with about a hundred *ands*. But the letter was filled with important news, and one particular paragraph-sentence held the best news I think I had ever received. I couldn't wait to tell Spud.

I have something very important to tell you and I know that you will be happy to hear that Rusty Jackson has moved to Alabama because his mama said the children in his school were always picking on him and she was tired of Rusty being picked on and she was tired of coming to school to talk to the principal and the principal always took the side of the other children anyway and poor Rusty never had a chance to explain his side of the story and so Rusty is going to live with his grandmother and all I can say is God have mercy on Alabama.

I'm sure that what she wrote was the truth, because our principal, Mrs. Elizabeth Williams, was her aunt.

That night I stood at the screen door in our kitchen and looked out across the field toward Gemma's house. When I saw the light shining in her bedroom window, its soft glow warmed me inside. I knew that Gemma was there and I would be okay.

I've decided that special memories are like lightning bugs. In the stillness of a summer evening, the little insects flash their lights here and there in the darkening air, and we never know exactly when or where to expect the next tiny light to glow suddenly before turning itself off as quickly as it had appeared. Special memories are just like that. In the darkest moments of our lives, they suddenly appear and bring a spot of light, and we never know when or where to expect them.

Sometimes now in the summer I catch a few lightning bugs

and put them into a Mason jar just to watch them light up the darkness. But I always set them free, because they aren't meant to stay captive. They are meant to fly freely in the darkness to bring a sudden point of joy and light into the world.

And when I'm writing or thinking about questions that need answers, a special memory of Grandpa suddenly lights up the darkness of the empty space his passing left in my heart, before suddenly slipping away until another special memory takes its place.

Grandpa loved to tell stories. They weren't fancy, filled with flowery language and big words. They were simple and straightforward. But he never talked down to me because I was a child, as if I was ignorant. He talked to me as if I was just as smart as he was, just in a different place in my life. Grandpa had the gift of storytelling. I hope he passed that gift down to me.